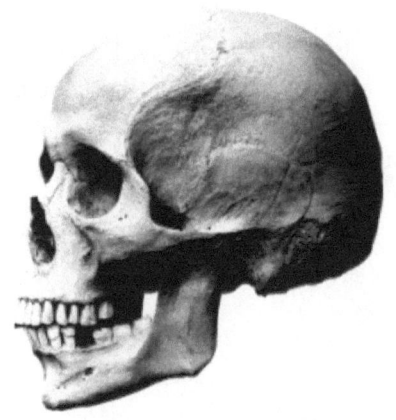

scribbled love dreams

five body blade books

2019

For my wife, who helped me begin the story, and for my children, who helped me finish

The plane shook and dropped from the sky. My stomach felt as if it were coming forward on a swing. I noticed Sara tensed as well, just a bit. She sat in the window seat with her hand cupped under her chin looking out the small oval window at a thick blanket of clouds spread beneath us. She told me she thought about playing in those clouds. She did this every time she flew—had done ever since she was a little girl. She'd imagine leaping from the plane, sliding down the perfect meringue slopes, and bouncing from one puff to the other.

The plane dropped again.

"Jesus Christ," I blurted. I gripped the armrest tight enough for my knuckles to pop.

Sara shifted her body toward me and put her hand on my arm. Our eyes met, and I smiled. I felt ridiculous, but I couldn't help myself.

"It's hard to get used to."

"I know," Sara said, her tone soft and calming, barely above a whisper. "It catches me off guard too, but it's perfectly normal."

"Is it, though?"

"Of course it is," she said, gently running her fingers along my forearm.

Father Paul had no problem with us getting married in St. Catherine, even though I was not a member of the congregation and Sara had not attended Mass in many years. The fact that I was at least raised Catholic made the decision easier for him. Before discussing it with the priest, Sara and I agreed it wasn't prudent to mention I had never been confirmed and had no plans to do so. I also hadn't been inside a church since my cousin Dominic had passed away over ten years ago. Father Paul's only stipulation was that we had to go through the marriage-preparation class. We expected this and had already signed up for classes at the church near our apartment in Orange.

During class that Thursday, which I believe was the second to last in the program, Sara brought up our trip back to St. Catherine to finalize some of the details for the wedding. I mentioned I wasn't looking forward to the flight. Charlotte, the wife half of the husband-and-wife team that led our group, asked me why. I admitted I wasn't a fan of flying.

"I can't get over the fact that it just doesn't seem natural for something that size and weight to be up in the air like that."

Henry, the husband part of the duo, looked at me with this half-lidded eyes and said, "It's physics."

To this, I nodded and thought, Well, yes, it is physics, which I believe means the knowledge of nature, or the study of matter moving through space and time. In other words, it's perfectly natural and I'm a fucking dumdum. Thank you very much.

I knew he was right, but it made no difference. That rational thinking, not to mention the science behind the safest travel known to man, did not make flying any easier.

I touched the outline of my father's dog tags beneath my T-shirt. I wanted to take them off and hold them in my hand, but I was already feeling embarrassed for carrying on too much. This wasn't a big deal. It was normal. It was turbulence, and it wasn't particularly bad turbulence either. It wasn't as if I believed the dog tags held some magical power, just as I didn't believe the grey Arizona State T-shirt was a shield protecting me from harm in case the plane went down. There wasn't anything to fear. This was simply air currents moving at different speeds and different directions smashing into one another. It was nature. Simple. No big deal. I knew this logically, intuitively, but the dog tags and the T-shirt still gave me comfort.

I don't remember why I started flying with the dog tags. It was an impulse, a fleeting thought right before leaving for the airport on some trip I no longer remember taking. It doesn't matter when or how it started, only that it had become an absolute requirement every time I got on a plane. It was the same with the damn T-shirt. I don't remember how it happened. On some flight some time ago, I wore a gray Arizona State T-shirt that Josh Ragsdale had left at my house one weekend. The shirt was comfortable and available when I needed it. It wasn't any more complicated than that. Regardless, it then became, along with a pair of khaki cargo shorts, my absolute must-have flight uniform.

It was a ridiculous observance, made even more so by the fact that I went to the University of Arizona. I don't hate the Sun Devils. I grew up in Phoenix, and my dad raised me on Sun Devil football, Frank Kush, and all that. It was by mere chance I found myself going to college in Tucson rather than Tempe. I rooted for both teams unless they played each other, but I would never bring myself to wear any of their garb in public. And yet somehow, a worn gray T-shirt with faded maroon-and-gold ASU lettering and a pitchfork had become my flight shirt. I only wore it when I was beating around the house or had to fly somewhere, and I always paired it with those raggedy shorts—even if we were flying back to St. Catherine in the winter with snow on the ground and the temperature walking out of the terminal hovering around forty degrees.

But on this flight, I wasn't wearing the T-shirt. It shouldn't have bothered me. I should not have cared. It was an old, ugly shirt made of cotton. The collar showed signs of wear. It probably wouldn't have made it too much longer. The shirt had no power—I knew it. It was an obvious enough fact. I kept trying to convince myself that not wearing the shirt was a good

3

thing. I was finally free from the burden of having to put the damn thing on every single time I had to step on an airplane. But the logical didn't matter a damn bit. It still bothered me. It bothered me a great deal, in fact, especially as the plane pitched and bobbed in the sky.

I wished I were wearing the shirt. I couldn't help it, and I was about to say as much out loud but decided against it. I didn't want to rehash it yet again with Sara. So I sat there, silent, eyes darting around the cabin, acid burning in my stomach and crawling up my esophagus. Pressure built in my head like a can of soda that had been vigorously shaken. My throat parched, I couldn't swallow. I was thirsty, suddenly incredibly thirsty, like if I didn't get a drink of something—water, anything—I would scream. There was a ding. My eyes went to the "Fasten Seat Belt" sign. That meant the turbulence would only get worse. I looked up the aisle, then behind me. I couldn't see a stewardess. Or flight attendant. Whatever they're supposed to be called, there wasn't anyone around. My mouth was dry. I couldn't produce any saliva. I desperately needed something to drink.

"I should have worn that goddamn shirt," I blurted out.

As soon as I said it, I turned my head so I wouldn't have to look at Sara. I waited a moment, not sure she had even heard me. I counted to five, then slowly turned back toward her. She was looking down at her hand on my arm.

"I'm sorry. I'm sorry for bringing it up again, but it's bugging me. I can't help it. I should have just washed the damn thing."

I glanced at her, trying to gauge her reaction. She kept a calm demeanor.

"It's stupid. I know. I'm sorry. All week long, I kept thinking I needed to make sure it's clean. I kept telling myself I needed to double-check and make sure, but every time I thought about it, I was at work, or we were out, and at home I never thought about it until it was too late. And then I would think, I have to remember to do that. And I never did."

The night before, I suddenly remembered I needed the shirt. It wasn't hanging in the closet or folded in the dresser. Anxiety and panic immediately began a whirling dervish in my chest.

"You haven't seen it?"

Sara told me she had not and that if it was clean, it would be hanging up. I tore through the closet again, flipping through the shirts on hangers, then going through the ones folded on the wire shelving. I went through the dresser a second time. When I didn't find it there, I went back to the closet and went through those shirts again. I pulled out all the dirty clothes in the canvas hanging bag in the closet. I couldn't find the shirt anywhere.

"Did we leave anything in the laundry room?"

"I don't believe so," Sara said.

I went down the stairs of our second-story apartment and across the courtyard to the laundry room. There was a load going in the washer. The dryer was off. I opened the door, and, no surprise, it was packed full with clothes. I launched into rage mode. Unless Sara and I did our laundry on an off night, late on a Tuesday or Wednesday, and even that wasn't a guarantee, without fail we would cart a basket full of clothes down to the laundry room only to find a load sitting unattended in either the washer or the dryer, often both. Some asshole had traipsed down, tossed their shit in, and gone back to their apartment. That's all well and good if they were conscientious enough to come back and take care of their clothes. That never happened. Ever. Not once. So Sara and I would have to come back every five, ten minutes to check whether these bastards had finally moved their stuff. Sometimes it would take an hour or so before we had an empty washer. The infuriating part of it was that we never messed with anyone's clothes. The other tenants were not so considerate. We always set a timer to remind ourselves to go back down and deal with our clothes, but on the off occurrence we were even two minutes late, there was a better-than-average chance we would find that someone waiting for us had not hesitated to pull our clothes from the machine and dump them in a pile on a shelf.

I checked the closet, the drawers, the dirty clothes, and the laundry room, my car, Sara's car, under the couches and chairs, wash, rinse, repeat. After an hour of this, I resigned myself to the idea I had somehow lost the shirt. I didn't know how it was possible, but it was clearly true. I couldn't think of anywhere I hadn't checked or where I might have left it. That's when Sara came into the living room and dropped the shirt into my lap.

"Where did you find it?"

"In the dirty clothes."

"Are you kidding me?"

Sara retreated into the bedroom, not saying anything. Her silence was always worse than if she openly teased me for stomping around the apartment like a maniac, missing what was right in front of me. I must have checked the dirty clothes five times. I'm not sure how I missed it.

The shirt was wrinkled and smelled sour. I checked the time. It was eleven, too late to start a load of laundry. It would be a pain in the ass. Even if I wanted to wash the shirt, I wouldn't finish the load until well after midnight. Plus, I couldn't justify spending three bucks—six quarters for the washer and six for the dryer—just to wash one shirt. We didn't have enough quarters anyway, so I would have needed to drive to the convenience store and hope I could get change. Sara offered to hand-wash it in the sink. I told her it wasn't worth the effort, even though she said over and over again that it wouldn't take long and it wasn't a big deal. I told her no. I could wear a different shirt. It wouldn't be a big deal, anyway. I could wear the navy-blue Huntington Beach surfing competition shirt she'd given me for my birthday. That shirt had a history and meaning branded to it. It could be my new flying shirt. Besides, I reasoned, I still had my dad's dog tags.

I had other rituals for flying. As soon I sat in my seat, I had to pray. It was a general prayer asking God to protect me (Sara too, if we were flying together) through the flight and make sure I made it safely to the other end. With that out of the way, I could get situated and relax a bit. Once the cabin doors closed and the plane was pushing away from the gate, I would tell myself I had to recite, say, ten Our Fathers and ten Hail Marys before the plane took off. I would alternate between the two prayers, and put myself under such incredible pressure to get through them in time that I would often confuse them or forget passages altogether. "Our Father, who art in heaven, hallowed be Thy name. And blessed our fruit among women, and blessed is the fruit of Thy womb, Jesus." It often happened that I'd get to the fifth or sixth recitation and my mind would go blank, inexplicably forgetting what came next, and I would begin to panic.

Why? What would happen? What would happen if I did not follow through with any of these observances? What would happen if I didn't wear the dog tags, or if I wasn't able to get through twenty prayers before takeoff? Would the plane go down in a fireball of death? At the time, I didn't know if there was a God. My parents raised me Catholic, but I had long since drifted from the Church and didn't know what I believed. But if there was a God, I didn't think he was looking down from heaven watching me fuck up these prayers and deciding to kill me and the rest of the passengers. I also didn't think if the plane was destined to crash that my lame prayers would stave off that disaster. I didn't think any of that would happen, but I still had to wear those dog tags and the gray ASU T-shirt, and I still needed to get those prayers in before the plane took off. And if I finished the prayers while we were still on the tarmac, I would tell myself, "Five more times," and I would have to go through the ritual and the stress all over again until the plane was racing down the runway and lifting into the air.

The plane dropped again. It was a big one this time. My body went rigid, and I closed my eyes.

Make this end. Please, get me on the ground and make this end.

Sara squeezed my arm, leaned in close, and whispered, "We're fine. We'll be down soon." She gave me a smile, one of her sweet and tender and understanding smiles. "We'll be on the ground and switching planes in no time."

I was fine once in the air. Anticipating the flight was always worse than the flight itself. The takeoff was the worst part, even though I knew statistically the descent was more dangerous. I know it doesn't make much sense that I would be less frightened of the thing that was more treacherous, but there you go.

After takeoff, I knew as soon as I heard the double chimes, I could relax. An attendant once told me that the double chime meant the plane was approaching ten thousand feet and everything in the flight was likely okay. When I heard those chimes, and perhaps saw the attendants unbuckle themselves and prepare the cabin for the beverage and peanut service, it was a clear sign I could now relax and breathe a little easier. I could enjoy the rest of the flight, as much as was possible. Once the plane was at a cruising altitude, I could handle, more or less, with varying degree, the bumps and unrest that sometimes came with the flight.

But that day was a carnival ride.

The plane dropped again, and there was the whirling sound of hydraulics as the wings adjusted. I leaned over Sara and looked out the window, half expecting to see a little gremlin sitting on the wing.

"Seems like we've been descending for a while now, doesn't it?"

"Not really," Sara said.

"No?"

She shook her head.

"Feels that way. Like it's taking forever for this thing to get on the ground."

"We'll be down soon."

"It's just taking forever."

The bell sounded twice. I looked at the panel above us. The "Fasten Seat Belt" sign was still on. I looked around me, bending my head to peer up and down the aisle. I couldn't see any of the flight attendants. What did that bell mean? Was it a signal we were getting close? Was it alerting the attendants to a problem? What the fuck was going on?

I caught Sara looking at me. She smiled. She had such an easy and open smile. I'd repeatedly seen over the two years we had known each other how that smile could light up a room and melt a heart in that cliché, love song kind of way. She had this innate ability to make people happy, and she did it in such an offhand, natural way, as if she couldn't help it.

"What?" She puckered her lips.

I leaned in and kissed her. "I love you," I told her.

"I love you too, Benny."

The plane rocked to the side and fell again.

I blew out air and said, "You can sing me something."

"What would you like me to sing?"

"I don't care. Anything."

Sara thought a moment. The plane dropped again, and my stomach flipped back around. I squeezed her hand and smiled. I feared it looked pained, as if I were trying to hold in gas.

Static came from the speakers as the intercom was switched on. We heard a pilot's deep voice say, "It looks as though the plane coming out of our gate is running a little late."

We had been on the tarmac for a good thirty minutes. They had switched off the air and the cabin had become a hot box of stale sweat and suffocating frustration.

The pilot came on the intercom for the third time.

"They're going to find us another gate to pull in to. It should only be a few more minutes. Again, I want to apologize for the inconvenience here. We should get going soon, then we'll get everyone off the plane as soon as we can. Thank you."

"Are we going to miss this connection?" I asked, looking for any chance to jump from our argument.

"We'll be okay," Sara assured me, although she didn't sound too sure. We didn't know what gate we would pull into and how far it would be from our connecting flight.

I wasn't in the mood to listen to her reassurances, no matter how encouraging she was trying to be.

"We should have paid the money for a direct flight," I said.

"The times didn't work out."

"What does that matter if we miss this flight?"

After a pause, Sara said, "I don't want to fight with you."

"Are you sure?"

"I'm pretty sure."

"It kind of seems as if you want to have a fight."

"Yes," Sara said, unable to keep the sarcasm from her tone, "that's exactly what I want. There's nothing I want more than to be on this plane fighting with you."

I shook my head. "I'm sorry I even brought it up."

"I'm sorry I was honest with you. Lesson learned."

"I don't know what you're so angry about."

Sara's brow furrowed. "I'm not the one getting angry."

"No?"

She shook her head.

"You're not? Is that what you're saying? This isn't angry?"

"I guess it's because I'm selfish." Her sarcasm was thick now. "I'm acting selfishly."

"You know, I said that one time. One time, and you relish any moment to throw it back at me."

I needed to get off this plane. What the fuck was taking so goddamn long? I hated this airport. I've always hated this airport. I had a history with the city. When I was a teenager, my dad was out here for work. He wasn't feeling well one night. He complained he was tired and had chest pains. He ended up in the emergency room with a massive heart attack that required immediate open-heart surgery. I remember flying in with my mom thinking that my dad might already be dead. Every time Sara and I flew anywhere, for some damn reason we had to connect through this airport, and every time there was some damn issue. The planes were consistently late to arrive and late to take off. The place was a monster, and we had to walk a mile, literally a fucking mile, to the Skylink to get from one terminal to the next and make the connection.

I told Sara, "You have this great ability to take that one thing I said one time in anger, focus on it, and never let it go, and you always forget all the other nice shit I've said to you."

"The nice shit?"

"That one thing you won't let be."

"Oh, okay," Sara said, nodding in an exaggerated way.

"Wait. I don't say nice things to you? Is that what you're saying? I never say anything nice to you?"

Sara said, "The problem, really, is that I never listen to you."

"Sometimes you don't."

"Fuck you."

"Why are you picking a fight with me?"

"You're the one picking a fight with me," Sara said, pointing from me to herself.

"You're the one."

Sara blew out air, shook her head, and said, "It's you. It's just a stupid piece to the ring. It's not the ring, just a piece."

"I didn't think it was so stupid."

Sara cocked her fist. "I want to punch you so bad sometimes."

"I know you do."

"I don't know how else I can explain this to you," she said. "It's not my band. It's not my wedding ring. It's just this little piece that gets attached to the ring. It's nothing."

"It's supposed to be the wedding band."

"No, it's not."

"Yes," I insisted. "That's exactly what it is. That's the whole point."

"It's not."

"That's what it was obviously designed to be."

"I don't know why it's so important to you anyway."

"Well," I said, trying to add a self-evident "duh" tone to my voice, "the reason why it's so important, Sara, is because it's part of the wedding ring."

"You didn't even buy the ring in the first place."

That stung. What she said was true, but it was a low blow and there was an awful lot more to the story.

I adjusted my position on the seat again, pulling away from Sara. I looked to the front of the plane. Two attendants chatted it up, laughing, without an outward care or stress in the world. They were not in a rush, had no place to be, getting paid either way.

I turned my attention back to Sara.

"You know," I said, "all I did was ask why you didn't want to get the fucking thing blessed when you had told me explicitly when we bought the ring that you wanted to. That's it. We talked about it, and you told me you were going to bring the rings with you. And I was just asking about it." I held up my hands. "That's all."

Sara pursed her lips. She wanted to say something, and I knew it was killing her to hold it back, but she did. She let it go, for the moment at least. I suppose she decided it wasn't worth it.

"I hate this airport," I said, looking to change the subject to a mutually experienced annoyance. "Every time we fly through here, it's something."

Sara sat with her legs crossed staring out the small window to the wing and the tarmac. She had a long neck, and her skin was bronze from our trips to the beach and our general knocking around town. She hooked her hair behind her ear, and I could see the small heart tattoo just behind her ear. I wanted to kiss her neck, but I didn't think she'd have appreciated the gesture just then. I reached over and touched her arm instead. It was clear she would not take my hand, so I ran the back of my fingers along her arm.

"How did we get onto this in the first place?"

"The cruise," she said, in a whisper so low I had a hard time hearing her.

It was a rhetorical question. I'm not sure why I said it at all. I wasn't looking for a reminder but hoping instead it might springboard us into a reconciliation.

The intercom crackled on, and the entire plane looked ahead in one simultaneous movement with hungry anticipation. The static hissed. It was as if the pilot were drawing out the suspense as long as possible.

Finally, he said, "It looks as if they've found us a gate. We'll be heading over in a couple of minutes." There came more cracking until he added, "We should have you at the gate shortly."

He didn't mention the gate number. I was just relieved we would be moving. I checked my phone. We had twenty-five minutes to get off this plane and rush to make our connecting flight. I thought it too much to hope that our flight would be in the same terminal.

"I really don't care," Sara said.

"I know," I told her, "but I want you to care."

She turned to face me. "Not that. The cruise. I care, but I really don't care, if that makes any sense. I'll be there with you. That's the point. That's the important thing. The details don't matter so much."

I moved my arm to take her hand into mine. We interlaced our fingers.

"I'm sorry," I told her.

"I'm sorry, too."

We kissed. It was soft, gentle. I could feel the tinge of something electric on the roof of my mouth. Sara's cinnamon lip balm made my lips tingle.

"I'm sorry about the tone of my voice," I said. "I'm sorry about it all."

"It's just the stress of everything."

"It's been tough."

"And it's not just the wedding," she said. I mean, it is the wedding, but it's everything else. It's trying to plan the thing from California, dealing with my sister and my mom. Making sure your family has rooms and they're going to be taken care of. I want everything to be perfect for your mom."

I wanted to tell her, as I had told her countless times before, that she didn't have to worry about my family, especially my mom, but I knew it wouldn't help ease her anxiety.

"We're at the end, and I think we're both just a little on edge," she said.

I gave her hand a little squeeze. "But we're getting married."

Sara smiled. "Indeed we are."

"Friday, we'll be married."

"Yes."

"We're getting married!" I said with a childlike excitement in my voice.

"It's happening."

"You'll be my wife."

"You'll be my husband."

I brought her hand to my lips. I didn't pucker or kiss her hand, but pressed it to my mouth.

"This is going to be an amazing weekend. Everything's set. We're lucky that we had your mom and sister helping us out. The details, like you said, don't really matter. We should just try to enjoy it."

"I know you're right. I do. It's just hard sometimes."

"I know, but it's going to be everything we wanted it to be, what we've talked about, what we've planned. It's going to be a party, a big party for our friends and family. And it's going to be fun. I mean, really, that's what it needs to be. Fun. No stress. No bullshit. None of that. It's all planned. We've done it. We've done all the work, and now we can enjoy it." This time I kissed the back of her hand, and said, "We need to enjoy it."

Sara's gaze went from her hand to my eyes.

"You're right," she said. Then, after a moment, with added emphasis, she repeated, "You're absolutely right."

"It's going to be the best."

"The week to remember."

"We'll have fun."

"We will."

"We'll relax and enjoy it."

"I promise," she said.

"You promise?"

"I absolutely promise."

Everything took much longer than it should have. It felt that while the clocked raced at an unnatural rate, people were moving as slowly as possible, getting in our way, going out of their way to keep us from making our connection. We were in an airport, for Christ's sake; these people must have had places to go, but they carried themselves as if they had no purpose.

The plane made it to the gate. As soon as the bell rung, the entire plane stood up in unison and opened the overhead compartments to search for and bring down their bags. I was up as if ejected from my seat. I was tired of sitting in that narrow space. I needed to stretch my legs, but with everyone else up and waiting on the doors to open, the plane felt choked and claustrophobic.

I pulled my backpack from under the seat in front of me and slung it over my shoulders. We had two smaller suitcases stored above. I pulled the one directly above me down and sat it on the seat. I had to reach back across the aisle for the second one. A shorter woman dressed as if she were headed for a yoga session had to step back, pushing against the man behind her, so I could pull my bag down. She seemed put out that I was being mildly aggressive getting our luggage, but I didn't care. I didn't have time to fuck around with proper manners. We also had two Build-A-Bear boxes containing a bride and a groom that we'd made two weeks ago and planned to set up at the reception.

While it was irritating butting up against people, having to nudge them to get enough room for ourselves, I couldn't understand the people who stayed seated and waited like they were in no hurry at all to get off this plane. I felt as if I were losing air, as if it were getting harder to breathe, but that dreadful feeling would only be compounded having to continue to sit in that goddamn chair, the back of my legs sweating, feeling caught, trapped, unable to move, unable to do anything, wanting to scream, with all these people sandwiched together, hovering over me.

We were two-thirds of the way to the back of the plane, row sixteen. It could have been worse, but there were still many people ahead of us that needed to file off the plane first. It felt like an interminable time waiting for the jet bridge to make it to the plane, and for the attendants to secure it before they could even open the door. At least, that's what I assumed was happening. Packed like a sardine, I couldn't see any of it. I knew these were the steps that needed to occur for us to get off the plane, and I could only hope the employees of this airline were acting accordingly. With every tick of the clock, they confirmed my undeniable conclusion that they were not in fact trying to get us off this plane in a timely manner. They were doing everything in their power to move as slowly as possible, and having a fun little snicker at the power they had over us.

The door opened. I could see people beginning to file out. This was an excruciatingly slow process. One would think after that martini shaker of a flight, plus baking on the tarmac for a half an hour, people would have a little get up and go in getting off the plane. That sure didn't appear to be the case. There was no rush at all. These people had spent the entire flight content to be by themselves, watching movies on their computer, or playing video games, reading books or magazines or the newspaper, or doing puzzles, crosswords, word searches, or sudoku. While we waited to taxi to a gate, there were some scattered conversations, but people mostly sat in silence. It was only now as we finally waited to get off this fucking plane that people became these incessant chatterboxes. They talked about the city and whether they lived here or were just passing through. They talked about sports and the weather and made other inane, insufferable chitchat. I stood there, hunched over, watching the front of the plane. People were leaving. I could see the exit, but it didn't appear as if it would be our turn anytime soon.

What was taking so damn long?

As the other passengers slowly trickled off the plane, my asshole began to itch. It was an almost overpowering irritation, and it came out of nowhere. I couldn't do anything about it. I couldn't scratch it, or do much to ease the problem. I gritted my teeth, praying I could be let off this plane soon. The guy in front of me had spent the entire flight with this head tilted back and his mouth open in a deep sleep. He smelled sour, as if he hadn't showered in days and deodorant were still a mystery. The woman who had sat next to him had a doughy, expressionless face. Couldn't she smell him? She had to. How could she not? The poor lady had had to endure the stinky bastard for the last three hours.

Sara figured out our connecting flight was in the same terminal. That was a nice bit of luck. We would walk out of the plane at B7 and only needed to get to B37. A small hike, and we still had to hurry, but we had a little breathing room.

My asshole was on fire and I couldn't do anything to relieve it.

An older man with a thick head of wavy silver hair had to walk back two rows to get his bag. At first it looked as if people were going to stand there and watch him struggle, not assisting him in any way. Then a short man wearing a Phoenix Giants ball cap pulled low on his head pointed to a flower-print bag and asked if it was the one. The old man said yes, and the younger man grabbed it and handed it over to him.

The last few rows ahead of us were quick to get their shit and get off the plane. We went from hurry up and wait to it finally being our turn to leave. The smelly man and the doughy-faced woman eased out and headed down the aisle. Sara and I had to wait for an Indian couple who had sat the entire time to stand and remove their bags from the overhead compartment and slowly make their way down the center aisle. I followed them, trying not to push them forward too much. The two flight attendants stood at the front of the plane smiling and nodding their heads and saying their robotic goodbyes and thank yous to everyone as they exited. I smiled at them, nodded, and turned around and gave Sara a high five as we walked off the plane.

I hurried up the bridge, turning my shoulders to ease past the Indian couple. I looked back to check on Sara. She was having a difficult time pulling the same maneuver. The woman moved a half a step to the left, and Sara was not aggressive enough to push past her.

I emerged out of the bridge into the chaos of the terminal. There was a line of people waiting to board the plane we had just exited. A woman was speaking on the intercom saying flight 8814 to Denver would board just as soon as they could get the other passengers off the plane and the plane cleaned. She apologized and thanked everyone for their patience. No one in line looked grateful or appreciative. They looked done, and they looked as if they were already tired of this entire adventure. Our plane switching gates meant these people had to switch gates too. I noticed a man asking his kids, who looked to be about six or seven, to please, please, for the love of God settle down. He was on the short side, five eight or there about, and had broad, thick shoulders and ropes of muscle on his neck. He looked like he was athletic at one point but now had a stomach created by whiskey and beer and bad food. He promised his children they would be on the plane in just a couple more minutes. The kids weren't misbehaving. They were perhaps a touch unruly and loud, but they weren't doing anything too out of bounds. I made eye contact with the man, just for a second, and saw in his face a mask of forlorn resignation. His daughter, the younger of the two, screamed out and cried because the son had done something to her. The man closed his eyes, shook his head, and looked down at the carpeted floor while a woman, who I assumed was the man's wife, tried to deal with the kids.

"We're at seven?" Sara asked.

She had a black canvas bag slung over her shoulder and across her chest, and she wheeled one of our lime-green suitcases behind her.

I walked about two feet in front of her and had to turn my head to tell her that was correct.

"And we have to get to?"

"Thirty-seven."

My asshole continued to itch like hell. I could feel wetness on my boxers from the sweat. I knew by the time we made it to the next plane, my cheeks would be chafed and it would be painful to walk.

The terminal was one big C-shaped curve. It was packed with people arriving or waiting to depart, the latter sitting around, reading, pacing, embalming themselves with twelve-dollar drinks in the bar, or checking the monitors for updates.

"How much time do we have?" Sara asked. She was having a hard time keeping up with me.

"We have time."

"I really have to use the bathroom."

I turned my head toward her and asked, "Why didn't you do that on the plane?"

"They wouldn't let us out of our seats."

I could tell by her tone it annoyed her she had to explain that.

We continued to hustle, sliding in and around people who were slower or were just standing in the middle of the walkway.

I checked the time on my phone. "We're not going to be able to eat for another few hours. Maybe we should try and get some food real quick. Are you hungry?"

"I just need to use the bathroom."

"You can't wait until we get on the other plane?"

"No."

My arms ached. It wasn't that the Build-A-Bear boxes were heavy, but they were awkward to hold with one hand. I eyed a sign indicating a men's restroom and another for the women's bathroom just beyond. I made my way to the side of the terminal, stopping on the way because a man wearing a suit with a leather bag slung over his shoulder wasn't paying the slightest bit attention and almost slammed right into me.

"I'll meet you here."

Sara nodded and headed to the women's bathroom.

"You can leave that," I said, referring to the suitcase and her bag.

"That's okay."

"We need to—" I began, but Sara cut me off.

"I'll be quick," she said, disappearing into the bathroom.

I figured if I had to wait for Sara, I should try to alleviate myself of this unceasing itch that was driving me crazy. The men's bathroom was lit with banks of bright fluorescent lights that bounced off the white tile floor and shining white tile walls. I moved past the sinks and urinals to a row of stalls in the back. I winced at the overpowering smell of shit. There were seven stalls. I was hoping for a handicapped one with its added room, but it was occupied. The other six stalls were quite a bit smaller. I checked for one that was empty and entered it.

The stall wasn't big enough for my suitcase and the two Build-A-Bear boxes. I worked my way inside and got the door shut and locked. I pushed the suitcase against the door and placed one of the boxes on top. The itch was so severe I couldn't take it anymore. I set the second box down on the bathroom floor, knowing it would disgust Sara and anger her to see me do it. I couldn't help it.

I unbuckled my belt, ripped the button free, and yanked down my shorts and boxers. I sat down on the toilet seat and sprang back up. I hadn't noticed before I sat down that the lowlife motherfucker who was in there before me had sprayed piss all over the seat and hadn't bothered to wipe it. I pulled a foot of toilet paper from the roll and wiped the seat clean. I sat down and ripped more paper from the roll. I reached underneath my legs and fingered my ass with the toilet paper. The relief was instant. My face went slack and my eyes rolled up. Holy Christ, the respite from that itch was welcome. I continued to scratch the damnable itch while trying not to think about the fact I was sitting in a stranger's piss and fingering my own asshole.

I wanted to sit for a moment and take a breath. The moment was fleeting because of a loud fart and the sound of chucks being poured into the toilet in the stall next to me. A foul stench hit me, something sick and diseased. Humans are repellent in so many ways. There is nothing noble or enlightened about man. We are dumb, lumbering animals whose sole purpose for existence is to eat, shit, and fuck.

I pulled up my boxers and shorts and buckled myself back up. I had to maneuver the Build-A-Bear boxes and suitcase so I could squeeze past and get the door open. I made my way to the sink. It was one with a motion sensor. I filled my hand with a foamy soap and waved it under the square black sensor under the faucet. Nothing happened. I did it again. Nothing. I tried again and again with the same result. If there was a trick to this thing, I wasn't figuring it out. I waved my hand across the sensor again. Still nothing. I tried various distances and angles to the sensor. It would not turn on. There were men on either side of me washing their hands with no problem at all. Was this sink broken, or was I simply a moron? I was about to move to another sink when the water came on as if by magic.

As I washed my hands, I realized I needed to pee. It wasn't bad. I could hold it—although I hated that feeling of needing to use the bathroom—but I figured I might as well do it now. I dried my hands and rolled the suitcase and the two bear boxes back to the rows of urinals. I unbuckled myself and worked my dick out of my boxers. I stood there, ready to urinate, but nothing happened. I had to go. I could feel it, but nothing was coming out. I didn't have time for this. We really needed to get going. Our plane would board soon. They might have started the process already.

I stood there a moment longer, closing my eyes, tightening my ass, trying to force the urine out. I could almost feel it working its way out of my bladder and into the urethra, but it was slow, like the mercury gradually rising in a thermometer. I closed my eyes and held my breath and tried to push it out. It was almost there, but I had to be careful. If I pushed too hard, I ran the risk of shitting my pants. It had happened before, and I sure as hell didn't have time to deal with that kind of situation now. I took a quick inhalation of breath and then pushed again. My face scrunched up, and I pushed as hard as I could. It was almost there. I could feel it. Just a little bit more, just a little bit harder. Urine trickled out of my penis and my shoulders slumped. Thank God.

I shook it off and put it back inside my boxers, still dribbling a little urine onto my hands. It happened every single time no matter how much I shook it. I dragged all my shit back to the sink. I pumped the foam soap into my cupped hand, then waved it under the faucet. Nothing happened.

I came out of the bathroom expecting to see Sara waiting for me. I didn't see her right away. I scanned the area. I couldn't see her and assumed she was still in the bathroom. This wasn't a surprise. It was too much to hope she would finish before me. Sara promised she would be quick, but bathrooms and speed were not something I associated with Sara. She always had issues with public restrooms. I'm not sure what it was all about. I know she had a particular hang-up with using the bathroom when someone could hear what she was doing. Whatever her issues, it typically took her much longer to take care of whatever she needed to take care of in there.

I worked my way across the terminal to the other side. I checked the bank of monitors suspended from the ceiling. They listed flight 2232 as on time. I checked my phone. We needed to get going.

I turned toward the women's bathroom and scanned the area again for Sara. I didn't see her. Here we go, I thought. In the three years we had known each other, how long had I waited for her to use a bathroom? Hours. At least a few hours. What would that time add up to after a lifetime together?

I heard shouting and turned my head. At the check-in counter nearest me, a fortyish man wearing a rumpled off-the-rack suit, face red, jaw tight, shook his head like an infant refusing to eat their carrots.

"No! No, no, no, no, no!"

A petite attendant with long auburn hair pulled back into a tight ponytail stood behind the counter looking at the man with as much patience as she could muster.

"You fail to understand what I'm saying," the man said.

"I understand you, sir," the attendant responded.

"No, no," the man insisted. "You nod your head. Yes. Yes. But no. Obviously not. Clearly, you don't understand. I need to be in Phoenix. That's the bottom line."

"I realize that, sir."

"Oh, do you now?" He could not mask the contempt in his voice.

"Yes, I do," she assured him. "The plane from Chicago was late due to weather, and—"

He cut her off there.

"Listen to me. I need you to listen to me and not just nod your head like a goddamn doll. Get me to Sacramento. Okay? All right? I don't care how you do it, but do it. Get me to Sacramento."

I turned back to the bathrooms. I didn't see Sara. How long had she been in there? My shenanigans in the bathroom must have taken five minutes, at least that long, and I'd been standing outside for another minute or two. We didn't have time for this.

A passenger cart carrying an older couple and their baggage tried to make its way through the river of people oblivious to it. It was a slow process, and the driver kept tapping an electronic horn, trying to split the sea, but the indifference made it difficult. Could we get a cart like that to get us to our gate? Would that be faster? Did you have to be old to get the service?

I sighed and blew out a long stream of air. I told myself to calm down. It was okay. We had time. We could make the plane. Sara would come out any moment now.

Two men dressed in full class-A army uniforms walked past me. They had various colored ribbons on their chests and patches on their arms. They stood ramrod straight, arms to their sides, and spoke in low tones as they walked. A tall, beefy man wearing a black button-down shirt filled with tiny Tabasco bottles broke away from a woman and two younger men, all about midtwenties, and walked over to the two soldiers. He stopped them and held out his hand and was saying something I presumed to be admiration as he shook their hands. The soldiers nodded, and the three talked a few moments longer before the man let them leave. I wondered how much of that man coming over was to thank those two soldiers and how much of it was to have people see him walk over there and shake their hands. My guess was a little of both.

It was a shitty thought to have.

I rubbed my temples with my fingers, then ran my fingers through my hair. I had a headache. I wondered if Sara had any ibuprofen with her. I needed to get a haircut before the wedding. When would I have time for that? I should have had it done before we left. I felt as if I needed to pee again. That was ridiculous. I barely had to go the last time. I couldn't have squeezed out any more drops with a gun to my head, but that fact didn't ease that feeling of needing to piss. I thought I could run back to the men's bathroom, try to pee, and be back before Sara made it out of the bathroom. Why was it taking her so long? It was getting ridiculous. Couldn't she recognize we were pressed for time and at least attempt to hurry?

Every time Sara and I had traveled through this airport, it was always incredibly busy with a deluge of people in a rush to wait. Where were these people coming from? Where were they going? What were their stories? What had led them to this point, to be in this airport at this time? There was always a wide variety of people, all unique yet with a certain sameness.

I checked the time on my phone again. As we'd waited to get off the plane, it had felt as if time had slowed. Now it felt as if time rushed by. It was an uncontrollable train heading for a dead end.

There was a high-pitched scream, loud enough to rise above the clamor of the terminal. I turned and saw a little girl no older than four, with a head of braids with tiny red, white, and blue beads on the end, shrieking that she did not need to use the bathroom. Her mother—at least, I assumed she was her mother—walked behind her and calmly insisted that the girl would need to use the potty before getting on the plane. The little girl wasn't having it, stomping her feet and turning her head up and wailing, tears streaking her face as she told her mom she already went potty and didn't need to go.

Two Hispanic men dressed in black pants and black collared shirts with white aprons tied around their waists tried in vain to a push a cart loaded with three kegs of beer through the crowd. They were patient, inching forward, not minding that it was taking so long.

I checked the time again. The digital display had not changed. How was that possible? Surely a minute had passed since I'd last checked.

I saw an older man walking bent over, as if searching for something he had lost on the ground. That had to be a bitch having a back so pained you had to hunch over like an over-the-top caricature of an old man. My dad injured his back when he was in his early twenties in an accident at work, and I knew from watching him struggle with constant pain and trips to the chiropractor to get realigned—only to sneeze and throw himself out again—that once hurt, an injured back never truly heals. It sticks with you until the end.

This was getting out of hand. There was no way it should take someone this goddamn long to use the bathroom. What was I going to do? There were too many people in this airport. It was insanity. It's no wonder why flights were always late coming in and out of here. It had to be damn near impossible to run this place with any efficiency.

How the fuck could she still be in that bathroom?

I looked around, searching for someone to assist me or at least give me some advice. I was surrounded by a mass of people utterly indifferent to my situation and my amped-up anxiety. I picked up the bears, grabbed the handle of the suitcase, and made my way back across the terminal. I steered through the crowd, hoping Sara would walk out of the bathroom looking for me. I had to thread myself between a field hockey team laughing and horsing around near the bathroom. I nodded and grimaced a lipless, pained smile as I pushed through.

I stood at the entrance to the women's bathroom. What now? I looked around again, lost, not knowing what I should do next. Women pushed past me, rushing in and out of the bathroom.

I walked across the entrance, turning to look back into the bathroom in a casual, nonchalant way, hoping I wasn't bringing attention to myself. I could hear voices coming from inside. I could hear water running and a dryer turning on and off.

A tall woman with frizzy hair done in a style twenty years old walked out of the bathroom wiping her still-damp hands on her pants. I averted my eyes as she passed before I looked back into the entrance. I leaned in and took a step forward. A woman in her fifties walked turned the corner and headed out of the bathroom. I wasn't able to react in time. I turned a little too late, and I thought it looked fairly obvious that I was hovering around this entrance like a pervert. If the woman noticed, however, she gave no sign as she walked by me.

I faced out toward the terminal. I felt nervous that someone was watching me. I knew I must look as if I were up to something.

I turned my shoulders sideways and glanced back into the bathroom. It sounded as if someone was laughing inside. Two more women walking one right after the other came out of the entrance.

What could Sara possibly be doing in there?

A small woman in her fifties with a full head of lacquered silver hair walked toward me. I gave her a smile, which she didn't see, and as she was about to go past me into the bathroom, I turned and said, "Excuse me?"

She didn't hear me, so I took a step forward and touched her shoulder. It startled her. She twisted around and looked up at me with wide eyes and an open mouth.

"I'm sorry. I didn't mean to scare you."

"You just caught me by surprise."

"I'm sorry," I said again. "I'm wondering if you can help me."

Her posture changed. She was guarded with suspicion.

"My wife has been in there"—I nodded to the bathroom—"for a while, and we're about to miss our plane if we don't get going."

The woman looked relieved. I'm not sure what she'd expected me to say.

She knew where I was going with this. "What does she look like?"

"She's, um, she's about five seven or so. Blondish hair. Dirty blonde. Kind of long, about to her shoulders. She's wearing blue pants. Navy-blue pants, and this red kind of tank top thing."

What was a tank top kind of thing? That made little sense. It was a tank top, simple and easy.

"I can tell her you're waiting."

"Thank you. Thank you so much. Her name is Sara. I really appreciate it."

"Of course," the woman said with a smile. "It's no problem."

She turned the corner and disappeared into the bathroom. I felt relief. I should have thought of asking someone to help me earlier.

I realized that I had referred to Sara as my wife. I don't know why I did it. It just came out naturally. I liked the way it sounded. Besides, in another few days she would be my wife. I hadn't quite wrapped my mind around the idea we'd be married soon. It didn't seem real, as if this entire time Sara and I had been performing in a skit about two people getting married.

"I don't think she's in there."

I turned and faced the small woman. At first, I didn't know if I'd heard her correctly, as if she were speaking a language that sounded like English but was something altogether different.

"What do you mean?"

The woman shook her head and said, "She's not in the bathroom."

"She's not in there?"

"I don't think so. There's no one in there wearing blue pants and a red shirt. I even called her name."

"You called out for Sara?

The woman nodded. "Yes. There was nothing."

"You called out?" I asked, and the woman's nose scrunched up at the question.

"I said there was a husband out here looking for his wife."

She's not in the bathroom. I considered that a moment. How could that be? It was impossible. How could she not be in there?

"I don't know," the woman said, and I realized I had asked that out loud. "I'm sorry."

The woman stood there looking up at me as if waiting for something. I looked away, trying to absorb this information and decide what it meant. The woman gave a slight shrug and then turned and headed back into the bathroom to handle her own business.

I looked out into the terminal. I half expected to see Sara standing in the crowd of other passengers. I had missed her coming out, and she was waiting and searching for me.

I didn't see her, though. I didn't see her anywhere.

"She's not in the bathroom." I kept saying it to myself over and over again. If she wasn't in the bathroom, then where the fuck was she? No. It didn't make sense. She had to be in there. I had been watching the bathroom with a vigilant eye. There's no possible way she could have walked out of it without me seeing her.

I took a step into the bathroom. I hesitated a moment. There was a brief flicker of doubt, but I took another step so I stood in the entryway but not far enough to see into the bathroom.

I leaned forward and called out, "Sara? Sara, we need to get going. We're going to miss our plane."

A short woman came around the corner and almost smacked right into me. She let out a high-pitched yelp of surprise and moved around me.

"Sara! Sara!"

I looked at my suitcase and the two Build-A-Bear boxes shaped like cottages for the bride and groom. I noticed a man in his late sixties walking by. He had pale legs, almost chalk white, with dark-purple veins etched into them. He wore a highlighter-pink T-shirt with "Life is the Question, Jesus is the Answer" written on it in black bubble lettering.

I walked past the entryway, around the wall, and into the bathroom itself.

There were two women at the sinks washing their hands, oblivious to me standing there. A toilet flushed in one stall and another stall door opened and a middle-aged woman still buckling her belt stepped out. When she saw me she screamed out, her body jerking her backward as if from an electric jolt.

The scream startled the women at the sink. Their attention went from the woman to me. They stood there, staring.

"Sara. Sweetheart, I'm sorry. We need to go."

"Who are you looking for?" one of the women at the sink asked.

"My wife," I said without looking at her, and then called out again, "Sara! Come on."

"I told you she wasn't in here."

The voice came from a stall. I could see pants and underwear bunched up by a pair of feet.

A woman walked into the bathroom and then did a silent-comedy double take, thinking she had walked into the wrong bathroom.

"It doesn't look as if your wife is in here," said a woman at the sink. I didn't know if this was the same woman as before or the other one. "You need to leave," she said, a little more stern. "She's not here. Will you please leave?"

I stood with what must have been a lost-little-boy look on my face.

"I'm sorry," I finally said. I then bowed my head and apologized again. I turned and walked out of the bathroom. I went back to the suitcase and the bears. If Sara wasn't in the bathroom, I must have missed her. She had be to out here somewhere.

I stood a little taller, cocking my head up, eyes darting around the terminal. She had to be here. I searched for red, anything red, scanning the surrounding area. My stomach was in knots, and I could feel my heart pounding in my chest.

Where was she?

I picked up the bears, grabbed the handle to my suitcase, and drifted out into the terminal. I spotted a couple kissing, looking as if they were trying to swallow each other.

She wasn't here. It was as simple as that. I knew I hadn't missed her. Sara was a hard woman to miss. She would stand out in this sea of mundanity.

I had suggested getting something to eat. Maybe she was at the food court. That was possible. She came out of the bathroom, somehow we didn't see each other, and she went to the food court thinking I might be there.

It didn't make complete sense. I still didn't think we could have missed each other, but okay, something had happened. I wasn't going to find her where I stood now.

I headed up the terminal, walking as fast as I could with my small suitcase and the two Build-A-Bears as anchors. I wanted to go faster and tried picking up the suitcase and walking with it. Instead of helping, this made my progress more cumbersome, and I had to go back to wheeling the case behind me. I stepped onto the moving walkway and sidled past the people walking at a slower pace, or the ones who stood to the right and simply rode the conveyer belt. I walked so fast that when the walkway ended, despite the constant warning from the electronic female voice coming from tiny speakers along the ceiling telling me to use caution, I still wasn't prepared for the sudden halt of movement, and I stumbled and damn near fell on my face.

I made it to the food court and frantically searched for Sara. Restaurants lined a back wall. There was a Burger King, an Arby's, a Cinnabon, and places selling wood-fired pizza, BBQ, chicken and waffles, sushi and ramen, and deli sandwiches and salads. Every restaurant had a line and a handful of people waiting for someone to call their order number. There was a common dining area packed with people eating and others holding trays of food, searching for a table to sit.

I made my way through the eating area to the restaurants. I had to push past unattended luggage and people bunched up in the small alley between the food counters and the dining tables. When I got to the other end, I walked around the outer edge of the eating area, hoping that I would spot Sara in her red tank top sitting at a table.

I couldn't find her anywhere. I looked back to the restaurants, didn't see her, then swept the area peripheral to the food court.

She wasn't here. I considered walking the line of restaurants again but didn't think I had time to do it.

I dialed Sara's number. I don't know why this didn't occur to me earlier. The call went straight to voice mail. It didn't ring once.

"Hello, this is Sara. I apologize for being away. Please leave your name and number, and I'll get back to you as soon as I can. Take care, and have a wonderful day."

A long beep followed the message.

"Hey, it's Ben. I'm in the food court area looking for you. Where are you?"

Going right to voice mail more than likely meant her phone was off or its battery was dead. Why would it be off? Had she turned it off before we made our way through security back in California? I couldn't remember. I'm sure she would have turned it back on. Maybe the battery was dead. It didn't matter.

I sent a text message: *Hey, where are you?*

The ache in my head had evolved to a dull but persistent pounding. I could feel my heart beating in my temples. I wanted to scream.

This wasn't helping. I took a deep breath, letting air come into my nose and slowly fill my lungs. I held it a moment, then exhaled in one long breath.

I needed to calm down and think about this a second. Sara wasn't in the bathroom or the area around the bathroom. She wasn't at the food court. The only other place she could be was the gate. That had to be it.

I checked the time again and sent another text message: *I'm heading for the gate.*

I rushed through the terminal at a pace between a fast walk and a jog, the green suitcase bouncing and tipping over. I struggled to deal with it, all the while continuing to look for Sara.

My headache continued to buzz, and my legs cramped. I could feel a tinge of something in my chest. I had become lazy about exercising ever since we'd moved to California. I was painfully out of shape. It's insane, really, that I spent so much time in the gym before, lifting weights and running like a hamster on the treadmill, hoping to look halfway attractive to someone from the opposite sex, and now that I was in a relationship, complacency had set in and working out had become less of a priority. I suppose that happens until the relationship ends and it's time to get back into shape again.

I made it to gate 39 and was relieved to see a small group of people gathered there with their carry-on bags, staring at a young black attendant dressed in the airline's uniform and standing behind a small podium near the entrance to the Jetway. There were more people loitering in the seating area with their bags at their feet.

I slowed down, although I kept on panting, and walked the rest of the way. I searched the area for Sara but didn't see her.

The attendant picked up a phone, punched a couple of buttons, and held the handset upside down as she spoke into the receiver.

"At this time, we're beginning general boarding. For safety purposes, we'd like to begin with the back of the plane. We invite those of you sitting in rows 21 and higher to please come forward. Rows 21 and higher, please."

I realized Sara had our boarding passes. I couldn't remember for sure, but I thought our seats were in row 24. Not that it mattered now.

Thankfully the inefficiency of the airline and this airport delayed this plane too.

The passengers crowded the attendant like a choked river, waiting to hand her their boarding passes. I walked around the gate area. I kept expecting to see Sara. She should be here. She should be in a panic searching for me. Now that I knew the flight staff had just begun the boarding process, I could relax a little. We wouldn't miss the plane. I wasn't mad or annoyed that Sara had taken off instead of waiting for me at the bathroom. I just wanted to find her and get to our seats.

I walked down to gate 38, and then up to 40, but didn't see her there either.

My headache was back with a vengeance, washing in like a poisonous tide. I took out my phone and dialed her again. The call went straight to voice mail.

"Sweetheart, where are you? The plane is boarding. I'm here at the gate."

I followed the call with another text.

I didn't know what to do. I had to wait. That was pretty much it. I was still working on the assumption we had somehow missed each other at the bathroom. Sara had to be looking for me too. I could rush back to the food court to look for her. I could even rush back to the bathrooms, but it would be more prudent to wait here. I had confidence Sara would come bopping along any moment now.

It felt as if someone was pounding on my head with a small, persistent hammer. She should be walking up the terminal. I should be able to see her, but all I saw was an endless sea of heads floating like aimless balloons, and no Sara.

I could envision her running toward me, out of breath, saying over and over again how sorry she was and telling me what had happened and how we'd missed each other. I wouldn't be angry. I wouldn't be upset. I would hug her and give her a kiss on the temple and tell her I was getting worried, and that I was happy we had finally found one another. We would kiss again, then we would walk to the gate. We might even hold hands. We would give our boarding passes to the attendant. There would be a loud beep as she scanned the passes, and she would tell us to have a good flight, and we would head down the Jetway and step aboard the plane that would get us to our wedding.

"We would now like to board rows 14 to 34. Rows 14 to 34 only, please."

People had already gathered around the gate, waiting for this announcement. They formed something resembling a line, and the attendant scanned their passes and welcomed them aboard.

I continued to look but did not see Sara anywhere. I kept checking my phone. There were no responses to my text messages. I began to think we might miss the plane. My knee-jerk reaction was anger. It annoyed me that there was a possibility we could be stuck in this airport. That quickly dissipated, however. I cared less about the plane than I did about finding Sara. I did not understand how we had missed each other, and I couldn't understand how we hadn't been able to reconnect. We'd lost each other. That was an obvious enough fact. We couldn't go back and figure out how it had happened and maybe have a do-over. But how were we not able to find the other again? The terminal was big and extremely busy, but we were both headed to the same destination and there were only a handful of places either of us could be between the bathroom and the gate. How had we not seen one another? I worried something might be wrong. Sara was a whip-smart, capable person, and what was happening right now made little sense at all. I knew no other way to describe it.

I watched the line of passengers hand in their passes and then disappear down the ramp. That was when I noticed the white paging phone. I walked to it and picked up the receiver. There was a click followed by white noise. Not a second later, I heard another click, and the line rang once.

A man answered. "Airport Services, how may I help you?"

I told him, "I need to have someone paged."

The attendant stood by herself behind the podium. The gate was empty. There were a few idlers, people early for the next flight, hanging around.

"Sir, no one is answering," the man from Airport Services said. "Would you like to continue to hold?"

"Yes, please," I said. "Would you mind paging her again?"

"Yes, sir."

There was a click, and they put me back on hold to the Muzak version of "I Won't Back Down."

The attendant picked up the phone at her podium, again turned it upside down, and said, "This will be the final boarding call for flight 2232."

I pinched the bridge of my nose with my thumb and forefinger.

"Would Sara Turner please pick up a white paging phone?" The page came over the intercom. "Sara Turner, please pick up a white paging phone."

I leaned against the wall and watched as the tall, thin ebony-skinned attendant closed the door to the bridge.

We would miss our flight.

I sent yet another text.

I picked up the Build-A-Bear boxes, grabbed the handle to the suitcase, and walked across the terminal, past the attendant's desk where they were shuffling paperwork and laughing about some inside joke, and on to a large window that looked out onto the tarmac. They'd probably closed the door and locked it for the flight by now. I looked through the large pane of glass and saw the plane I should have been on, its light pouring through the small porthole windows. I could see people on the plane sitting, talking, putting their luggage away. Our assigned seats were somewhere near the wing, but I didn't know what side of the plane they were on. I caught my image in the window. My reflection looked like a faded Polaroid. I looked tired. The recessed fluorescent lights gave my eyes a sunken, blacked-out look, like two hollowed-out caves. I thought again that I needed to get a haircut before the wedding—I couldn't get married looking like this. I stood there watching as a small tractor-looking thing pushed the 737 back. Once it was away from the gate, the handler disconnected the tractor and removed the bypass pin. He then stepped back and held up the pin for the pilots, who signaled they saw it. The handler got back into the tractor and scurried away. The plane sat looking like a giant prehistoric bird resting on the ground. Was there someone sitting in our seats? Had anyone on the plane realized that there were two empty spaces, an aisle and a middle seat, and moved to them to make the flight more comfortable?

The plane taxied forward on the tarmac. I stood and watched as it rolled away and vanished behind the other gates.

That was it.

I had a thought perhaps the plane would go down. Maybe this would be one of those stories, like Waylon Jennings giving up his seat on the plane to J. P. Richardson, "the Big Bopper," on that fateful night near Clear Lake, Iowa. Perhaps us missing this plane was a fortuitous bit of luck. It was a terrible thought.

I did not know what my next step should be. Sara had answered none of the pages. Where was she? What in the hell was going on? I could accept missing the plane. That was easy enough. There wasn't a damn thing I could do about it now, and there would be other flights, for sure. One way or another, we would get back. If I was being honest, I wasn't in much of a hurry to arrive anyway, but I didn't want to spend my time trapped in this goddamn airport either. I didn't want our trip delayed this way.

I turned away from the window and drifted through the rows of seats around the gate back to the terminal. I noticed a tall, broad-shouldered woman with a severe chin and the forearms and hands of a meat cutter. I did a double take, not knowing if it was a woman or man coming toward me.

I walked back down the terminal against a wave of passengers heading the other way. I searched the food court area again and then walked back to the bathrooms.

There was something wrong. There was something clearly wrong. Something must have happened. It was the only explanation. Something had happened to Sara. But what? And what should I do now?

I called her cell phone again. I was just going through the motions, but it couldn't hurt to try. It went to voicemail. It was strange that she hadn't tried to call me.

Yes, there would be other planes. I didn't care about that anymore. I wanted to find Sara. I wanted to see her smile, feel her embrace, smell that sweet scent that was her, and know she was all right. She had to be all right. I didn't know where she was or what was going on, but I was sure Sara was okay. She wasn't hurt, lying somewhere, in a ditch or a dumpster or who knew where, perhaps unconscious, bleeding, needing me, needing her fiancé—her love, the man to whom she was about to pledge the rest of her life—to help her.

It was easy to jump to the most extreme possibility.

I shook my dark thoughts away. Things weren't as dramatic as that. Not yet. I didn't think we were at that stage, and I didn't need my imagination running wild.

I sent another text message letting her know I would be sitting in the food court.

I wasn't hungry, but I'd skipped breakfast and I didn't know what I was going to do next, so I walked back to the food court to get something to eat. I decided on Grandma Moore's Chicken and Waffles. I ordered the Grandma Moore's special: two southern-fried breasts, two waffles, two eggs (which I ordered over easy on a separate plate), and a small bowl of grits. The chicken was good, tender and almost bursting with juice, and the waffles were tasty. There was a hint of something I couldn't quite place. It was either vanilla or almond. I picked away at the chicken, and cut the waffles into large sections that I slathered with generous amounts of butter, real butter, and loads of syrup, which the waffles soaked up like a delicious sponge. For someone who wasn't hungry, I ate almost everything. I kept the phone on the table in case Sara called or responded to a text. She should have called. Maybe her phone had died. That was the only explanation that made any sense. I couldn't imagine she was out there looking for me and hadn't thought to turn the phone on. Maybe she had lost the phone. Maybe she was in a situation where she couldn't get to it. What kind of situation would that be? If I thought about it too long, it would paralyze me with dread.

I was full, but I still had a second breast left, along with a bowl of grits that had congealed into snot. I didn't want to get a box for the chicken—I wasn't about to carry a box of leftovers around the airport—but it would be a shame to throw it away.

I felt tethered to something, trapped. I needed to take some kind of action, but I didn't know what that should be. I kept hoping that I would see Sara wandering through the terminal, dragging our other small green suitcase behind her, with her black satchel slung across her chest. I kept telling myself I would give it a minute, just another minute, maybe two, and then I would get up and do something.

I began picking at the second piece of chicken, first peeling the skin from the meat and setting it aside. I'd already eaten the skin from the first breast, and I thought it would be too unhealthy to indulge in the skin from the second. I pulled the flesh from the bone and ripped it into smaller pieces and ate them. It was no longer hot, but it still tasted good.

Please, let her walk by. Please. Please. Please, let her walk by.

We could get another flight without too much hassle. We might have to pay a fee. Hell, we probably would have to pay a fee. The airline might act empathetic, but they wouldn't hesitate to take advantage of our mistake. That was fine. If there wasn't a flight or a way we could connect to a flight that would get us back tonight, we could always stay the night. That was okay, too. We could make a night of it, find a nice place for dinner, a local spot with good reviews, maybe some music and drinks. We could turn this into an unexpected adventure. We could handle it. We would make it work.

I finished the second breast and then ate the skin.

I checked the time.

I would give it a minute. Another minute. Just a minute. One more. One more.

I sat in a plastic chair that made my lower back ache. I stared at a picture on the desk. It showed the man in charge of airport operations who had just introduced himself and whose name I had already forgotten—Patrick or Rick or Ricky, something like that—with a woman who had a perfectly coiffed helmet of blonde hair. They sat in a field of thick green grass holding a child of about two with thick ringlets of spun-gold hair and eyes the color of the Caribbean Sea. With the hair, the kid looked like a girl, but the blue outfit embroidered with a cute smiling whale spouting a fountain of water from its blowhole signified it was a boy. They all had bright smiles, and the parents had impossibly white teeth. They looked happy, unbearably happy, the kind of happy that was annoying and made you hate them and their stupid, perfect fucking lives.

"Okay, then," the man in the picture said as he came around the corner and sat behind the desk. He wore black slacks and a white button-down shirt that was a touch too small for him, stretched tight across his stomach and budding breasts. He reached into his desk and pulled out a yellow legal pad. He took a pen from a ceramic bowl that held a variety of pens, tried writing something, found the pen out of ink, scratched vigorously on the pad just to make sure, then tried another.

"I apologize. It was Sara, right?"

I looked at him a moment, then opened my mouth to speak and found I had no voice. I swallowed and tried again. "It's Sara."

"Last name Peterson?"

"No. Turner."

The man nodded and wrote it down. He leaned back as if inspecting the name, made a sound kind of like a "Huh, imagine that," and looked across the desk.

"You live in California?"

"Yes. We live in Orange."

"Near Anaheim, right?"

I nodded.

"Disneyland," the man said.

"Yes."

"What's the address?"

"725 Indian Hill Boulevard."

"How tall is Sara?"

I looked at my hands, laced in front of me, and took a breath. "I'd say five sevenish."

"Weight?"

I considered this a moment. "I'm not sure."

The man looked at me. "You don't know how much your wife weighs?"

"Is that common information to know?"

"I guess not," the man said, then laughed. "Truth is, I probably couldn't tell you how much my wife weighs either. They like to keep that a guarded secret. What would you guess, though?"

"One twenty. Maybe."

He nodded and noted it.

"Kyle," the woman from the adjacent cube called out.

"Yes, ma'am," the man said.

Kyle? That wasn't anywhere close to Patrick.

The voice said, "We're getting more complaints about the connectivity issues with the Wi-Fi."

"We have to call Chris and get that guy to come back out here. There's not much more we can do in the office, and whatever they did didn't do the trick."

Kyle eyed me with a slight smile and a "What can you do?" expression. He then sighed, looked at his notepad, and asked, "Was your wife ill at all?"

"Ill?"

"Sick."

"What do you mean?"

"Cold. Flu. Anything."

"No."

"She has a cell phone?"

"Yes."

"I guess you've tried to call her."

"Of course."

"Texted?"

"Yes."

"But she's not answering either?"

I couldn't tell if that was a question he expected an answer to.

"Was she taking any medications?"

"Yes," I said. I couldn't think of what they were. I kept looking at my hands as if this were a quiz and the answers were written on my palms. "She took something for anxiety."

"What kind of anxiety?"

I shrugged and said, "I don't know. The general kind."

"What did she take for that?"

"Like the specific name?"

"Yes."

"I don't know."

Kyle nodded and jotted that down. "Is that it?" he asked.

"Just general, over-the-counter type stuff. For allergies, mostly."

"And nothing like this has ever happened before?"

"Has she ever disappeared before?" I couldn't help but laugh at that. "No, she hasn't disappeared before."

"Okay," he said, making a few more notes. I tried to read the scribbling upside down, but his handwriting looked more like it was in Arabic than English. "Well, I'll get this information out to the guys around the terminals. I'll tell you one thing, if she's still here, if she's still in the airport, we'll find her. We'll also be looking at the cameras."

The Skylink tram emerged from the cement tunnel into the sunlight. I had to squint and turn my head until my eyes got used to the extreme brightness. The tram connected the terminals, and I was riding it to get a change of scenery. I needed something different to occupy my time. Two parents sat across from me trying to settle their three kids, a boy and two younger girls. The kids were bursting with excitement and energy for their trip to Disney World. The kids went back and forth on what rides they wanted to ride and how many times they wanted to ride them and in what order they would ride them.

Sara had booked our honeymoon as part of a timeshare presentation package. If we toured a facility and listened to the pitch about purchasing a timeshare that there was no possible way we could afford, we received two nights in Orlando with tickets to either Disney World or Universal Studios, along with a couple of nights in a hotel on the beach in Hollywood, Florida, and a two-day cruise to the Bahamas. Since our brief stint living in Orange County, Sara and I had been to both Disneyland and Universal Studios. Our initial plan was to bail on both the Florida parks. Why bother since we have our own version practically in our backyards? But there was something about the unabashed enthusiasm emanating from these kids that had me reconsidering. Maybe we had dismissed the idea too quickly. I made a note to bring it up with Sara and see what she thought.

I needed to call Sara's sister, Michelle. I had put it off, still hopeful Sara would turn up, or some beatific intervention would occur, making it unnecessary. Michelle was set to pick us up and lived about an hour from the airport in a small town on the west side of the state. I checked the time. She had probably left the house by now.

I scrolled through my contacts list. I didn't have Michelle's number. Shit. I thought Sara had put it in my phone for me. I looked for Sara's mother's number. I didn't have that either. Or her cousin's number. Or any of her family's. Dammit. I didn't have anyone's damn number.

I considered this a moment. Would my mom have Sara's mother's phone number? She probably had her address for her yearly Christmas card, but I didn't know about the phone number. I didn't want to call my mom. I didn't want to get into why I needed it. But did I really have to tell her? I could probably come up with some excuse, but I didn't want to. I wanted to exhaust any other options I had before I got my mom involved.

I dialed the number for information and hit "Send."

There was a moment of dead air, then an electronic-sounding female voice said, "CalLink Wireless, 411 search, connecting you to anywhere in the United States." There was a pause, the phone rang twice, and a woman, a live woman, said, "What city, please?"

"St. Catherine."

I could hear the woman typing.

"Michelle Turner," I said.

"I have the number. Would you like it?"

I realized I had nothing to write it down with, and there was a really good chance I wouldn't be able to remember the entire number.

"Are you able to just connect me?"

"Absolutely. Thank you for using CalLink."

There was a click and then silence.

I bit my lower lip. What was I going to tell Michelle? The truth, I suppose—what else was there? But how would I tell her? Was there a way to tell her what was going on without panicking her? Why shouldn't she panic? Why wasn't I more panicked?

The phone rang: once, twice, three times. I thought Michelle wouldn't answer, and I didn't know if I should leave a voice mail or not. If I did, what should I say?

On the fifth ring, the phone picked up and a female voice said, "Hello?"

As soon as I heard the voice, I knew I had made a mistake. The woman's voice wasn't Michelle. I knew that much. But why should it be? Michelle was married. Her last name wasn't Turner.

I hung up on the woman, cursed myself, and dialed information again.

That was probably a cousin, or someone married to a cousin of Sara. I had a vague memory of a squat woman named Michelle that Sara had introduced me to at some point. One could hardly turn around in that town without running into someone Sara was related to, and it was impossible to remember everyone.

"What city and state, please?" This time it was a male voice.

I froze, realizing I couldn't remember Michelle's last name, and hung up.

Fuck.

It was something Italian. The man she'd married was decidedly not Italian in any way, but his last name sounded Italian. It started with an *M*. I knew that. It had something to do with a cookie. What was it?

Maybe it was Bonaparte. Was it Bonaparte? No. Bonaparte is French, like Napoleon, but it was something like that.

Why couldn't I remember this?

I'd heard the name about a thousand times in the last year and a half. It was a cookie. It was one my favorite cookies. They were delicious. I loved to put them in the freezer. I could never eat just one or two. If I opened the bag, I was pretty much committing to eating the entire thing. What was it? A cookie. The name of a goddamn cookie.

I dialed information again. The town had fifteen hundred people—how many residents were named Michelle and had a last name that began with *M* and was the same name as a cookie?

"What city and state, please?"

"St. Catherine."

"Okay."

"Yes, I'm looking for a Michelle. I'm not one hundred percent sure of the last name, but I know it begins with an *M*, and it might sound like a cookie. Or it might be the same as a type of cookie."

I winced at how stupid I sounded.

There was silence on the other end. I could hear the buzz of a call center in the background.

"I don't have a listing that matches that."

"You sure? Nothing close?"

"No, sir."

"No Michelle with a last name that begins with the letter *M*?"

"No, sir."

I wanted to ask if he was sure but decided against it. What was the point? I tried to think. Did Michelle not live in St. Catherine?

"You're searching for St. Catherine, correct?"

"Yes, sir. That is correct."

"Are you able to search surrounding areas?"

More typing.

"I have a Michelle Milano."

"Yes!" I almost shouted. "That's it."

"Would you like the number?"

"Could you connect me, please?"

"Thank you for using CalLink."

A click, silence, then the phone rang.

Again, one ring, two, three, four, five.

The line picked up and a young male voice said, "Hello?"

"Hey, is this Matthew or Jeffrey?"

"Matthew."

"Matthew, this is Ben." Silence. "Your aunt Sara's fiancé."

"Uh-huh," Matthew said. There wasn't a hint of recognition in his voice.

"Is your mom home?"

"No, she left."

"She left for the airport?"

"I don't know."

"She didn't say?"

"I wasn't here when she left."

"Your mom has a cell phone, right?"

"Yeah."

"Do you know the number?"

"Yeah."

I waited for an answer, but there was only silence. I might have thought Matthew had hung up if it weren't for the sound of the television in the background.

"Can you give it to me?"

"Sure."

Matthew rattled off the number. I closed his eyes and took it in, trying to envision the number in bright neon. I thanked him, hung up, and quickly dialed the number and hit the call button.

The other line picked up before the end of the first ring. "Hello?"

"Michelle, it's Ben."

"Who?"

That threw me. "I'm sorry. Ben. Benjamin Baca." When my name didn't do anything, I added, "Sara," as if her name would do the trick.

"This isn't Michelle."

"This isn't Michelle Milano?"

"No."

"It's not?"

"I'm fairly certain."

I said, "Okay," and hung up the phone.

I didn't have Michelle's home phone number. When you called information, they were supposed to text you the number you're asking for. They hadn't.

I had to call information again, which connected me to Michelle's home number. When Matthew answered, he had a tone like "Didn't we just do this?" as he gave me the phone number again.

I must have switched a digit, but I wasn't totally sure. I dialed the number again. Michelle picked up on the third ring. She sounded as if she were in a car.

"Hello?"

I stood there, mouth open, unable to talk, unable to breathe.

"Hello?"

I closed my eyes and had to force the words out of my mouth.

"Michelle, it's Ben. Yes. Yeah, well, no. That's it. That's . . . Right. That's what I'm calling about. There's a problem. Yes. It's about Sara."

It was late. The sun had long since retreated for the day, and the constant waves of travelers racing to their final destinations had thinned. It happened abruptly too. It felt as if one moment it was loud chaos and bustle, and the next it was empty and quiet. There were a few wayward people scattered about waiting to board their red-eye flights. The stores and snack shops were closed for the night. A middle-aged man in dark gray pants and a gray button-down shirt moved a vacuum cleaner back and forth and back and forth between a row of seats between two gates. He looked as if he hadn't slept in days and the rhythm of his monotonous work had hypnotized him.

I walked the terminal, exhausted, a shell of myself. My feet hurt, but when I sat I felt restless and couldn't get comfortable in any chair I found. I would wander to the window and stare at the traffic passing through the airport or look to the twinkling lights of the city. It was hard not to feel as if I had become trapped within some hallucinatory dream from which I could not wake.

The man who introduced himself as Detective Saeid Farr sat across from me, hunched over, forearms resting on the corner of the worn pressboard and laminate desk, gazing at the stapled document. His face was about eighteen inches from the paper, close enough he had to lean back to give himself room when he turned the page. He made periodic noises as he read whatever was in front of him.

I tore off the tops of three sugar packs and poured them into a small Styrofoam cup of pitch-black coffee. I stirred the coffee with a thin red straw.

Detective Farr straightened up and raised his glasses so they rested on his forehead above his eyes.

"Did you have many arguments?" he asked. He had a soft, nonthreatening voice.

I considered the question. Not that I didn't know the answer. I was so tired and my head was in such a fog, I was having a difficult time concentrating. I knew how I wanted to answer, but the words eluded me, just out of reach. Besides, I didn't know how I could possibly explain the complexities of our relationship in this little room. From the beginning of the interview, I kept thinking I was rambling, or coming off inarticulate and loopy— or worse, drunk, maybe even drugged up with some prescription medication. The more conscious I was of my behavior and answers, the worse it became. I had to remind myself to pause, think of the answer, and choose my words carefully. But this didn't seem to work, and in fact, made me look more conspicuous.

"We had some arguments," I said. "Like any couple."

"Anything of note lately?"

After a pause, I said, "The wedding, I guess."

"What about the wedding?"

He rubbed the bridge of his nose with his thumb and index finger. I felt as if I had gone from tired, to wide awake, and back to bleary.

"Being in California. Planning it from fifteen hundred miles away. Dealing with her family. The general stress of it all."

"So, you're not married?"

"No. That's what this trip is for."

The detective leaned forward and double-checked the document, flipping to the second page.

"They have you down as already married."

I shrugged. "I don't know."

"Sara's not your wife?"

"Not yet."

"Ah," the detective said, as if this were an ah-ha moment. There was something about his manner, a little too forced, that made me think he already knew this.

"And she was taking medication for anxiety?"

I regretted having told the other guy this. I'd offered it up easily, with no thought it might be a point the authorities would focus on.

"Yes," I said, "but I don't think it was an all the time, everyday type of thing."

"She didn't take the medication every day?"

"I don't believe so."

"Planning the wedding was causing problems?"

"Not problems exactly."

"Anxiety?"

"I guess so."

"She was under pressure? Stressed?"

I nodded. "Sure. I mean, of course. It's a wedding."

"Of course," the detective said. "We had a little wedding, and my wife drove me crazy with every little detail. It almost made me reconsider." Detective Farr smiled. It was a gentle, empathetic smile. "What was she dealing with in regards to her family?"

"I don't imagine planning a wedding is easy under the best circumstances. Planning a wedding from California has its own particular challenges."

"What kind of challenges would that be?"

What kind of question was that? Wasn't the answer self-evident?

"Well, I mean, just everything. We were planning a wedding."

I thought the emphasis would bring the point home. But Detective Farr just sat there, hands interlaced in front of him, and stared at me with his calm eyes.

"It's every detail," I said. "I mean, there are so many things. The church. Decorating the church. Reception. Food. Music. Picking the songs. Invitations. Party favors for your guests, which I didn't even know was a thing we had to do. It's every little detail. And it's a big wedding. We pretty much had to have a large wedding because it's a big family on both sides. There's six aunts and uncles, and I don't even know how many cousins, second and third. And we can't invite one without inviting the entire clan. Plus, there's my family. Only a few could make the trip, but we had to deal with those that did. Hotels and transportation, and just making sure they're taken care of. And we're doing it from California. Her mom and sister are helping, but that doesn't always work because they have their own opinions on how things should go. Half the time, they're good ideas, but half the time it's stuff we don't want, or don't care about, but we have to entertain because they are helping us, like really helping us. We couldn't do it without their help, and so we feel like we kind of have to listen to their opinions."

I stopped. I felt like I was nattering on, but didn't know if I was, or if it was just in my head.

"It's just, you know, it's a lot of stuff to deal with."

"Yes," Detective Farr said, his mouth turned down, with a thoughtful nod. "I can see where it can be quite the challenge. How was Sara dealing with the stress?"

There was a moment, a fraction of a second, when I didn't know what the detective was asking me. Who was Sara?

"We're dealing with it. As best we can. What else can you do?"

"Quite right," he said. "How was the relationship with her mom and sister?"

What did this have to do with anything?

"I'm not sure I know what you mean."

"Were there fights? Did she argue much with her mom or her sister?"

"No," I answered, although this wasn't exactly true.

"No?"

"Not really."

"Not even with all that stress?"

"Maybe about little things. Normal things. Nothing too bad."

"What about you?"

"What about me?"

"Have you and Sara had any arguments?"

Hadn't we already talked about this? I shook my head and said, "No, not really."

"Not at all?"

"Again, like any couple, there were little things here and there. Nothing major."

"She looked forward to getting married?"

"Looked forward?" I asked.

"She was excited about it? She wanted to get married?"

"Yes, I would say so. Very much. We both were."

"Good," the detective said. He studied the legal pad a moment, then asked, "Would you describe her as happy?"

"Happy?" I turned the question in my mind. "I would say yes, overall. She was happy. Yes."

I tried to say it as if it were a "duh" answer to an overly simplistic question, as if saying, I know where you're going with this, and what you're thinking didn't happen.

Detective Farr nodded. He exhaled through his nose and looked down at his hands. "What would you argue with her about?"

"What do you mean?"

"I asked you if you had arguments with Sara, and you answered that there were some."

I said that? I couldn't remember saying that.

"Did you argue about the wedding?"

"No," I said, a little too defensively. "I don't know. A little. Of course, there were little things, but it wasn't anything big. They were just normal arguments all couples have."

"No reason she would want to leave?

There it was: the question we had danced around this entire time. Why hadn't he just come out with it from the beginning?

"No," I replied.

"You sure?"

"I'm pretty positive."

"Pretty positive?" the detective said with a slightly arched
   eyebrow.

"Yes," I said, then after a pause I added, "sir."

"Nothing against you of course," Detective Farr said. "It
would be the most reasonable explanation."

I adjusted my position in the chair, wincing a bit at the pain.
They hadn't built the seat for comfort.

"I've seen it before," he continued. "Not just with weddings.
In general. A high-pressure, high-stress situation, fight or
flight—some people get overwhelmed. It's not that uncommon."

"I don't think that's what's going on here."

"No?"

"Of course not."

"You don't?" Detective Farr asked with his same gentle
smile, although this time I sensed a tinge of grimness to it, as if
he felt sorry for me.

"No," I said, raising my voice a touch, almost to a whine.
"No. That's not what happened here."

"What do you think happened?"

"I don't know, but she's not going to up and run away."

"You're sure about that?"

What the fuck kind of question was that?

I moved my position again in the chair and made a face
between a sarcastic and dismissive expression. "Yes, I'm sure.
She didn't leave."

"Then what did happen?"

"I don't know."

My tone was more aggressive than I meant it to be, but I was
worn out and tired of these questions.

"Do you think perhaps something more nefarious
happened?"

My eyes went to the detective. My mind was blank, like television snow, and I tried to remember what *nefarious* meant. I knew the word, but right then, at that moment, I couldn't think. I knew it was bad, but I couldn't for the life of me remember the meaning.

"Is that what you think?" I asked. It came out like a croak, as if I were still trapped in puberty.

Detective Farr held up his hands in a gesture that reminded me of a picture my grandma had hanging in the hallway of her home. It depicted Christ standing on a hill, presumably during the Sermon on the Mount, speaking to a small crowd of people with his hands held up in the exact same way.

"That's what we're trying to find out," he said.

It was a possibility, an obvious and dreadful possibility, all too real, that up to that point I had pushed away as best I could and not dwelled on too much.

The detective went on. "There's a camera that's focused on that bathroom area exclusively, the entrance at least, and apparently it's been broken for some time."

"Broken?" How was that possible?

"There's been a work requisition order to get it fixed or replaced, and for some reason that hasn't been done." The detective lifted his shoulders and gave a flippant "What can you do?" shrug. "We're going through the periphery cameras now. Eventually, we'll start looking at everything in that terminal and, if necessary, the entire airport. I expect to see her on one of the cameras, but that might take a little time."

The door for the gate opened, and almost immediately weary travelers exited the bridge. Friends, relatives, wives and girlfriends, boyfriends holding flowers, families, and children who'd created "Welcome Home" signs waited for them. When the travelers emerged from the tunnel and saw their loved ones eager to greet them, they came alive with bright smiles and outstretched arms. There were hugs and kisses, and a couple wiped tears from the corners of their eyes.

A steady stream of people materialized, almost like the prestige of a magic trick. I stood back, watching them. I felt nervous. I wanted a drink—*needed* a drink—some salve to calm my nerves. The faces in the crowd were different but the same, always different and the same, indistinct and blurred together.

There was a moment when I was sure I saw Sara. My heart damn near jumped into my throat. It wasn't Sara, however. Sara's sister, Michelle, and her mother, Sheryl, stepped off the bridge. They didn't see me at first, and I stayed back behind the crowd. They looked tired. Sheryl had the open mouthed look of a bass pulled from the river. When they woke up yesterday morning, neither of them could have conceived they'd be taking a red-eye flight.

I took a few steps forward. Michelle saw me push through the crowd and made her way toward me. She looked relieved, but I noticed a pained expression on her face. Sara's family was not as a rule outwardly affectionate. They were not huggers, and even though they might be excited to see you, they never wanted to make a production out of it. Michelle surprised me by opening her arms and taking me in. It was a limp hug, and I stood rigid, not knowing how to respond. I could smell cigarettes mixed with her subtly sweet perfume.

"I'm sorry," I said, and then I said it again to make sure she'd heard me.

We broke apart. I leaned in to give Sheryl a hug but quickly realized the gesture was unwanted. I was past the point where I could reverse my course, so I put my arm around Sheryl's back and gave her a little pat on the shoulder.

This is it, I thought. This is the left turn my life has taken.

"Did you check any bags?" I asked.

"Mom had to check one," Michelle said.

"It's this way," I said.

We headed down the terminal. We walked in silence until I asked, "How was the flight?"

We stood at the baggage claim with the rest of the passengers and waited. Sheryl stood about three feet from Michelle and me with her arms crossed over her chest. She looked as if she were in a trance and not in the mood for conversation. Michelle and I were close, shoulders brushing against one another. I leaned in and told her everything that had happened, this time in much more detail that I was able to on the phone. I also told her about the conversation I'd had with Detective Farr.

"I told him what time you were coming in. I don't know if he's still here or not. We can maybe try and call him."

"I want to get her to the hotel first," Michelle said, nodding toward her mother.

"How's she doing?"

"I don't know. She hasn't said much. I don't think she knows what to think of this. I don't know what to think of this. Ever since you called, it feels as if we've been acting, like going through the motions of two people trying to deal with the situation. We haven't had time to let any of it sink in."

"It hasn't sunk in with me yet," I said.

An alarm sounded. I tensed and readied myself. A yellow light began to flash, and the belt began to move. Sheryl moved toward the carousel. I sidled up beside her.

"I can get these."

She eyed me as if considering my trustworthiness, before nodding. "They have purple and gold ribbons on the handles."

I smiled and nodded, attempting some bit of good attitude, however strained and false it was. Sheryl didn't notice one way or the other.

I guessed Sheryl to be in her late forties. I was pretty sure she'd had Michelle when she was eighteen. I remember someone telling me that. Michelle turned thirty last year. That would put Sheryl in the forty-seven, forty-eight ballpark. She looked much older than that.

She had a hard life. There was a first husband. I didn't know his name. This was Michelle's father. I got the impression he was abusive, but I don't know if it was physical, emotional, or a combination of the two. Sheryl divorced the man when Michelle was young, maybe two or three, despite the vehement objections of her own mom. She was a single, divorced mom trying to make her way through secretarial school while raising her daughter. Sometime after the divorce, this first husband had a sudden massive coronary while he was on his way home from work. It sent him into a ditch off the side of the road. It was an unexpected and joyously welcomed turn of providence—divine or otherwise, Sheryl did not much care. There was an insurance policy, and Sheryl was still listed as the primary beneficiary. The money allowed her to pay her tuition for the rest of her program and put a down payment on a small house in the country back in the town where she was raised.

Sheryl met, or rather reunited, with Sara's father, James, when she moved back home. James's mom called him Jamey, a variation he tolerated but did not care for and discouraged if anyone else gave it a try. To his friends he was known as Jimmy or sometimes Jimbo. Sheryl called him Jim.

Sheryl and James's parents were old friends. Both fathers were farmers, corn and beans. They also raised cattle and pigs. They had children at about the same time. Both Sheryl and

James were the second born, and James was two years older than Sheryl. There was never a time when they were not a part of each other's lives. The kids all played together: James's two brothers, and Sheryl's older sister and three younger brothers. They went to the same schools through elementary, middle, and high school. Although not best friends, James and Sheryl were close, and their friendship slowly evolved into a summer romance between the seventh and eighth grade. It was an on-again, off-again, hot-and-cold courtship that continued throughout high school, and it ended rather abruptly in the summer of '71, July 1 to be exact, when James's draft number was called and overnight he transmuted from a boy working on his father's farm to a man being shipped to the Quang Nam Province in South Vietnam as a Marine.

The trajectory of Sheryl's life drastically changed. She'd just graduated high school, and she'd thought, planned even, that she and James would soon get married. She begged him not to go to Vietnam. She said they could move to Canada, or Mexico, or even head to Europe like they had endlessly talked and dreamt about, but James was steadfast in his resolution to do what he thought was the right thing. I guess it was just like James to stand by the notion to honor a country willing to sacrifice its own for what was, at the very least, a misguided cause.

They didn't break up exactly. They did not have a dramatic parting of ways at a train station or an airport. They spent their last day together at the park, sitting under a large elm tree near some railroad tracks, not really saying much, content to just be in each other's company. They kissed goodbye and Sheryl gave James a crushing hug, trying to take all of him in—his touch, his feel, his scent. She felt sure she would never see him again.

She was pregnant then married to another man by the end of the year, and before the summer came round again, while James was trying to survive in the jungle half a world away, Sheryl was trying to figure out a way to divorce her new husband without upsetting her mother, who, as a strict Catholic, did not believe in divorce and would not tolerate it from her daughter. It was bad enough that Sheryl had gotten pregnant before she was married, showing a hint of a bump under her modest dress the day of her wedding. Her mom could not handle the shame of having a daughter who was divorced before she was twenty.

Life has a way of working itself out, and Sheryl found herself back in her hometown only to find that James was also back, having been honorably discharged from the Marines. He was married, and worked part-time as a mailman and as a bartender at the King of Clubs, one of two bars in town. He planned to someday buy the bar from Will Logan.

Sheryl and James had changed, irrevocably changed, both of them scarred, wholly different people than when they were together. But when they met again for the first time in many years at the Labor Day picnic at the golf course, and Sheryl introduced James to her daughter, Michelle, and James smiled and crouched down and touched the tip of the girl's nose with his index finger and smiled and called her sweetheart, it was as if they'd never separated, and the time apart, what they experienced and endured and survived in those years, had brought them closer together. They could pick up pretty much where they'd left off.

They had an affair, and Sara was the result. Sara didn't give up too much about her dad, and I wasn't made to feel comfortable asking too many questions. She never spoke about it directly. I figured out bits and pieces over the last year and a half. It was an open secret that James was Sara's father. Soon after she was born, he sold the bar and he and his wife moved. I'm not sure where. When Sara was little, he sent money, but over time that became less frequent. The calls and letters eventually stopped as well. It had been years since Sara had heard or spoken to her father.

When Sara was thirteen, Sheryl married a shade tree mechanic—a handyman of sorts and by all accounts a genuine, all-around asshole—named Sydney Youngdahl, or Sid. This was a tectonic event for Sara, and its aftershocks would never stop reverberating. The fault line between mother and daughters, especially her youngest, already tender from the general day-to-day drama of being a teenage girl, split open to an enormous rift that I often thought would never heal.

"Here it comes," Michelle said.

The enormous black suitcase slid down the belt and knocked into a set of golf clubs. The bunches of purple and gold ribbon tightly curled on the handle made it look like a giant birthday present. I stepped forward and waited for it, leaning over just a little, ready to snatch it as soon as it was within reach. But I didn't expect how heavy the bag would be, and I wasn't able to get it on my first try. The weight of it jerked me back. I had to walk a few steps with the bag down the conveyor belt. A shorter, stocky man wearing a big straw cowboy hat and impossibly tight Wranglers with a perfect crease down the front of the legs was annoyed he had to step out of the way. I got a better grip on the bag and jerked it up. I knew Sheryl would be watching me, and I wanted to hide any difficulty I was having. It was unwieldy maneuvering the bag off the belt, but I got it on the floor and pulled the handle up.

I asked, "Is this the only one?" even though I already knew the answer. We already had a variation of the "How many bags did you check in?" conversation three times already.

We made our way to the area for rental cars. There were seven different car companies renting cars, but it seemed as if everyone had chosen the same one. There was a long line waiting and only one person behind the desk to assist.

We waited. After twenty insufferable minutes that felt like hours, I think we were all done with this shit. Any equanimity had vanished by the time we stepped to the counter. Michelle gave the man her first and last name. He typed the information into the computer, studied the screen, pursed his lips, and shook his head and told her they didn't have a reservation on file. Michelle gave him the confirmation email with the confirmation number, but that didn't make a bit of difference. After some back and forth in which the man appeared nonchalant, with no sense of urgency, he typed on his keyboard, checking one system and then another, then made a call to someone and asked questions in a hushed tone, all the while stating more to himself than to us there wasn't a reservation on file. Michelle kept pointing out that whether the reservation was in the computer or not, she had made the reservation. She had the email and the confirmation number. How hard was it to give us a car? That the reservation wasn't in the system was irrelevant. The man behind the counter did not share this view.

"Listen," Michelle said in a voice I had heard her use on her children many times before, "do you have a car for us, or don't you? Are you going to honor the reservation or not?"

The man stopped typing and gave her a look that could not hide his disdain. Didn't we realize he was doing everything he could to help us? Couldn't we be just a little more grateful for what he was trying to do?

There was more typing and another phone call. The man said they had a midsize for them. "That's great," Michelle said, "but I already paid for an SUV or something similar."

The man shrugged in an "I don't know what to tell you" kind of way and explained that he could give them the midsize rental and then they would have to call a number and talk to someone about getting the difference credited back to their card. Through gritted teeth Michelle asked why he couldn't credit her card the difference. He said something about his system not allowing him to refund cards—although it was easy peasy to charge them. Michelle decided it wasn't worth the argument and said the midsize would be fine.

There was more typing, and paperwork was printed and signed. No apology for the inconvenience. No thank you for their business. The man handed over a set of keys.

We made our way outside and had to find the stop where we could pick up the shuttle that would take us to the rental car lot. We didn't know whether we needed to go to the left or right. We decided on the left for no particular reason, and after walking two hundred feet, I figured out we were going in the wrong direction. We reversed course and headed back the other way. Sheryl kept saying we needed to ask someone, and I reassured her we were now going the right way. She still asked a young woman who was cleaning the used cigarette butts from the black sand ashtrays, and the woman pointed her in the direction we were headed.

We reached the stop, and there were four other groups waiting. Sheryl and Michelle took this downtime as an opportunity to have a cigarette. I stood to the side, wanting to get far enough away where I didn't have to smell their smoke, and leaned against the suitcase.

Both of my parents smoked, so I grew up in a house fogged with their thick gray clouds. I remember stinking of it as a kid, and having to go to school with my clothes, skin, and hair reeking of cigarettes.

I had only tried a cigarette once before. It was that last winter. Sara and I had gone back to St. Catherine for Christmas, and one night we were invited to Kelly's house, a childhood friend of Sara's, with a group of girls and their husbands and boyfriends, who had all grown up together. We played cards, drank, smoked a tremendous amount of really good weed that Kelly's husband, Rob, had gotten from some guy he worked with. At some point, we went out back where the farm land began and set off fireworks in an early New Year's celebration. Later, we were back inside listening to records and bullshitting nonsense. I sat in an old wooden rocking chair. Sara sat on the floor between my legs. I was more an observer, not taking part too much in the conversation. They played "Remember when?" and I knew none of the people or history that was being discussed. I sipped my drink—vodka and cranberry juice, which was met with derision and mild teasing from the others—and took the occasional hit from the endless joints that cycled the room. Sara was fired up about someone they all went to school with who had slighted her friend, Anna, talking a mile a minute, punctuating everything with hand movements, smoking a cigarette she had bummed from someone. She had been trying to quit and only smoked when we went out drinking. I reached over and took the cigarette from her, took a shallow drag, and then handed it back to her. I promptly forgot all about it, and in fact had a hard time remembering I'd done it at all when Sara told me the next morning she didn't like it. I didn't know what she meant. She admonished me, saying she felt as if I were trying to impress her friends. I confessed I didn't know why I had taken the cigarette. It was an offhand, seemed-like-a-good-idea-at-the-time thing, but I told her I wasn't trying to impress anyone. We went back and forth about it, and it surprised me that it bothered her so much. I promised I wouldn't do it again.

"That's not you," she told me. "I just want you to be you."

I didn't intend to smoke again. It was a disgusting habit, and that one impulsive moment notwithstanding, I could not wrap my head around why anyone would do it. Even though it was the early morning now, it was still very hot. Waves of heat radiated off the asphalt and the wake of passing cars and buses. I didn't think there was any way Michelle and Sheryl were getting much pleasure sucking hot smoke into their bodies. Sheryl was particularly aggressive, holding her cigarette between her middle and index finger so tight it was as if she were trying to cut it in half. She had imprinted her burgundy lipstick onto the tip of the filter, and when she exhaled, the smoke plumed out of her nose, making her look like an ancient dragon.

When the shuttle arrived, I had to muscle the suitcases and the bears up the stairs. The man at the rental counter had told us that our car was in parking space number three. I thought that meant it would be closer to the shuttle drop-off; however, with the way the parking lot was laid out, number three was actually on the far side.

Nothing would be easy about that day.

We could finally get into the car and make our way out of the airport. I had been up for almost twenty-four hours now. I was hungry. I needed a shower. I feared that when we got to the hotel I would get a second wind, or more like a fourth or fifth wind, and wouldn't be able to sleep.

We found a hotel not too far from the airport. Michelle checked us in. I stood back and thought I could lie down right there on the travertine-tile floor and fall asleep.

Why were we here? How the fuck had this happened?

Where was Sara?

Michelle thanked the woman behind the check-in counter and handed me a key card.

"Thanks for the room," I said. "You didn't have to do that."

"Hopefully, it will only be the one night," Michelle replied.

We waited what felt like an interminable amount of time for the elevator to make it from the fifth floor to the lobby. When we were in the elevator and the door closed, it felt as if we were barely inching to the top floor. I caught my reflection in the metal door. It looked stretched out of proportion, grotesque, as if my face had been ripped off and haphazardly stitched back. I looked like a monster.

Michelle told me she and Sheryl would call later. Sheryl had already gone into the room without saying goodbye. I gave Michelle a hug and told her again how sorry I was. She thanked me for everything. I didn't know what she was referring to, but I nodded and said goodbye, then walked four doors down to my room.

I slid the key card into the metal slot and pulled it out. I tried the door, but it was locked. I tried it again, but the door would not open. I checked the card to make sure I was putting the right side in. I was, but I spun the card around anyway and tried it again. No luck. I closed my eyes and took a breath and imagined taking an ax to the fucking door. I tried the key again, and again, and again. I tried variations. I tried putting it in and pulling it out slowly. I tried doing it quickly. I tried easing the card in and rapidly pulling it out. Nothing worked.

I left my suitcases and the bears and went back to the elevator, waited for it, and rode it back down to the lobby. I told the woman behind the desk that the key wasn't working. She eyed me, then turned the card over in her hand. She ended up coding a new card and apologized in a clipped tone.

When I made it back to my room, I tried the new key. The red light on the lock flared, and the door would not open. I threw my head back and made the sound of a three-year-old being told it was time to go to bed. I almost collapsed right there in the hallway. Throughout the day, I had done a pretty good job keeping my emotions in check, but now I was done. I wanted to lash out. I wanted to scream. I wanted to break something. I wanted to fucking cry. More than anything, I simply wanted to get into this room.

I took a breath and then tried the key again. The red light came on, and the door remained locked. I thought I would have to go to Michelle's room and knock on the door and somehow tell her I wasn't able to get inside my room. As embarrassing as that would be, I didn't know what else to do.

I slid the key in again, waited a moment, and then pulled it out. The green light came on, and a split second later I heard the lock unlatch. I pushed the door opened to a dark room.

I felt a tingling elation as I stepped inside. I flicked a light on, left the suitcase and bears at the door, and dropped my backpack onto the floor. I walked across the room to the air-conditioning unit on the floor and cranked it to the lowest temperature it would go. I fell onto the bed and pulled a pillow into my arms. It felt so good to lie down. The frigid air blew against my face. I smiled. I still needed to take a shower and wash the dirt of the day from my body and my mind, but I wanted to lie there, just for a minute.

I was asleep almost immediately.

Six hours later, I was back in the airport security offices. Detective Saeid Farr sat behind the desk. The guy who'd first taken information from me the day before, Kyle, stood behind him, leaning on a long sideboard against the wall. Michelle and Sheryl sat in the chairs across the desk. They had to bring in a plastic number for me. It was a smaller office, so they squeezed me into the side.

Detective Farr recapped what they knew at that point, which wasn't much more than the previous night. The camera that covered the bathroom area was not working properly, and the airport had yet to fix it. Michelle asked if there was only one camera covering the area. Detective Farr told her that was correct. He said they were still going through the footage from the other security cameras. They'd started working their way out from the bathroom and going through the outside cameras as well. They expected to finish going through everything by the end of the day, possibly the next day. They had not seen Sara on any of the cameras, but as Farr put it, there was "an awful lot of footage to go through."

Michelle said, "So, what you're telling us is that she up and disappeared. She vanished without a trace, is that it?"

Detective Farr laughed and said, "No, I don't think that's what happened. I'm simply saying we haven't been able to locate her on any of the footage."

"I don't understand," Sheryl said. "None of this makes sense to me."

Detective Farr looked at her with sympathetic eyes and said, "Well, Ms. Youngdahl, to be honest, it doesn't make much sense to me either, but I promise you we're going to do everything we can to figure it out. We're going to do everything in our power to find your daughter."

We decided to get breakfast and found a diner near the airport. It was an old greasy spoon that had the smell of comfort as soon as you walked in. We sat at a booth near a large window that looked out to the parking lot and the highway beyond. Michelle and Sheryl sat on one side, and I sat on the other. A young high-energy waitress handed us menus and took our drinks order. We studied the menu in a silence that was both deafening and uncomfortable.

What was I doing here? These women were essentially strangers. Sara and I met in California. I'd been to St. Catherine three times since then. During those trips, I'd had two dinners with Sheryl, both of which were pretty cold going on the friendly meter, and hung out with Michelle and her husband, Nick, a little. That time was cordial, but it was also people going out of their way to make nice. It's not like we were friends. It wasn't as if they liked me. If they claimed to like me, it was only because of Sara. I'd called Sheryl to get her permission before I asked Sara to marry me. I remember a frigid silence on the other end before Sheryl said, "You two are very young for that kind of thing." We ended the call with an "I guess if that's what you two want, I can't stop you" blessing.

Sheryl visited us in California once, and it was a painful four days. Sara put forth minimal effort to be a good host to her mom, but I got the distinct feeling that no matter what she did, it wouldn't have been appreciated. I felt obligated to make conversation, which was never not awkward. I organized day trips to Hollywood, Olvera Street, the Griffith Observatory, the farmers market, and the Santa Monica Pier. Sheryl then told me she didn't like doing touristy things. I made sure we were plenty stocked with Diet Pepsi and that we watched the shows she wanted to watch at night. She spent most of the time chain-smoking, with the disgruntled look of someone sitting in a dentist's waiting room. I couldn't understand why she'd bothered to come out at all unless it was because of some misguided sense of obligation.

The waitress took our food order, and we waited.

"I talked to Todd about the alcohol order," Sheryl said. She was looking for anything to break the uncomfortable silence. "I think we'll have enough."

"That's good," I said. "Sara will be happy about that, for sure."

I thought about getting a paper. That would at least keep me occupied and free from the obligation to talk.

"We finished the music list for the DJ," I said. "I think we have a mix of different types of things for everyone."

Silenced descended on us again. I couldn't escape. I stared outside. Sheryl unrolled the silverware from her paper napkin. She then folded the napkin as if it belonged in a restaurant with tablecloths. Michelle was content to stir her iced tea. I thought about excusing myself and going to the bathroom. I didn't have to go, but I could sit in the stall and wait for five or ten minutes. It would at least relieve me of this torture.

These were my in-laws. I would have to deal with these people for the rest of my life. While that might be tolerable in fits and starts with Sara as a buffer, left on my own that idea was unimaginable. How long were we going to be forced to do this? Not simply sitting in a booth at a roadside greasy spoon but meeting without Sara there. How would that work? My assumption, and I would have guessed it was the collective assumption, was that Sara would turn up sometime soon, but if she didn't, how long could we keep this routine going?

The waitress swooped in just in time with a big tray filled with food. We at least had something else to focus on.

We met Detective Farr at the police station. He asked more questions about Sara, but they were essentially the same questions as before, only phrased slightly differently. He explained that the more detail they had on her and her life, the better chance they had of finding her. I assumed I was being suspected of something. I didn't know what that would be, and I didn't much care. The story was so crazy, and since I was the one telling it, it stood to reason they would be skeptical and would try to figure out if I was lying or had any motive to do something terrible to Sara. Great, I thought. Knock yourself out.

Farr quickly confirmed that Sara had boarded the flight from John Wayne Airport. If I'd done something, it had to have been once we landed. I answered Farr's questions to the best of my knowledge—I had nothing to hide, so there was no reason to be anything but honest—and any theories I was involved in Sara's disappearance were swiftly eliminated.

"We've contacted the other divisions and the surrounding stations," the detective said.

"And why would you do that?" Sheryl asked.

"On the chance she was picked up."

Sheryl nodded. I could tell she didn't know what to do with this information.

"There's no one in custody that matches her description."

"I wish she'd been arrested," Michelle said. The detective gave an understanding nod, but Sheryl looked confused. Michelle explained, "At least we would know where she was."

At one point, Sheryl excused herself to use the bathroom. Michelle asked the detective if they'd contacted the morgue.

"Yes," he said. "Nothing."

This did not comfort me as much as it should have.

That afternoon, we were back at the airport. Michelle received a call from a producer from a local news channel. I don't know how they got her phone number. They wanted to do a story on Sara. After some discussion, we agreed to meet at the airport.

"They're going to need a photo of Sara," Michelle said. "Do you have one?"

"No," I said.

"You don't have a photo of her?"

"Not on me," I said. "We have pictures back at our apartment."

"You don't carry a photo in your wallet?"

"No," I said. "Do people still do that?"

She gave me a disapproving look, which I thought unfair. Sheryl had a photo of Sara in her senior year of high school. She obviously looked younger, with long hair, fuller cheeks, and more makeup than Sara would ever wear now. It would have to do.

A tiny plastic-looking woman wearing thick, vaguely orange makeup greeted us and introduced herself as a reporter named Heather Hardenburg. A slovenly cameraman, who did not give his name, accompanied her. They taped an interview with us outside the terminal. Michelle did most of the talking, pleading that anyone with any information please contact the police. All the while, Sheryl stood next to her, wiping away tears. I stood in the back, not knowing what to do with my hands. At the end, the reporter gave the number for the missing persons hotline. After we'd wrapped, Heather said she wanted to get some footage inside the terminal, especially the bathroom where Sara was last seen, to help complete the story.

"And this is going to air tonight?" Michelle asked.

"That's right," Heather said. "It'll air at five and at six. It could make it onto the eleven o'clock broadcast, too."

When we got back to the hotel, Michelle thought we should try calling hospitals. We pulled out the phone book and were shocked to find there were thirty-six hospitals in the area. Michelle and I divided the list, starting with the hospitals closest to the airport and working our way out, and started calling. Sheryl went outside to smoke.

Every conversation I had went along these lines:

"Hello?"

"Yes, I'm looking to see if a patient is at your hospital."

"May I have the name?"

"Sara Turner."

"Hold on."

A click, Muzak, waiting.

"Sir?"

"Yes?"

"There's no one checked in under that name."

"Okay. Thank you. And you were able to check the emergency room as well?"

"Yes, sir."

"Okay. Thank you."

"You're welcome."

Then I would hang up and move on to the next hospital.

We worked our way through a dozen hospitals when Michelle said, "There's a possibility she could be at one of these hospitals as an unidentified patient. She could have come in unconscious. She might not remember her name. Who the hell knows what the situation could be?"

I called another five hospitals, with similar results. I didn't want to do this anymore. I didn't see the point, but I didn't know how I could tell Michelle this without dealing with her judgment.

I called one more hospital. I saw the name in the phone book, and I heard the receptionist say, "St. Joseph's Memorial, how may I help you?" But it wasn't until I was on hold listening to the Muzak version of "Let it Be" that I realized this was the St. Joseph's Memorial where they'd brought my dad after his heart attack. I remembered being twelve years old in that fifth-floor waiting room with my mom chain-smoking, wiping away tears, teetering on the verge of frenzied panic, trying to balance herself with whatever combination of drugs she took, while my dad lay in an operating room with his chest cut open and doctors tried to save his life. I could never forget the smell of that hospital, the antiseptic scent of alcohol and bleach that had an underlying hint of death and shit. It was the first time I realized my dad was mortal. He would die. If not that day, then someday. It would happen. I would die. Everyone I knew would die. This was not an abstract idea, it was very real, tangible, and there was no way to avoid it.

The memory made me feel overwhelmed and lightheaded, trapped, as if the walls in this little hotel room were closing in on me. I needed to flee, escape, just leave as quickly as possible.

"Sir? We don't have anyone listed under that name."

I hung up without thanking her. I stood from the bed and thought my knees might buckle and I would fall to the old and dirty carpet. I knew if I fell, the carpet would swallow me and I'd fall into a black, inescapable pit.

"I need to step out," I said. "Get some fresh air."

Michelle didn't so much as acknowledge me. I hurried out of the room as if escaping a poison chamber. I didn't want to cross paths with Sheryl, so I raced down the stairs. I burst through the door at the bottom into the sunshine, and a sticky hot fist of humidity punched me in the face.

I found my way to the hotel bar, where I propped myself on a stool and ordered a beer.

"Bottle or draft?" the bartender asked.

"Draft is fine."

He rattled off what they had on tap. I didn't care and just picked the first one he mentioned. It tasted so fucking good, exactly what I needed. I downed it and ordered another. I left my wallet upstairs, so I made sure I could charge everything to the room.

By the fourth beer, time had slipped away. My head swam in a gloriously numb haze. I hit that target of perfect intoxication, just on the other side of tipsy, where you're riding a nice wave, feeling good, still clear-headed and aware, your words crisp, your tongue sharp, and you feel strong and invincible. I could never stay on this wave for long, not content until I broke through to blotto. I wasn't there yet. I graduated from beer to vodka to whiskey, but remained in relative control of myself.

I stewed, content to pickle myself on that stool. I watched a ball game but didn't pay much attention to it. I watched others come in and sit at the bar, order drinks and food, have conversations with one another, laugh, or sit in silence. Once again, I began to wonder where they were going. Where were they from? What was going on in their lives to bring them to this bar and this moment? What were their stories? Once the whiskey began to do its job, I started to think everyone here had been a baby at some point. Everyone had been a kid once. They'd played, not caring about anything except that moment, whatever they were doing, whatever was in front of them right then, right there.

This bar had no video games, not even a pinball machine. I didn't know the time. I didn't care. Music was playing. Someone must have fed money into the jukebox. I wasn't paying much attention to it. It was just noise that played in the background.

I ordered drink after drink. I don't know how many. I lost track. I couldn't taste the whiskey anymore. I realized I had eaten nothing since breakfast except bits of candy and chips. I gazed at a menu. Nothing looked appealing. I ordered a burger and fries and knew I didn't want it.

And then I heard the song. I knew it from the first few bars. It broke my trance. I sat up and looked around. Otis Redding sang, "For your precious love . . ." Who chose this song? I scanned the bar. I had the crazy idea it could be Sara who'd picked it. That first time I visited her in St. Catherine, Sara drove me up to Black Angel Park, which overlooked the small town where she grew up. We drank and got high. The radio was playing, and this song came on. Sara closed her eyes and moved her head to the rhythm of the music and sang along. I couldn't help but smile. I knew I wanted to love her, and I knew I wanted her to love me. I didn't know how I could make that happen. This was the song. This was our song. We picked it as the song we would dance to at our wedding.

The elevator door opened, and I stumbled out. Even though I was walking into an empty hallway, I didn't want to show just how drunk I was. The patterns in the carpet, blue airplanes morphing into red birds like an M. C. Escher parody, made me dizzy. I fumbled the key card out of my pocket. I had to prop myself up with my hand on the wall as I slid the key into the lock and quickly withdrew it. The red light on the handle didn't switch to green. Good God, not this again. I slid the card in and withdrew it. The light was still red, the door locked. I turned the card over and went through the process one more time. The light turned green, and I popped the door open and fell inside.

I emptied my pockets onto the dresser. I had left the television on all day. A local commercial played for a husband-and-wife lawyer team who looked more like brother and sister. I kicked off my shoes and plopped onto the bed. The ceiling texture had flecks of sparkles. I closed my eyes and tried to get the room to stop spinning. It didn't work. I rolled off the bed, peeled off my shirt, and kicked off my pants like a child. I caught my reflection in the mirror. I'd developed a gut. I'd meant to do something about it, lose fifteen to twenty pounds before the wedding, but it didn't work out. My chest and shoulders were pale, pasty white, my forearms tan. I growled at my reflection, then stumbled into the bathroom.

I was in the middle of washing my face when I heard, "A desperate search as we speak right now for a missing woman from Southern California. Take a look. This is Sara Turner. She was on her way back home to get married when she disappeared at the airport."

I went back into the room, the soapy lather drying on my face. They'd pieced together shots of the airport, the terminal, and the bathroom where Sara was last seen as the reporter painted the scene of the story. They cut to a shot of me as I recounted what happened. I looked like a bloated pig. Then a shot of Michelle and Sheryl with me in the background, followed by a shot of Detective Farr giving the police's point of view. Back to the reporter standing outside the terminal tagging the story by saying police are confident that someone at the airport saw Sara, or had information about her whereabouts, and asking anyone with information to contact the number on the screen.

The next story concerned a water-rights dispute between ranchers.

It didn't seem real, as if I were watching a story from a parallel version of our lives. I needed a drink, but I had nothing in the room and I wasn't about to step outside again. I turned the television off and rinsed the dried soap from my face. I crawled onto the bed. My eyes ached from exhaustion. I cradled a pillow and closed my eyes, but it was a long while before I fell asleep.

Time moved at a glacial pace, and I often felt trapped in an out-of-focus movie. Detective Farr told us that Sara's name and vital information had been entered into a national database of missing-person cases. In theory, it sent alerts out to all precincts, and if an officer came into contact with someone they suspected as being missing, they could cross-check it with the database.

A nonprofit organization dedicated to finding missing persons contacted us. The head of the organization, a guy with slicked-back hair and bug eyes named Robert Flores, claimed to provide critical resources to families with missing loved ones. Most of their work comprised safety education for children through school programs. Robert told Michelle they were a group of passionate volunteers willing to help us find Sara. They had a revolving team of about twenty people. They organized a canvassing operation that went door to door, asking if anyone had seen or knew anything concerning Sara's whereabouts. They handed out flyers and hung them up at businesses, the bus station, the train station, and wherever else they could. Two local newspapers and the all-news radio station conducted interviews with Michelle and Sheryl. Michelle easily stepped into the role of family spokesperson. Updated stories ran on all the television stations. The story was even picked up by the national news circuit. The police set up an anonymous telephone hotline for people to call if they had any information. Sheryl put up a ten-thousand-dollar reward, though Michelle thought her mother could have offered much more. Hundreds of volunteers participated in organized searches: more of Sara's family flew in for a few days, or extended weekends, National Guard troops, firefighters, students and faculty from the local university, and everyday people who just wanted to help all searched for Sara, to no avail.

One day led to the next, one week to the next. It was exhausting. We sometimes worked nineteen- or twenty-hour days. I kept in contact with my job, letting them know I had no idea how long I would be out. My manager said he understood, but I sensed a tone in his voice that he considered this an inconvenience he'd rather not deal with.

I didn't know how long I could afford to stay here. Not only was there the expense of being in a different city, but I still had to deal with bills back home. Sara and I didn't have a hell of a lot saved. Michelle paid for my hotel room for the first week, but it became clear I needed to step up and take over the expense. I tried to pay it on my own, but eventually had to call my parents and ask for money. The days took a physical toll, but also an enormous mental toll. I woke up every morning feeling confident that today was the day. Today would be the day we would find her, or at least a lead—something, some bit of evidence that would either get us closer to finding Sara or give us hope to continue the fight. As the days wore on, that optimism would be slowly eaten away until I felt such hopelessness it was hard to function. Each passing day increased the dread we might never find Sara. I tried to push those thoughts away, but they always dug their way back up. Drinking helped. I was a casual drinker before, a weekend drinker, but I began to drink every day. At first it was only at night, but by the end of the second week I'd also started drinking vodka during the day. It thinned the pain, dulled the nerves, opened the door for a needed fog to roll in and sink its claws into my head. It became necessary for me to get through each day.

We had just spent a painfully long day canvassing a neighborhood we had already been through the week earlier. The idea was to hit the houses we missed the last time because the residents were not at home, or, much more likely, hadn't bothered to answer the door. Sheryl and I sat at a small round table in her hotel room playing alligator rummy, racing to inebriation. After we finished our hand, I shuffled the two decks while Sheryl poured the last of her chardonnay into one of the hotel glasses. Sheryl sniffed the wine like it was some high-end expensive bottle and not something bought for five bucks at the corner convenience store.

She closed her eyes and said, "My mom used to say that no one ever died saying they should have done less."

"We'll find her," I said. "Something's going to break."

"Will it?"

"Yes."

"I'm not so sure."

"She's alive, Sheryl. Sara is alive, and we're going to find her."

She looked at me with blank eyes and sipped her wine. "I hope you're right," she said. "I pray you're right. My heart, though . . . in my heart I know you're not."

That stopped me. I had to take it in and turn it over.

"Why would you say something like that?"

She turned her head as if she couldn't take my disapproving look and made a noise of mild contempt.

"She's my little girl. I made her. She came from me. I've known every pain she's ever had. I mended her. I felt the pain along with her. It didn't matter you two had run off to California. I could still feel her when she was hurt, or sick, or alone. I could feel her in my heart, in the pit of my stomach. I can't feel her anymore. I can't feel her presence. It's not there anymore. It's gone. And I'm afraid she's gone too."

I held the decks and looked at her, not knowing what to say or how to react.

"Do you still want to play?" she asked.

We sat in Detective Farr's office. He wore a green-and-blue argyle tie so ugly it had to be a shitty gift from his kids.

"I understand what you're saying, but that's just the sad fact with the way the news works. At a certain point, they are not going to cover it unless there's something new to report."

"The paper hasn't mentioned Sara or the search for days," Sheryl said.

"I know," the detective said with a sympathetic expression. "They look at it as old news."

"Old news?" Michelle asked.

"I'm not saying it is, of course. We're still working as hard as we can on this. We're following up every lead we have."

"What leads?" Michelle asked. "There are no leads."

"We're doing everything we can," the detective said. "That's what I'm saying."

"I don't understand how it works," Michelle said. "Some blonde goes down to Aruba and disappears and they can't keep her picture out of the news for months. Sara is already forgotten. How does that work?"

"She's not forgotten," the detective said.

"It seems that way."

"I know it does, and I wish I could say something that gave more consolation than that."

"What are we supposed to do?" Sheryl asked.

"We're investigating every single lead that we have."

"Again," Michelle said, "what leads? Unless there's something we're not aware of."

Detective Farr nodded. His eyes glanced briefly out the window, and I wondered if he wished he could escape. He must have been tired of dealing with us by now.

"It's true," he said. "We don't have much to go on. So far, it's been nothing but frustrating dead ends. There's not much to explore that we haven't already explored. I'm not quite sure where we can go from here. Now, that doesn't mean we've given up. Not by a long shot. Please don't ever think that. We don't know what can happen. We don't know what the next phone call or new bit of evidence or discovery can bring. You can't give up. We haven't. That I promise you. We are not giving up on finding your sister."

Sometime later, Michelle and I sat across from each other in a booth at Hermie's Big Breakfast. Discovering that small diner was one of the few bright spots in all this misery.

Michelle and I had reached a point in our relationship where we did not feel the need nor did we bother to make small talk to fill the silences. We had evolved, but also didn't have much to say to each other.

"I don't know how much longer I can keep my mom here," Michelle said.

"How's that?"

"There's nothing here," she said. "Nothing. Even the cops are saying there's nothing we can do here."

"That's not exactly what they're saying."

"My mom's not doing well. She needs to be home."

The waitress bopped to the table. She set pancakes the size of a frying pan in front of me and an omelet in front of Michelle. "Ketchup or Tabasco?" she asked.

Michelle shook her head and stared at food she no longer wanted to eat. The waitress walked off.

"My mom's not doing well," she continued. "All she does is cry. She's not sleeping. She can't take much more of this. I want to take her back, at least for a while. Maybe I'll come back. I don't know. But I don't know how much more I can take with her and everything back home on top of this whole damn thing here."

I listened, slathering butter on the pancakes and coating them with thick, real maple syrup. I nodded and said, "Yeah" and

"Right," as I cut my pancakes. I needed them to soak up the vodka churning in my stomach.

"There's nothing we can do here."

I put a forkful of the pancakes in my mouth. They were so fucking good I had to close my eyes.

"There's nothing we can do," Michelle repeated.

"We can help," I said. "We can wait for her."

"Is that what we're waiting for? Are we really waiting for her? And how can we help, exactly? What can we do?"

She pushed her plate away. She took the cup and went to drink it but remembered she needed it refilled. She turned her head, looking for the waitress.

"How long?" she asked. "How long are we supposed to wait for something to turn up? The search goes on for, what? Months? It's been this long and there's not really much of anything to go on. There's nothing."

"She didn't just up and disappear."

"She didn't?"

"No."

"Sure feels like it."

"She didn't."

The waitress glided over with a pot of coffee and quietly filled Michelle's cup before slipping away.

"I know she didn't just disappear," Michelle said, ripping open four sugar packets and pouring them into the pitch-black liquid. "But how long do we wait? Another week? Is a month long enough? How long?"

This talk made it near impossible for me to enjoy the pancakes. I looked out the window to the parking lot and the traffic. How long had we been here? Not the restaurant, this town. I couldn't remember. Life had long since taken a left turn into the absurd. I couldn't tell what was real and what was a nightmare.

"What happened that day?" Michelle asked.

"What do you mean?"

"What happened?"

"I don't understand what you're asking me."

Michelle stirred the coffee, the metal spooning tinking on the sides. "I never asked you," she said.

"What do you mean?"

"At the airport. I never asked you directly. What happened?"

I stared at her, her face blank, expressionless, green eyes peering at me.

"What kind of question is that?" I asked.

"I don't understand it. She's not going to up and walk away from you."

"That's right. She's not."

"Do you think she was kidnapped?"

"I don't know."

"Do you think Sara's the type of person who would allow herself to be taken?"

"No."

"No. She's not. She would have fought. If she was put in a situation like that, she would fight. She would fight like hell."

I wasn't hungry anymore.

"I don't think that would be possible," she said.

"I know."

"It wouldn't be possible."

"I agree with you."

"The idea is just wrong."

"Michelle, what are you asking me?"

Michelle put her hands to her face as if washing herself. She then ran her fingers through her long, thick hair and exhaled.

"I don't know," she said. "I don't know. I'm sorry. I'm tired. I don't think a week of sleep could make up for how tired I feel. I don't know what to do."

"Get on a plane, and get the fuck out of here," I said with a tone much harsher than I wanted.

"Wait a second," she said, holding up her hand as if trying to stop me. "Who the hell do you think you're talking to?"

"You can leave," I said. I'd already showed my cards. There was no point in pretense now. "I'm staying. You can go. Do whatever you have to do, but I'm staying right here until she's found, or there is some kind of fucking answer."

"Like you're the hero? You're the only one who cares? She's my sister."

"Half sister."

"Right. And what the hell does that have to do with anything?"

I shook her off and said, "Forget it."

"What?" she insisted. "What did you mean by that?"

"I know the story, Michelle. I know everything about you two, so don't act as if you and her are best of fucking friends."

"She's still my sister."

"Okay. Whatever."

"You don't know half of what you think you know."

"I know enough to know your bullshit."

"What bullshit?"

"Please," I said, voice dripping with contempt. I couldn't take it anymore. "Get on the next plane and get the fuck out of here. Insincere fucking asshole. Sara wouldn't want your fake, disingenuous ass here anyway."

Michelle's lips quivered. I noticed an old man sitting at a table by himself with the newspaper spread out before him watching us over his thick glasses. I wished I had stormed off and left her. I looked across the table to Michelle, already regretting I had lashed out with such venom.

She sat with her face contorted, trying not to cry. I knew she didn't want to give me the satisfaction. I turned to the window again.

"It's . . . this situation," she said. She pulled out a twenty and dropped it on the table. She scooted out of the booth. "I'll call you later."

I nodded and waited until I was sure Michelle had walked out of the diner. Then I pulled the plate back in front of me and finished my pancakes.

I sat on what had become my nightly stool at the corner of the hotel bar. I smoked a cigarette and nursed a whiskey. The sun hung low, and light the color of raw steak bled through the lowered blinds.

"Today would've been my wedding day," I told Willie. "Today was the day. I should be married now."

"You're still going to get your chance," Willie said.

Willie was a semiregular of the bar. Somewhere in his seventies, Willie grew up in some small town in Minnesota. After four years in the army, including time in Italy during the war, he came home to his wife and daughter and decided he no longer belonged in that small town. After puttering around the country trying to find sustainable work, Willie followed his brother here and worked for a rancher, doing all kinds of various jobs. When the rancher died of a heart attack, dropping dead right there in the fields, the brothers pooled their money and got a loan to buy the ranch and everything in it.

Willie was an amiable guy, easy to talk to, with a generous laugh. He liked to buy my drinks, too, which didn't hurt. The bartender, Mike, told me one night that Willie was easily one of the richest men in the county. One wouldn't tell by looking at the modest western-style clothes he wore and the '86 Chevy pickup he drove. When he learned about Sara, Willie offered to kick fifty grand into the reward. It was such a mind-boggling act of kindness and generosity, given to someone who was a stranger, someone to that point he knew only as a fat drunk on a stool, that when he told me about the money I wept.

"Her mom and sister want to head back," I said with a shrug.

"I wish I had words of wisdom for you," Willie said. "I don't. I just, I don't know. The pain they must be enduring is unimaginable."

Yes, I thought, that's true. But what about my pain? Why doesn't anybody consider that?

"I don't mean to take anything from you," Willie said.

I shook him off. "I know that. It's not a big deal."

"Are you going to have to go home?"

"Not without her I'm not. I'm not leaving without her."

I downed the rest of my drink and motioned for another.

"One thing I can tell you," Willie said with his calm, graveled voice. "One thing I know for certain is that nothing stops. It never ends."

"What do you mean?"

"My wife died almost eleven years ago. I knew it was coming. The cancer had been eating at her for a long time. But when it happened, it was still quite a kick. You might have thought my world had ended. In a way, it did. But it also didn't end at all. I just wished it had. Nothing stops. Your life goes on. And the thing I learned is that you can't just live your life in limbo."

The bartender placed a new drink in front of me. I stirred it with a red plastic straw.

"It took me too many years to figure that one out," Willie finished.

"California was because of her," I said. "I never wanted to live there. That apartment, that's ours. We share it. If I went back, I'd be going to our home. Without her. I don't know how I can do that. I mean, how could I do that? I don't know how that would work."

"You just do it," Willie said, straightforward. "It has to be done. It's as simple as that."

I sipped my whiskey. "I know you're right," I said. "I know that, but I wouldn't know how. How am I going to sleep in that bed? Our bed. How am I going to cook myself dinner? Go back to work? How do I just carry on like none of this has happened?"

"What's the alternative?"

The hotel phone screamed a piercing caterwaul over and over again. It yanked me from my coma-like sleep. I spun in bed, and reached out into the darkness.

"Hello?"

I sat in a plastic chair. The only vent blasted such bitterly cold air it was almost painful to sit in the waiting room. Michelle and Sheryl sat a couple seats away from me. They both wore chiseled stone faces.

Detective Farr led us down a long hallway. The walls were painted a light mint green, and the white tile had flecks of black. I could see the door at the end of the corridor. Death surrounded us. I could feel it. Panic pounded in my chest like a bird trying to escape. I didn't want to go through that door. I wanted to run. I wanted to run away screaming. I didn't think I could do this. I didn't think I could face what would be on the other side of that door. I didn't want the answers. I could not face it. This was impossible. No one could ask me to do this.

We stood around a steel gurney on the far side of the room where a body lay with a baby-blue sheet covering it. Detective Farr said a few words, but I couldn't hear him. Michelle nodded. Sheryl wiped away tears. The smell of formaldehyde and alcohol damn near buckled my knees. Michelle held her mother in her arms, their bodies tense, rigid, anxious. I stood to the side trying not to fall.

A tall, spindly coroner slowly walked around the table. He said something to Detective Farr, but again I couldn't hear him. The coroner looked from Michelle to Sheryl, then to me. I averted my eyes, looking at the floor. The coroner took the sheet and pulled it back.

Sheryl sobbed, a big, loud, wailing sound. I looked at her and saw Michelle had to fight to keep her mom from falling. She looked at Detective Farr and shook her head.

I made myself look down at the table. The body wasn't Sara's.

I didn't realize I was holding my breath. I gasped for air.

I sat with Michelle and Sheryl at their gate. The surrounding sound was muted, slightly metallic, otherworldly. People moved around us slower than they should, as if caught in a dream or walking underwater.

Michelle tapped her mother on the knee. They stood. We gave each other one-armed hugs and talked about phone calls and went over plans for future action. Sheryl kissed me on the cheek.

I watched them walk to the gate. They handed the attendant their ticket, then walked down the long corridor toward the plane.

Five days later, I sat in the window seat and touched the outline of my father's dog tags beneath my T-shirt. The flight attendant handed me a Coke and a small packet of peanuts. I thanked her and looked out the window to the whipped clouds. I imagined what it would be like to dive into those clouds, and to laugh like mad and play.

"This thing is a dream," he said. "It was your dream."

Richard crushed out a cigarette and immediately shook another from the pack and lit it.

"I know," he continued. "I know all about it. And just so there's no misunderstanding, I admire the tenacity with which you've tried to keep it afloat. It's truly commendable. Let's be honest here, Ben, the restaurant has been a sinkhole from the beginning."

"That's not true."

"Yes, it has. I take responsibility for some of it, too. I think maybe I've protected you a little more than I should have. It's hard to say. Despite what you say, though, I wanted this to succeed as much as anybody, but all the hope in the world can't replace the fact that you're facing bankruptcy. I'm sorry, but it's as simple as that."

I couldn't look at him. I stared out the office window and the view of the expansive city. It had mutated at an exponential rate. The city where I grew up was almost unrecognizable. There was no sign of it slowing down anytime soon. Where were these people coming from? Why did they decide on here? Weather was the most likely answer. They were tired of dealing with the winters. It was also cheap to live here, relatively speaking. A family could get more bang for their housing dollar. Both fair points, I suppose, but this was still a desert, and while the winters were mild, the summers could turn uninhabitable. When I drove past the endless subdivisions of cookie-cutter tract houses, I kept thinking, We're in a desert with finite resources. How in the fuck will there be enough water for all these people? It seemed impossible.

"What can I do?" I asked.

"Honestly?"

I finally looked at Richard, sitting in his chair with a wry smile and a smug air of conviction.

"Yes, honestly," I said. "Why would I want something else?"

"There's nothing."

"What do you mean by that?"

"There is nothing."

"I understand the words you're saying. But what do you mean?"

He sighed. "I've known you, what, fifteen years?"

"Something like that."

"We've known each other a while. That's the point. We've been in business a long time, but aside from that, we're also friends. I consider you a dear, close friend, and I'm telling you, as a friend, as someone who loves you and is worried about you, there is nothing that can be done. It's time to walk away from this."

"What are you worried about?" I asked.

He didn't know what to think about that. "Is that a joke?"

I shook him off, not wanting to elaborate. My point was that it wasn't his ass on the line. He had nothing invested. He wasn't losing anything. What the fuck did he care if I walked away or not?

"This place is it," I told him. "There isn't anything else."

"I know it was."

"What do you mean was? It still is, *Richard*." I put the emphasis on my lawyer's name as if it were a slur. "It hasn't fucking gone anywhere yet."

"I know it hasn't."

"We're still open for business. We're serving lunch right now."

"I get it."

"This is all I have. This is all I am."

Richard sat in that leather chair, aggressively sucking down one cigarette after another. There was pity in his eyes. I couldn't take that. I didn't need his fucking pity. I wanted to leap across the desk and pummel his face to a bloody mush. I wanted to scream, to rage, to rage against the world, but I was pinned down and helpless.

"I can't afford another failure."

Richard said nothing to that. What could he say? For that moment anyway, he had the sense to sit there and wait for me to continue.

"My dad, he'd say to me, when a man works hard, he will achieve that thing he's after. Whatever it is. That piece of whatever. It'll be yours."

"Ben, listen to me." Richard crushed out his second cigarette, and I saw his eyes go to the pack as he thought of another.

"Tenacity. This is what he told me. Tenacity is the key. It's the key to life. It's the secret."

"I'm paying you the respect of being honest with you."

"Is that what I pay you for? My dad, he gave thirty-five years and a crippled body to a union that let him fucking rot in a hospital. They didn't give a fuck about him. He busted his ass every single day of his life and ended up with cancer from asbestos and jack shit."

Richard held up his arms and asked, "What do you want me to do?"

"I want you to do your job."

"I am doing my job. That's what I'm doing. So, what do you want? What would you have me do?"

I sighed. My gaze turned to the window and the view. I wondered if I'd die instantly if I were to jump from this height.

"What is there?" I asked. "Tell me what's left. What are my options? And how much time do I have?"

I stepped out of the glass high-rise into a wave of heat so intense I winced. The sidewalk was thick with the lunchtime crowd hurrying to stuff food down their faces, or trying to squeeze a few errands into their allotted hour.

I walked over to the meter I'd parked beside and spotted the bright-yellow rectangle of a parking ticket on the windshield of my car. I hopped into the lane of oncoming traffic and ripped the ticket from the wiper. It was a sixty-five-dollar fine. I looked up to the meter, whose red flashing light showed that the time had indeed expired. I couldn't have been more than a minute or two late, though. That fucking meter maid must have been waiting to pounce. I scanned up and down the street but saw no one. Sixty-five goddamn dollars.

I folded the ticket and put it in my back pocket. I then dug in my front pocket for my keys, but my fat sausage fingers struggled to pull them out. I could feel the tension in my face, pulsing in my temples. Traffic buzzed past me. I picked up the keys and got the door open and squeezed into the car. It was like an oven inside, and I immediately broke out into beads of sweat. I turned the key, thinking it would be a perfect capper to this afternoon if the fucking car refused to start. Thankfully, it started, and I turned on the air conditioner. The blast of cold air quickly cooled the car.

I sat there a moment, staring out, not focusing on anything. I didn't want to go back to the restaurant. I didn't want to deal with anything anymore. I wanted to go see a movie. I wanted a drink. I wanted somehow to escape.

I waited for a break in the river of traffic, then pulled out. The lanes were open both ways, so I flipped the car around, making a wide U-turn and nearly missing a car parked on the street. I didn't notice the Lincoln sitting in the turn lane at the intersection. I wasn't paying attention to it at all. The light turned yellow. I gunned it, heading into the intersection, confident I would make the light. I imagine the driver of that big boat of a Lincoln hesitated, not sure what I was going to do, before turning. I plowed into the passenger-side door. The impact was like a cannon. I slammed against the steering wheel. The Lincoln spun around, ending up on the other side of the street. A green Pinto had to hit the brakes to avoid slamming into it. I could hear a horn blare. I closed my eyes, and the sound went on and on and on.

They blocked the intersection off with flares and small orange cones. An officer in a blue uniform wearing a neon-yellow vest directed traffic. There was a group of EMTs attending to an elderly man, a guy at least in his seventies, whom they pulled out of the driver's side of the Lincoln. Dark blood streaked his face. He looked disoriented and confused. A second group of EMTs worked to assist a woman around the same age as the man. She was still in the passenger side, still strapped in by the seat belt. She appeared lifeless.

I stood near the back of an ambulance with a tall, beefy middle-aged police officer whose rectangular gold name badge tagged him as "B. Boyd."

"No," I said for the third time.

"It wasn't a red light?"

"No. As I said, it had turned yellow as I was entering the intersection."

"You had already entered the intersection before the light turned yellow?"

I nodded. "Yes."

"The light wasn't red?"

"No."

"You didn't run the light?"

"No."

"Are you sure?"

"Yes. I'm sure. I'm positive."

"We're talking to witnesses."

"Good."

"You think they'll say the same thing?"

"Without a doubt."

"Without any doubt."

"That's right."

"You did not run a red light?"

"No. I did not. Not a chance."

"No chance, huh? Well, that's pretty confident."

One of the EMTs turned away from the woman in the Lincoln. There were smears of blood on his light-blue latex gloves. It was hard to see what was going on with the woman in the car.

"Do you think they are going to be all right?" I asked.

Thirty minutes later, I stood on the sidewalk with a group of spectators as we watched the EMTs pull the woman from the Lincoln. They lifted her limp body onto a metal gurney, then wheeled her across the street to an ambulance. The elderly man, his head wrapped in gauze and bandages, his left arm in a sling, could walk on his own, but he needed help stepping up into the back of the ambulance.

Joslyn lit a cigarette as she rolled down the window.

"Since when do you smoke?" I asked her.

"Since a while ago."

"What's a while?"

"A year or so."

"Your mom know about that?"

"No," she said. "Are you kidding?"

I watched my daughter take a drag from the cigarette and wondered what else she was doing I didn't know about. I didn't want to dwell on it too much. It was too depressing. My daughters were quickly becoming strangers, especially since the divorce.

"I'm sorry about this," I said.

Joslyn shook her head. "I'm glad you were able to get ahold of me. That one paramedic said you should've gone to the hospital."

"I'm fine."

"Of course you are. It wasn't like it was a violent car accident."

"I'm still fine."

"You feel okay now, but who knows how you'll feel tonight, tomorrow, in a couple of days? It's best to get it checked out now."

These were all things I knew, plus the EMT had already admonished me for being a dumbass by choosing to not go to the hospital.

"You think that woman is going to be okay?" Joslyn asked.

I took a moment, then I told her I didn't know. I wasn't sure if she was looking for an answer or not. She finished her cigarette and tossed the butt out the window. My instinct was to scold her, but I didn't feel like it.

We made our way through downtown to the freeway. I stared at the traffic and the industrial buildings, various machine shops, places to get something welded, or get your car painted, or buy travertine pavers for your backyard. This was my dad's neighborhood when he was a teenager. He ran with a gang that called themselves the Mighty Horsemen. It was more a car club than a dangerous gang. I could imagine him racing up and down these streets, drinking, chasing girls, and raising hell.

"How's school?"

"It's school," Joslyn said. "I'm going to be happy to finally get out of that place."

"I thought you liked school."

"What? No. Jesus, no. I hate school."

"You do?"

"I can't wait to get out of there."

I couldn't argue with her. I'd hated school. I barely earned the grades to graduate. I had to beg my Spanish teacher to pass me. I didn't bother going to the ceremony. It wasn't something I wanted to celebrate.

"What about prom?" I asked.

"What about it?"

"It's coming up, isn't it? Your mom said something about it."

"I don't think I'm going to go," Joslyn said. "We all might go as a group-like thing. All us girls and maybe Bobby."

"I guess prom isn't a big deal with kids anymore."

She shrugged. "It is for some. It's not a big deal for me anyway."

We drove the rest of the way mostly in silence. Joslyn hunted for the perfect song on the radio, and there was sporadic small talk. It seemed like the accident had happened much longer than only an hour ago. I was grateful when we pulled into the restaurant parking lot.

"Thanks again for picking me up."

"Of course. I'm glad you remembered my number."

I couldn't tell if that was a dig or not.

"Thank God you weren't hurt," she said.

I smiled. "Not a scratch."

"You're goddamn lucky. You have to promise me to see a doctor if you start feeling any pain."

"I will."

"I'm serious. It could take a few days before you really feel anything."

"I told you, I will."

"You promise?"

"I promise. Are you going to tell your mom about this?"

"I suppose I don't have to."

"I would prefer if you didn't. I mean, I don't want you to lie exactly . . ."

"I don't see why she has to know. Not right now anyway."

"Do you want to come in? I can have Ernie whip you up something to eat."

"I could always crush some tacos, but I best be going. There won't be a graduation if I don't study this chemistry."

I nodded and opened the door. I leaned over and kissed my daughter on the cheek. It took some effort to pull myself out of the car, and I had a bad feeling there would be residual pain. I closed the door. Joslyn rolled down the passenger window, and I bent down.

"You doing okay with money?" I asked.

"I'm fine."

"You sure?"

"I'm sure."

I reached out, and she took my hand and gave it a squeeze. I told her to be careful.

"I will, Daddy."

"I love you."

"I love you, too."

I stepped back and Joslyn pulled away. I watched her make her way through the parking lot, then pull into traffic and disappear.

I turned and faced the exterior of the restaurant. An overwhelming sense of doom hit me like a crashing wave. I didn't want to go in. I didn't want to face what was inside. But I had no choice.

I took a deep breath, opened the ornately carved front door, and stepped inside.

I loved the kitchen of my restaurant. It was large, probably bigger than it needed to be, and it was all pristine white tile and steel. I greeted the crew, who were just finishing cleaning up from lunch and beginning the prep work for dinner. I nodded hello but kept my head down, trying to avoid eye contact, and bulled my way to Art's station near the back of the kitchen.

He saw me coming, and his face lit up with that big, beautifully contagious smile of his.

"Que pasó, comandante?"

Art was a big man, both in size and personality. Technically he was my sous chef, but in the last year or so I suppose he'd effectively been the head chef. I admired him. He ran the kitchen with an amiable authority, always serious about the food and exacting in the work but not a demanding taskmaster. He might have spoken directly, but he never needed to raise his voice. He also genuinely cared about the staff. In fact, to him they weren't staff but members of a family that was Casa de Baca. He took the time, even if it was only a fleeting moment or two, to find out how people were doing, asking if there was anything they may need from him. It wasn't lip service either; there wasn't an action or word that was not sincere. He weighed upward of three hundred pounds, but he moved with surprising grace and dexterity in the kitchen. He was a monster cook, and had been married nineteen years and was a dedicated father of five—two boys and three girls.

In other words, he was everything I was not.

He worked a three-inch spackle knife, spreading corn masa onto large corn husks. He did this with delicate, machine-like speed.

"How goes the good fight?" I asked.

"Busy."

"Lunch was busy?"

"Lunch was incredibly busy. We turned . . . I don't know how many we turned actually, but it was busy. We've barely been able to catch our breath getting ready for tonight."

That was a pleasant bit of news I hadn't been expecting.

"Good," I said, patting him on the shoulder. "I'll be out in a bit."

"We'll be here."

I walked into the office and found Mark sitting behind a cluttered desk, going through receipts and paperwork.

He looked up at me. "There he is."

"Here I am. How was lunch?"

"Nice. Busy."

"That's what I heard."

I sat in the chair in front of the desk. I had a sudden, near-overpowering need to have a drink.

"It was very busy indeed," Mark said.

"There's been an uptick lately," I said.

"There has," Mark agreed.

"I wonder why that is?"

"Listen," Mark said, blowing past the question. "I'm having a problem with that bastard Marty and the booze. I know we've been with him for a while, but he's giving me shit about that last order. He doesn't want to admit the mistake."

I leaned forward and reached across the desk for the phone. I picked up the handset and quickly dialed.

"I've been talking with Stapley. I think we should meet with him, like in a more formal way."

I nodded, only half listening. I got the voice mail again. I listened to my wife's overly sweet and upbeat greeting and waited for the beep.

"It's me again. I was hoping to . . ." I didn't know what else to add to the other messages I had left. "I'll hopefully see you tonight."

I set the phone back into the cradle and sat back in the chair.

"So," Mark said. "What have you been up to today?"

After fighting with my insurance company for the better part of an hour, finally getting them to agree to deliver a rental car sometime that day, I felt restless, trapped in this office. I got them to agree to deliver me a rental car that evening. I needed to get out. I took off my blue button-down shirt and put on my black chef's jacket. It had been a while since I had suited up. On the left side of the jacket, right above the heart, was my father's name, my name, and the name of the restaurant—Baca's—embroidered in bright-red thread beneath the head and horns of a bull created by two simple lines.

I opened my knife roll and picked the eight-and-a-half-inch chef knife I had bought on my first trip to Kyoto. The history of the knife was almost comically mythic. Kinji Ozu, a master craftsman, made it. Ozu's father made knives, as did his grandfather. At the time I purchased the knife, Ozu was seventy-eight years old. He started when he was ten, learning the craft from his father. He owned a small shop in the Western Kyoto district, not too far from the Togetsukyo Bridge. Sakai worked with his son and three assistants. Every knife was hand-forged and topped off with a birchwood handle. They were beautiful knives, the work exquisite, beyond anything I had ever seen.

I didn't want to get in the way of the kitchen. I decided on something simple and busied myself cleaning tomatillos. It was impossible for the staff not to know I was cooking, but they knew me well enough to know to keep their distance.

I roasted the tomatillos and made a quick salsa. It was an easy recipe, a few simple ingredients, but it was a punch in the face in terms of flavor. When I finished, I brought people over and asked for opinions. It went over well.

I felt good and didn't want to stop. I roamed the kitchen, looking at the dry goods, stepping into the large walk-in cooler, searching for inspiration. I pulled a beautiful big snapper, an amazing-looking fish, and carried it over to my workstation. I broke the fish down. My knife skills were still on point, and I worked with speed and precision. I noticed that a couple of the prep cooks stopped what they were doing to watch. I cut the fish into cubes and combined it in a steel bowl with some onion and lemon juice.

"A ceviche," Art enthused.

"We can push it as a special. If it doesn't sell, we'll keep it for the kitchen."

"Kind of hoping it doesn't sell then."

I worked up a sweat. It felt good. I had almost forgotten the meeting with Richard and the accident, but I couldn't completely outrun it. My adrenaline was up. I enjoyed the work. It had been far too long since I had been in the kitchen like this. That needed to change. I needed to be more involved. I realized I had missed the camaraderie of the kitchen. Why had I allowed myself to become increasingly removed from the day-to-day operations and cooking? It was hard to remember. Actually, that wasn't true. It was easy to remember, I just didn't want to.

I stood outside the restaurant on the edge of the parking lot. The sun had retreated for the day, but I could still feel heat radiating from the concrete and asphalt. It wasn't even summer yet. I'd changed into a black suit, and I could feel sweat on my back. I wanted a cigarette. I wanted a drink even more. The parking lot was full, and people had to park across the street at the dirt lot. They milled near the entrance, waiting for a table. I didn't want to go back inside. I'd given up the day-to-day kitchen to become a half-assed front-of-the-house stooge. I spent most nights fluttering from the kitchen, to the dining room with Mark and our hostess, Deborah, to the bar, and back to the kitchen. I spent a lot of time walking, chatting to the regulars, putting on a face, shaking hands, and blowing smoke up our customers' asses. I hung out, pretending to be in charge, pretending to decide, pretending to be engaged. I also spent a lot of time hiding in the office.

I walked out of the office into the kitchen. The dishwashers were almost done. One of the prep cooks, Carlos, a shorter ex-army guy who had forearms disproportionately thick with muscle, mopped the floor. He whistled as he worked. I asked if everyone had gotten themselves something to eat. They assured me they had.

I loosened my tie and struggled with the top button of my shirt. When I got it, the relief was instant. I popped through the door leading into the dining room. The waitstaff was cleaning the room, getting the tables cleared and ready for tomorrow. I asked again if everyone had gotten something to eat and told them if they were hungry, they needed to get a plate before they left.

I went up to the bar. Mark stood at the far end going through the receipts for the night. Mingo, one of the bartenders, silently cleaned.

"Another busy night," Mark said, and took a sip from his beer.

"That seems to be the consensus."

I walked behind the bar and took out an old-fashioned glass. I poured myself a healthy shot of tequila. I kept my eye on Mark, still looking through the receipts. I sipped the drink at first and then tossed the entire thing back. I poured another and stared at Mark with his thick, wavy hair showing touches of gray and his permanent two-day stubble. He wore designer clothes, clothes whose intention was to give an air of casualness but that were a touch too calculated, and reading glasses on the end of his nose. His wife, Rebecca, was younger than him, but close enough to his age to not look unseemly. She had an unforced geniality and was a consummate host who loved dinner parties and nights out at the Herberger Theater. She came from money. Mark came from nothing. They lived in a nice ranch house in North Scottsdale. She leased a new Mercedes every December. Last week, Mark was talking about the new range of Corvettes. He wanted one. They looked nice. Nothing like the older Vettes, mind you. Nothing like those old '70s Vettes, like a '77, but they still looked mean enough to get the job done. What would one of those new ones cost, brand new, right off the lot? Anything better than the base model would run seventy or eighty grand.

My eyes bored into that bottle. I wanted another. I already felt warm and lightheaded. I eased myself around the bar to stand across from Mark, dragging the bottle of tequila along the bar with me. I could see Mingo turn around, and I knew he caught something in me, a look, a tone that radiated. He knew enough to give us room and busy himself putting away clean glasses, but he kept glancing sideways toward us.

"How good was it?" I asked.

He said, "The bar is really kicking it up lately."

"Why is that, you think?"

"The happy hour, my man." Mark took another sip of his beer. "We altered the hours. I knew that was going to work. And I think folks are staying a little longer, too."

"It's working?" I asked.

"Indeed, it is. I think it's starting to come together."

"You do?"

"We're finally starting to turn the corner again."

"You really think so?"

Mark held up the receipts and said, "The proof is here."

I nodded and asked, "Are you stealing from me?"

Mark swallowed and turned his head to the side so as to hear me better.

"Are you stealing from the restaurant?"

He stared at me, looking above his glasses, confused. He adjusted his stance and asked, "What do you mean?"

"I don't know how I can be more clear. Have you been stealing from the restaurant?"

He continued to look at me like he was trying to figure out a puzzle. "What do you mean?"

I locked my eyes on his. I didn't want to give him any room to maneuver from my question.

"How can you ask me something like that?" he asked. "Where does that come from? How can you seriously ask me something like that?"

"What do I look like to you?"

"What is going on?"

"Did you steal from me? Are you stealing from this restaurant?"

"How can you ask me that? Where do you get off asking me something like that?"

I would not avert my gaze. I would not let him off the hook.

"Where is this coming from?" he asked again.

"It's coming from the fact that we're going to have to close this restaurant."

"And you're laying that on my doorstep? That's my fault?"

"Answer the question. Tell me the truth."

"I told you the truth the first time. You don't have to ask again. It's a bullshit question, and you should know better."

"You haven't been stealing from me?"

"What happened to you? That's some balls you have laying this on me."

"So, the answer is no?"

"Fuck you. That's the answer. Fuck you, and go fuck yourself. You don't trust me."

"I thought I did."

"Seriously, go fuck yourself."

"You still haven't answered my question."

"And I'm not going to answer it. You need to look in the mirror, my friend."

"What does that mean?"

"That means the problem is not with me."

"Who's the problem with then?"

"I'm not doing this," Mark said. "I'm not doing this with you."

"You're not doing what with me?"

"I feel sorry for you," Mark said. "I really do feel sorry for you."

"I don't need your sympathy. Take it and shove it up your ass."

Mark dropped the receipts and clapped his hands like a dealer ending his shift. "I'm done."

"That it?"

"I'm done with your bullshit."

"Take the money and run, huh?"

"You know that's not true. You goddamn well know that's not true."

"Is that what I know? Tell me what I know."

"You're sick. You're paranoid."

"Why did you steal from me?"

"You checked out a long time ago."

"Tell me why you did it."

"You don't cook. You don't give a shit. You haven't for a while now."

"How long has it been going on?"

"I'm not going to let you lay this on me. It's not going to happen."

"Why did you steal from me?"

Mark backhanded his glass, spilling beer all over himself and the bar.

"How long have you been stealing?"

"I've never done anything to hurt you or this restaurant."

"Why did you do it?"

"What do you want me to tell you?" Mark asked. "I've been stealing from the beginning. Is that what you want? From the fucking beginning, okay? It was easy, too. Is that what you want to hear? You're nothing but a drunk, selfish fool."

I threw my glass point blank at Mark's head. It missed, instead bouncing off his shoulder. He screamed out. I leaped onto the bar and had to wiggle my way across to the other side. Mark rubbed his shoulder. I attacked him with punches, not connecting in any substantial way. I hadn't been in a real fight since junior high. Mark stood back, bringing his hands to his face to block any blows. I grabbed Mark around the neck and wrestled him to the ground. He didn't put up much of a fight. We clumsily grappled on the floor, rolling around, gnashing our teeth. Mark screamed for me to get the fuck off him. He hit me in the side with small rabbit punches that didn't have much bite. I grabbed a fistful of his hair and tried to slam his head onto the floor.

Art ran in from the dining room. This prompted Mingo, who up to this point had stood watching with his mouth open, into action. He lunged for us.

"Get him the fuck off me!" Mark yelled.

Art and Mingo yanked me off Mark. I stood, fists clenched, little bits of spit in the corners of my mouth, ready to beat the shit out of him. Art kept a hand on my chest, and Mingo stood in front of Mark.

"The fuck is wrong with you?" Mark asked.

I reached around Art and slapped Mark as hard as I could in the face. He exploded in an uncontrolled rage, and screamed, "I'm going to kill you! I'm going to fucking kill you!" repeatedly. Mingo held him back.

"Come on," I said. "Come on, cocksucker. Do it. Fucking do it."

He kept screaming and fought to break free of Mingo.

"You're bleeding me dry," I said. "Might as well put a gun to my head."

"Never, never happened."

I picked up the beer glass on the floor and threw it at him. The glass hit the edge of the bar and bounced off.

"Piss on you," I said and walked away.

"Never happened," Mark yelled.

As I walked away from the bar and into the dining room, I could hear Mingo ask Mark if he was all right.

"What the fuck is wrong with him?" Mark asked.

The rental car was some mid-level sedan, nothing fancy, a functional, somewhat comfortable ride. I kept hitting the "Scan" button on the radio, moving from channel to channel. I couldn't find a song I liked, something that fit my mood. I settled on some hair metal ballad from a band I didn't remember. I only remembered the song being in constant rotation my sophomore year of high school. It now played on the oldies station.

I lived in an upper-middle-class bordering on wealthy neighborhood in East Mesa. Intermittent streetlights, and the periodic porch light, irradiated the dark and quiet neighborhood. Many of the houses looked abandoned instead of locked up and alarmed for the night.

I hit the garage door button on the visor as I pulled into the driveway. I waited for the door to rise. I saw my wife's Buick parked inside. It surprised me although I'm not sure why—she didn't mention having plans for the evening, but that didn't mean much. Our communication had been lacking of late. That was an understatement. I didn't expect her to be there, so it was a pleasant surprise to see she was home.

I eased the car into the garage, gathered my stuff, and walked into the house. The lights were off. It was as dark as a cave. I punched the code to disarm the alarm and flipped the lights on in the kitchen and living room.

"Christine?"

No answer.

I walked through the kitchen and down into the sunken living room. The television was off. The stereo played no music. My wife was not home. I knew it, but I still felt the need to walk down the hall and check our bedroom. It was dark, but I could see a soft white light coming from the bathroom.

I pressed the button for the answering machine on the small desk in the bedroom. I heard a woman's voice confirming a dental appointment for Christine. There were no other messages. This meant that she had been home at some point. She'd listened to all of my messages, deleted them, and not even tried to call me back.

I walked into the bathroom. Christine left her makeup on the counter along with her hair dryer and a bottle of hairspray.

I peed and didn't bother to flush the toilet. I washed my hands and splashed water onto my face. Driving home, I'd been dead tired, ready for a beer and a good trashy movie on cable. But now, I didn't feel like being in the house anymore.

I changed my shirt and put on a sports coat. Not five minutes later, I pulled out of the garage and headed back into the night.

I handed my keys to a college-aged valet dressed in black pants and a black button-down shirt. He handed me a claim ticket, and I walked into the club.

The entry was a black room decorated with white Christmas lights. I felt the vibration of music coming from the main room. A very large Mexican man with thick sideburns and a brown cigarette dangling from the corner of his mouth checked the IDs of four antsy young men, all tightly coiled with nervous energy. They looked like kids. As the Mexican cleared them, they walked to Victoria, a tiny woman perched on a stool behind the counter, and paid her the cover charge. Victoria wore a strategically placed faux-leather outfit, her white hair piled on top of her head in big loopy curls.

The Mexican recognized me and nodded me through. I pushed through the double doors. The music hit me like a wave. The room was like smoked chocolate. It looked to be a slow night, with a handful of customers spread thinly throughout the room. A petite blonde who wore the tiniest bikini bottoms danced on the main stage. A man sitting at a small table next to the stage tossed a five-dollar bill toward her. The dancer saw it. She spun and slid over to the man. She twirled around, giving him a complete view, then bent down and flicked the bill behind her. She then crouched down in front of him, slithered from side to side, and pressed her enormous breasts together.

Another young girl danced by herself on a smaller stage nearer the bar.

"*Compa*, how in the hell are you?"

Ernie appeared at my side as if by a magic trick. As usual, he was dressed in a beautifully tailored suit with a black wool cowboy hat. He held out his hand. I looked at him and smiled. I couldn't help myself. I shook his hand.

"It's been too long," he said. "Where have you been?"

"About and away," I told him. "How's my credit?"

"How's your luck?"

In the middle of the small stock room, surrounded by boxes of liquor and T-shirts for the club, five men sat on metal folding chairs around a round oak table chain-smoking cigars and cigarettes and trying to play poker. The game played seven days a week. Ernie did not impose rules for the game. It remained fast and loose. It began around eight and went until there were not enough players to continue, typically around dawn. It would not be unusual to see games last two or three days straight. The players rotated in and out depending on their schedules, but there was a core group of regulars.

Everyone at the table knew me, and when I walked in with Ernie, they gave me a wave or a perfunctory hello. I shook a few hands and peeled off my sports coat. A young kid emerged from the shadows of the room.

"May I take that for you, Mr. Baca?"

I handed him the coat and told the kid I wanted a whiskey, neat. He nodded and disappeared back into the shadows.

The dealer, a small man, a retired teacher named Hadid, gave me a slight bow of his head and asked, "You want in?"

"I'm in."

I stood at the urinal unable to pee. James, the bathroom attendant, a tall black kid who kept his hair like Dr. J circa the ABA years, stood beside a small table filled with various cigarettes, cigars, fragrances, mints, gums, and condoms. He handed paper towels to customers washing their hands. Friendly to a fault, James enjoyed the small talk and the dumb jokes with the customers.

I shook it off, still dribbling on my hands, and zipped up. I stepped up to the sink.

"How's the action out there?" James asked.

"A pot of piss thus far."

He laughed. "By chance, would some gold help?"

I lathered my hands with soap and said, "It might at that."

I lingered, taking as long as possible to dry my hands. I studied James's spread as if trying to figure out what I wanted to buy. When I was the only one left in the bathroom, I handed a folded bill to James. He took the money and lifted a basket filled with hard candy. Under the basket was a tiny Ziploc pouch of cocaine.

I snatched it up and retreated into a stall. People kept coming into the bathroom. The door opened, the music boomed, and James greeted them with small talk. I unfolded the top of the baggy and ripped the corner with my teeth. I sprinkled the powder on my hand in the area near the index finger and thumb. I looked at the powder and considered whether this was a good idea, then snorted the cocaine.

The effect was instant, like a kick from a horse. I shook my head and rubbed my nose as if taking care of a ferocious itch. My brain opened. A current of electricity coursed through me. The fluorescent lights above me shined brighter and I could see them pulse.

I flushed the toilet for no reason and stepped from the stall.

"My man," James said with a wide smile. "Better?"

"Much better," I said. "Much better indeed."

I went to the sink and washed my hands again. I caught my reflection in the mirror. I didn't look quite as good as I felt, with bloodshot eyes and waxen skin. I splashed water on my face and gave myself a couple of quick slaps. I took a paper towel from James.

"Thank you, good sir."

James gave me a slight tilt of the head and said, "Always a pleasure."

I opened the door. A surge of sound punched me. The intense thump of the bass felt good. I felt energized. I moved through the tables. It was busier now and I had to push through men and dancers to get to the bar. I lit a cigarette and caught Marina's eye. I waved. She finished making a drink, handed it off to a waitress, and walked over.

"Stranger in a strange land," she said.

"I've been meaning to call you."

"Really?"

"It's the truth."

"You're always meaning to call," she said.

"That's not entirely fair."

She let it go.

"You want a drink?" she asked.

"I need a hell of a lot more than that."

"We'll start with the drink and go from there."

"The woman of my dreams."

Marina smiled. "You're finally realizing that?"

I'd told her the truth. I really had meant to call her. I'd missed her and found her presence now immediately comforting.

She brought me a double whiskey, neat. I reached out and took her wrist. She made eye contact with me. I smiled, but she gave nothing back.

"We'll talk later," I said.

"Sure," she replied, and someone called her away to make another drink.

Ernie and I stood outside smoking.

"Maybe you can start by erasing what I owe you," I said.

"Maybe you can start by fucking yourself. What else can I do?"

I shrugged and took a deep drag from the cigarette. A nice cool breeze surprised us.

"There's no doubt of the money situation," I said. "I'm staring in the face of bankruptcy. I'm fucked."

"That's a shame," Ernie said. "It doesn't make any sense. It's the best goddamn place in the city. I'm not just saying that either. It's better than that snobby froufrou first joint you had. It's the best, but—and I told you this, I told you this before—the last thing this city needed was another goddamn Mexican restaurant. I don't care how good it is."

The effects of the coke had dimmed. I weighed up whether I wanted to go back to James for another round.

"Do you have a plan?" Ernie asked.

"I just found out the extent of the nightmare this very day."

"What are you going to do?"

"I'm going to try and hold on," I told him. "I don't know how I'm going to do that exactly, but that's the plan, as it were."

"How's the wife taking it?"

I looked up at the starless sky. "I haven't had a chance to talk to her about it yet." I took the cigarette down to the filter and flicked it away. "You know she's fucking a tennis instructor?"

"That's a nice little situation you have," Ernie said.

"It's so goddamn cliché it makes me sick."

I lit another cigarette.

"How's it going in there?" Ernie asked, nodding toward the door.

"You damn well know your guys are knocking my dick into the dirt."

"You can always walk away."

"What fun is that?"

"Hey, listen," Ernie said. "We're friends and all. We have this little relationship going, but you know I'll still take whatever money you have left."

"I know you will."

"I'm more than happy to take it from you."

"I'm going to take my chances on you having to give it over to me."

Ernie laughed. "Oh, I know you will. That's what I love about you, *compadre*. You're at least consistent."

"You going to sign me over some money?" I asked.

"How much are you down?"

"Don't ask like you don't already know to the fucking penny."

The fierceness of my tone gave Ernie pause. "What are you doing?"

"What do you mean?" I asked, a bit too defensive.

"What are you doing?" Ernie asked again.

"If you're going to give me the money, give me the money. If not, then don't. Stop with the concerned, nice-guy act. You know you've never had a problem with me paying my debt. So, do what you're going to do."

Ernie took a step back and looked at me as if he couldn't believe my insolence. I felt a ripple of shame, but I also didn't want a guilt trip from him. I could see he wanted to say something. He gave it a thought and decided against it.

"Have the kid set you up," he said.

"Ten?" I asked.

He held up his hands. "You're the boss."

I sat at the table in the stockroom and unwrapped a new pack of cigarettes. I knew I should leave. I should have pushed away from the table, thanked everyone, said good night, and walked away. Staying was a bad idea, but I didn't want to leave.

The same kid who took my coat brought over a small clipboard. I signed the slip without looking at it. The kid disappeared and not a minute later returned with a rack of chips. I took the chips from the rack and organized them.

"In again, sir?" the dealer asked.

I eyed the other players at the table and knew I could take every last one.

I smiled and said, "Let's give it a go."

Marina rested her head on my bare chest. She felt good, like she belonged here. I traced patterns on her back with my fingers. We passed a joint back and forth.

"No, no, no," she said. "I wanted to be an actress."

"An actress?" I asked. "I didn't know you ever had an interest in acting."

"You learn all kinds of things when we actually have a conversation."

I let the much deserved jab go.

"Did you act?"

"In high school, sure. I was a big theater rat."

"And you acted, like, in plays?"

"Why is that so hard to believe?"

"It's not."

"I was in the theater department. We did all kinds of plays. It was probably the most pure fun of my life. I wanted to study acting in college."

"Why didn't you?"

She shrugged. "I was never the one with the talent."

"Why do you say that?"

"My sister was the talented one."

"What?"

"It's true. It's not false modesty. She was something. She was beautiful and talented. You could see it even in those dumb high school productions."

"This is Julie?"

Marina nodded.

"I find that hard to imagine," I said.

"She always had something I never had. She had a presence. An aura people were drawn to. I didn't have that."

I wanted to remind her that all that talent and beauty did not mean much. Marina's older sister, Julie, married a Mormon who worked for his father's construction company. She was a housewife and a stay-at-home mom who was already working on a litter of kids. That was all well and good, but Julie didn't exactly light the world on fire.

Marina held the joint between her finger and thumb. She seemed to drift off, lost in a faded memory. I gave her time to come back on her own.

"Whatever," she said. "It was never really a possibility anyway. A kid's dream. I had my son and had to put that away. Besides, if I can ever finish up and get this damn degree, I'll be on my own doing something closer to what I want."

"I always wanted to be a shortstop," I said.

"What happened with that?"

I pointed to the scars on both my knees.

"Never quite works out, does it?" she said.

"It does for some."

"Was the baseball thing serious?"

"I don't know how serious it was. I was pretty serious about playing. I was good enough for All State. I probably could have gotten some scholarships. At least division two."

"But in the end, it worked out," she said.

"How so?"

"You found your passion wasn't baseball. Or if it was baseball, you found something to replace it."

"Which was what?"

"Food. You became a chef. An award-winning chef. Best in the valley."

I groaned as if I had just stepped in dog shit.

"Multiple categories. Multiple years. Best overall restaurant."

"Stop," I said. "Please."

"Rising Star Chef of the Year," Marina said. "James Beard. I know all about that too."

"Enough," I pleaded. "I'm serious."

"Oh, you're being serious now?"

"I'm asking. Please."

"The point," Marina said, "is that you found something else. You found something you were meant to do."

I admired Marina's hopeful outlook. She was still young, twenty-three years old, and had already had to deal with some heavy challenges in her life. She liked to joke that her life was a jumble of after-school specials. There was truth to that. Some of her circumstances were vague. She didn't always like talking about her past. Her father was both physically and verbally abusive. He vanished when she was still young. Her mother wandered from one asshole to the next until she had a severe heart attack one night and never woke up. Marina was sure the death was drug related, but there was never an autopsy so she could never know for sure. She and her sister, Sasha, and their younger brother, Joel, went to live with their grandparents. The details from there on were fuzzy, but I got the impression it was not an ideal situation for anyone. When he was sixteen, Joel flipped his jeep out in the desert and broke his neck. He died on the helicopter ride to the hospital. Marina became interested in boys early. She picked up on her mother's habits, drifting from one toxic relationship to another, and eventually became pregnant when she was fifteen. Even though her grandparents were very devout evangelical Christians, her grandmother damn near ordered Marina to have an abortion. She refused. The baby was due in June, and Marina made it through the entire school year. I couldn't imagine that was easy. Once she had the baby, a boy Marina named Daniel, her grandparents asked her to move out. She didn't fight it. She did not argue. She just packed her things and left and had been on her own ever since.

She had overcome far more hardship than me, and she remained almost naively optimistic about her future. Meanwhile, I couldn't clear myself of my overwhelming dyspeptic view of my life and what lay ahead. Maybe the bankruptcy and the possibility, the very real possibility, of losing the restaurant were too fresh for me to see any bright side. I could not see a way out.

"What time is it?" I asked, wanting to change the subject.

Marina looked back to the digital clock on the nightstand.

"Three."

"Is it really?"

"A quarter after."

I tightened my arm around her and said, "I hate to leave."

"Then don't."

"I should."

"That's disappointing."

I didn't move right away. It wasn't a lie. I did not want to leave. I never took the time to figure out my relationship with Marina. Perhaps I was afraid of what I might find, or I didn't want to face it. My attraction to Marina was obvious. It was a well-worn stereotype. Her heartbreaking beauty aside, she was young, fun, and energetic. She made me laugh. My time with her was stress free. I didn't think about the restaurant, or money troubles, my failing marriage, my ex-wife, her new husband, my relationship with my kids, or any of the annoying banalities and petty frustrations that devour you. She was a great hang.

I never asked Marina why she was interested in me. You didn't have to be a therapist to unpack some of her issues. I wouldn't categorize the relationship as toxic, but it was unhealthy. She would have been better off without me, but I didn't have it in me to break it off.

I eased myself out from under Marina and swung my legs over the side of the bed. I stood, self-conscious of my nakedness, hoping Marina wasn't watching me, and dressed.

"Who is this?" she asked.

I turned. Marina had my wallet. It must have fallen out of my pocket. She'd opened it and pulled out an old, faded photograph. It was the size of a photo one would get from a booth. I looked at Marina holding the photograph and froze, not knowing what I wanted to say.

"She was going to be my first wife."

"Really?" She brought the picture closer.

"It was a long time ago."

"And you still keep her picture with you?"

"I guess so."

She seemed to study the photo as though it were an artwork in an exhibit. "What happened?"

I finished buttoning my shirt and tucked it into my pants. "It's a long story."

"I'd like to hear it."

"I don't know if that's a bridge I want to cross."

I could tell that stung a little. I looped my belt through my pants and reached out for the wallet.

Marina handed it to me and asked, "When am I going to see you again?"

"I don't know."

"I want to do something. I want us to go out."

"Like on a date?"

"Not a date. It could even be something with Danny."

"I can call you next week."

"Is that a promise?"

"It's a promise."

"Do I have to walk you out?"

"No," I said. "I think I can handle it. Besides, I want this image of you right now lying in that bed to linger in my head."

She smiled and stretched. She was sexy, and she was smart. She had goals and a plan. She was damaged and for some damn reason felt she needed me. It felt good to be needed.

I leaned in and kissed her.

"Be careful," she said.

"I will."

I entered the house through the garage and tossed my keys onto the kitchen table. I saw a black purse on the table, but I didn't need it to tell me my wife was home. I could smell her perfume as soon as I walked in.

I went through the living room and down the hallway to the bedroom. Christine was asleep in the king-sized bed. I walked into our large closet and undressed. I considered a shower to wash the smoke and the smell of Marina and sex off of me, but decided it could wait until tomorrow. I kept my boxers and T-shirt on and slipped under the covers. I closed my eyes and meditated.

"It's late," Christine said. "Even for you."

"Did I wake you?"

"No. I was up."

"I tried calling you a couple of times."

"What did Richard have to say?"

"He told me basically everything we already knew." I let that linger in the darkness for as long as I could before asking, "Did you expect something different?"

"I hoped it wasn't quite so dire."

"It is."

Christine sighed. It sounded pained, as if she were trying to expel something from her body.

"It's so goddamn embarrassing," she said, and I realized she was trying to hold off tears.

"What's embarrassing?"

I waited. Christine didn't answer, so I tried again with more force.

"What is so embarrassing?"

Again, she didn't answer.

"I'm sorry you might lose your chair at the country club."

"Fuck you," she hissed.

"That's nice."

"This isn't what I wanted."

"It's what I wanted, right?"

"This isn't what I agreed to when I married you."

"There was an agreement? What did you agree to? I don't remember that. Did we agree to things? I'm sorry it didn't work out for you."

"You're so smug," Christine said. She was crying now.

"It's not as if I'm not working my ass off to do everything I can to not lose that restaurant. That restaurant is everything I have. It's my life."

"It's not just the restaurant," she said. "It's not the money. It is that, but that's not all of it. We were having problems long before the restaurant."

She was right, but I didn't want to go round and around about it. We wouldn't solve anything right then, and I was exhausted. I needed sleep, and I wished I had stayed with Marina.

"There was a time when we were happy," Christine said. "It's hard to remember now, but we were."

"Were we?"

"Don't say that. Please, don't do that. We were, at one time."

"Well, you're right," I said. "It's just been so long, I can't really remember."

Christine sat up in bed. Her outline was a shadow among the shadows. She took her time before speaking. I adjusted my breathing so she might think I had fallen asleep.

"I'm not perfect, Benjamin, but it hasn't been just me. I'm not the only one at fault." She wiped the tears from her eyes. "I'm going to call Richard myself tomorrow. I don't think I can deal with this anymore."

I said nothing. I lay there, breathing heavily. She was pissing me off, and I wanted to be angry. I wanted to lash out at her, but I didn't have it in me. I should not have come home. I should have stayed with Marina, or got a room somewhere. It had been one long goddamn day, and I wanted it to end.

"What have you had to deal with?" I asked. I couldn't help myself. "I'm curious. I really want to know what you've had to deal with."

"Now you're just being mean."

What was she doing? What was her end game here? I couldn't figure out this soft, beaten-down voice, the victim act. I couldn't let that pass. I would not tolerate it.

"This is pointless," I said. "You never loved me anyway."

"There's no way you believe that."

"Tell me what I believe."

She sighed again and wiped her tears. Everything she said or did angered me, and I knew I would never get to sleep now.

"We've been married all these years," she said. "It's a shame we never got to know one another."

That was rich. I laughed, or thought I laughed. Was it in my head? I didn't know. I should have laughed. It was such a ridiculous thing to say. I turned away and closed my eyes. I was asleep not ten seconds later.

I sat at the desk, still hungover. That morning, I'd shaved and taken a long, scalding-hot shower. I still felt unclean, as if the alcohol and drugs continued to seep through my pores.

Mark had worked himself up and was pacing the office like a caged predator. He seethed in anger, fists ready, his jaw so tight I thought his teeth would crack. I'd watched him do this same routine a few times over the years. He had a little bite to his bark, but it was an amusing act. I had Art waiting outside just in case.

"We're partners," Mark said.

"You don't have any money in this thing," I told him. "The restaurant goes down, it's not you that needs a life jacket."

"That's not fair."

"But it's true."

Mark waved the point away like it was an annoying fly. "I still can't conceive where you would get off accusing me of stealing from you."

"How many times are we going to rehash this?"

I waited two days after our fight to give Mark a call. I'd had to leave a message telling him I wanted to talk about what had happened. He didn't, and I'd had to call twice more before he called me back. The conversation was strained. I apologized for what happened and how I'd reacted. I blamed it on the stress of possibly losing the restaurant. He didn't say much. I told him we needed to discuss how we would proceed, and he said he needed to think about it. I had Deborah call him as well. She made the case that I sincerely regretted what happened and that I hoped Mark would come back. She told him we needed him back. It took the rest of the week before Mark agreed to come in and talk. I didn't know if I wanted Mark back, but I felt guilty about how I'd acted.

"I don't care," Mark said. "I'm still pissed. We built this place, you and I. I've been here since the beginning. We fucking built this place together, and you accuse me of stealing. I should have left your spic ass last year. Victor offered me a spot up at the Rock. I should have taken it. But for some insane fucking reason, I felt obligated to stick with you."

"You're the one that stuck with me?"

"You're goddamn right," he said. "I had options."

I wanted to challenge this but bit my tongue. Instead, I pulled out a bottle of whiskey from my desk drawer and added some to my coffee.

"And then to accuse me of stealing without any evidence, without any evidence at all."

"I'll tell you this again: I was out of line with that. I told you I'm sorry."

"I should sue you for assault."

I leaned forward, and wrapped both hands around the cup of coffee.

"In the pit of my stomach, the pit of my fucking stomach, I knew this was never going to make it," he said.

"When did you know that?"

"I knew it from the beginning."

"Is that a fact?"

"You're goddamn right that's a fact."

"The blame is mine," I said. "I gave you too much responsibility. You were in over your head. I put too much trust in you."

"Trust?"

"That's right."

"You trusted me?"

"I trusted you like a son."

"What son?" Marked asked, incredulous. "Isaac maybe. You're so full of shit."

"I trusted you enough to let you run me into the fucking ground."

Mark laughed. "That's rich, my man. That's balls blaming me. It's my fault, right? It's not the fact that you checked out long ago. It's not the fact that you don't show up for work, and when you are here, you're not really here. It's not that. It can't be that. Or it couldn't be the food. It couldn't be the marketing. It couldn't be this location you forced on us. It couldn't be you lost your fucking passion a long time ago. It has to be me. My fault."

He took a moment to catch his breath. He sounded on the verge of an asthma attack.

I took it all in, keeping a vise-like grip on the coffee mug. I wanted to scream and yell and fight back, but Mark was more right than he was wrong. I was still self-aware enough to recognize that. Also, as much as I hated to admit it, if I was going to keep this restaurant going, I needed him. I might fire his ass as soon as we crawled our way to soluble again, but right now I needed him.

"Are you done?" I asked.

Mark considered it, then nodded.

I downed the rest of my coffee and whiskey. I debated pouring more whiskey into the cup but decided to wait until Mark left.

"I'm glad you came down here," I said. "I mean that. You're right, we've been together a long time, since the beginning—of this place, anyway—and I don't want to see that end because of a stupid moment. The fact is that this restaurant is in a lot of trouble. We're going to lose it. I have a plan to keep it going. I don't know if we can do it, but I think I have a way out. But I need you. I need your help. I'm asking if you can come back and help me."

Mark stared at me, but it was like he was looking right through me. I waited, not wanting to rush him. It felt like a long time although I'm sure it wasn't even a minute. He blinked, and the trance was broken.

"I can't do it," he said.

I fully expected him to accept my apology and come back to work. He gave me a look as if I had just pissed on the carpet.

"This has been building for some time now. It's not just the other day. It's so many things that have happened. You're a fundamentally broken person."

"Is that a fact?"

"Yes, it is a fact. It's the restaurant. It's the food. It's the fact that you're an alcoholic. It's all that shit you blow up your nose. It's all the money you drop on that fat fuck degenerate bookie. This place has been toxic for a long time. You're a toxic fucking person, and I have to get away from you."

"Okay," I said. "I have work to do. I have a restaurant I'm trying to save. I don't have time to suck your dick anymore. I've sat here and indulged you long enough."

"Indulged me?"

"I let you rant. I let you spout your bullshit. Get your shit and get out."

"Fuck you."

"Fuck you!" I rose from my chair.

"You!"

"Get out!"

"I'm going to sue you for assault."

"Shove it up your ass."

I charged around the desk. Mark flinched, arms up just in case. I shook my head, wagged my index finger, and dismissively tutted. I walked past him and stuck my head out the door.

"Art?"

"Yes, sir."

"Get this asshole out of my office."

Mark turned his head and looked past me out into the kitchen. The phone on the desk rang.

"Artie," Mark said. "Don't you think about making a move."

Art was already heading our way, wiping his hands on his apron.

Mark looked me in the eyes and said, "Fuck you."

"Fuck you."

Art stood in the doorway.

"I'm not leaving without my shit," Mark said.

Art reached out for him. "Let's go."

"Don't touch me," Mark said. "I'm not kidding. Don't."

I picked up the ringing phone. "Hello?"

"Just come back when he's not around," Art said to Mark. "It's not worth the trouble right now."

"Hello?" I could hear a voice on the other end, but it was too soft to make out.

"It's the principle," Mark said.

"What principle?" Art asked.

"I'm not letting him have one over on me."

"What difference does it make?" Art asked. "It's not a board game. You're not scoring points."

"That's not the point."

"Hold on, please," I said. I covered the phone and told Art, "Get him out of this office. Please. Now. Get him out of here."

Art pulled on Mark's arm, but Mark jerked it away.

"Hello?" I said again.

"Don't fucking touch me," Mark said.

Art pointed at Mark. "Don't you get rough. I'm trying to be nice and help you out."

Mark turned back to me. I saw he was overcome with emotion. He looked like a boy.

"What happened to you, man?" he asked.

I gave Art a look he read right away.

"Mark," Art said. "I'm going to ask you nice only once more."

Mark turned his head back to Art.

"Come back later," Art said again.

"Fuck you," Mark said. "Fuck you both."

He pushed past Art and stormed through the kitchen.

I thanked Art. He nodded, held up his hand, and went back to the kitchen.

"I'm sorry," I said into the receiver. "Go ahead."

There was a knock on the office door. I ignored it as I listened to a chipper young woman tell me she was looking to extend me a line of business credit. I let her get halfway through her pitch before I told her I wasn't interested and hung up.

A man stood in the doorway. He was shorter, with skin the color of sweet chestnut, and thinning hair. It was hard to pin his age, but I would have guessed he was somewhere in his fifties.

"May I help you?"

"Are you Benjamin?"

"How did you get back here?"

"You're Benjamin Baca?"

"That's right."

"You killed my mom."

It felt as if I had been slapped. The man had big, piercing eyes. When I looked at him, really looked at him for the first time, I couldn't take his gaze and had to look away.

"She died last night. At the hospital. She was alone. She died last night, and you killed her."

His eyes welled up with tears. He couldn't fight it.

"You killed my mom, and I thought you should know that."

Art appeared behind the man. "He was waiting in the main room. I told him he couldn't come back here, but then everything happened with Mark."

"You'll remember my face," the man said. "You'll see me again."

The man then turned and walked back through the kitchen. Art and I watched him exit through the door that led into the dining room.

"I'm sorry about that," Art said.

I looked at him as if he'd spoken a foreign language. I didn't have my bearings. If I didn't sit, I might fall down. I worked my way around the desk and fell into the chair.

"You want to talk greens now or later?"

I didn't know what to say. Art stood there looking down at me, waiting for me to say something. After some time, I can't remember how long it was, he finally let me be, and he walked out of the office.

The bartender set a whiskey in front of me, my third, and again asked Richard if he wanted another beer. Richard shook his head and the bartender walked back to the other end of the bar and resumed cutting limes.

I held the glass with both hands, hunched over, my body in a knot.

"They could charge you with vehicular manslaughter," Richard said, "but I don't think that's likely."

"Why not?" I asked, staring at the amber liquor in front of me.

"There's nothing criminal in what happened. It was a clear accident. I'd be surprised if you were charged with anything. I suppose there could be a wrongful death suit. Maybe the family could be persuaded that it wouldn't be a good idea."

I didn't want to hear an elaboration on what he meant by that.

"Can we talk about the restaurant?" I asked.

"Yes, by all means. What do you want to talk about?"

"Is the restaurant protected?"

"If they decided to come after it, you mean?"

I nodded.

"They could try. The financial situation won't make it easy for them."

"Is that supposed to make me feel better or worse?" I asked.

"Listen, I don't know what you want me to tell you. The restaurant's not the only problem."

I blew out air as if trying to expel the bitterness.

"It's the debt. There's money owed all over the place."

"Richard, you're real good at telling me what I already know."

"Then what do you want? I don't know what you want me to tell you."

"I want some answers," I said, speaking as deliberately as I could. "I don't want to give up the restaurant. I want to fight to keep the place open, and I'm looking for some solutions. Isn't that part of what I pay you for?"

"I'm sorry to say it, but that ship might have sailed. I don't know if there's a way to make a U-turn."

"Then what?"

Richard shrugged and held out his hands.

"That's it?" I asked. "That's all you got?"

"What do you expect, for Christ's sake?"

"Tell me something."

"I keep telling you. I've been telling you for months. You don't want to listen. We're past the point of no return."

"What we?"

"Fine. You are, okay? It's a bust. I'm sorry. I know what this meant to you."

"With respect, I don't know if you do."

"With respect, there's no need to be an asshole. I'm on your side."

I downed my drink in a single gulp and held up the glass, signaling for another.

"What are you trying to do with that?" Richard asked.

"I might as well drink. At this point, what difference does it make?"

Richard nodded. He kept looking to the television mounted near the bar. It showed a replay of last night's game. He wasn't interested in the conversation and was probably wishing he'd never agreed to come, eyes darting around the bar as if looking for an excuse to leave. It annoyed me to no end. He worked for me. I had paid him tens of thousands of dollars over the years. He could at least feign concern and empathy a little better.

I realized how much I hated this man.

"I built that place," I said. "It was nothing. It was a vacant lot. I designed it. I built it from nothing.

"I know you did."

The bartender set a fresh drink in front of me. Richard's attention kept going back to the game. He found it difficult to look at me anymore.

"Now you want to take it away from me."

"Come on," Richard said. "Don't start with that shit again. This isn't my fault. If you care so goddamn much, you should have taken a bigger interest nine months ago. That was the time to try to turn this around. Not now."

I wanted to flip the table over and strangle this motherfucker, with his heat-lamp artificially bronzed skin and veneer smile, his waterfront condo across the street from the Scottsdale Fashion Square, his foreign, overpriced, whatever the fuck it was car, his haughty attitude, and his condescending voice. He grew up with a silver spoon up his ass. His family handed him his clientele. He was good at what he did, but he never worked for it, he never knew what it was like to build something from the ground up. And here he was giving me the fucking high hat.

"You'll be able to keep the house, at least," he said. I could see in his face that he knew he'd made a mistake as soon as he said it. He couldn't rewind and try again.

"That's Christine's house." I told him what he already knew. "I never wanted that damn thing."

Richard took a sip of his beer and grimaced. It had to be warm by now.

"I might as well tell you," he said. "Christine came to me today."

That stopped me. "Isn't that some kind of conflict of interest?"

"She came in as a friend looking for a recommendation." He took another sip of his piss-warm beer before adding, "She's suing you for divorce."

There it was. The possibility had loomed for at least the past year, and while hearing it was not a surprise, it still made my heart ache.

"Was that your recommendation?" I asked.

"Don't be ridiculous," Richard said. "She'd already made up her mind."

I let that seep in. I took a sip of my drink and said, "Good."

"I see," Richard said, clearly tired of the conversation. "Well, I don't know how it's going to play out, but it doesn't sound as if she's going to be as vicious about it as she could be."

"I should probably applaud."

"It's a little surprising," Richard said. He brought the beer to his lips but didn't drink. He couldn't do it again. "What happened to the counseling? I thought you were trying to patch things up."

"It didn't take."

"She wants to do it clean. She knows there's no money to get, so it's not about that."

I downed the rest of my drink and held up the glass.

"That's not a good idea," Richard said.

I nodded to the bartender that, yes, I did want another drink.

"On our first date, Christine wore this sundress," I said. "It was a blue thing with these tiny white flowers. It had these straps over the shoulders. She was amazing. So beautiful. Sort of delicate, but still strong, if that makes sense."

The bartender set a new drink in front of me and took away the empty glass.

"We ducked into this little pub down by the Old Town, just to get out of the heat. We sat there drinking beer and eating peanuts, the kind you have to shell first. She told the filthiest joke I had ever heard. I damn near pissed myself laughing."

Richard waited, and when it was clear I wouldn't tell him, he asked, "What was the joke?"

"I don't remember."

I stood in the middle of the dining room. I had called a mandatory meeting, and every employee, everyone who worked at the restaurant in any capacity, stood in front of me. They stared, waiting for me to begin. They knew I had an announcement to make, and gossip being what it was, most of them already knew what I would say. The restaurant couldn't keep secrets for too long. News always got out and spread with rapid efficiency.

I still didn't know how to begin. The last few months had been a slow-motion nightmare from which I couldn't shake myself awake. I felt pinned down like a bug in an experiment. I had few options left, and the little hope I had of being able to keep the restaurant open was eroding.

I felt sweat rolling down my back. My head throbbed, in sync with my pounding heart.

"I want to thank everyone for coming in, especially those who have the day off."

My mouth was dry. I needed a drink.

Many of these people had been with me since my first restaurant. After that place closed, it took five years to open Casa de Baca. They'd followed me, quitting their jobs, taking a chance, taking a risk on me, believing in what we planned to do with this new restaurant. When I called the meeting, I'd looked at this speech as a perfunctory obligation, a pain-in-the-ass responsibility that was mine because I was the boss. I didn't think they would give a shit. Why would they? They would move on, find other jobs, do something else. They might be disappointed, and maybe feel inconvenienced, but this would not be a life-altering change for them. Standing there, I realized for the first time how the closing would affect them, perhaps even more than it would affect my life. My failure would hurt quite a few people.

"I know there has been a lot of speculation about what's going on. Instead of getting the news from gossip and rumors, I thought it would be best for you to hear it from me."

I gasped like a swimmer coming up for air. Emotion overwhelmed me. I cried. I wasn't going to fight it. I didn't care how it looked.

"This restaurant was a dream. It was my second chance. In many ways, it was a way to redeem myself. And now it looks as if it will be coming to an end. I don't have an exact end date yet. We're trying to maneuver a bit and keep it open, but it doesn't look good. I'm hoping, I'm sincerely hoping, that the closing will only be for a short time. This should be temporary."

I searched the faces before me for some bit of empathy, but found blank eyes. Maybe they didn't care. Maybe this restaurant meant nothing to them. They would move on. They would find new jobs and forget about this place.

"That being said, when we do close, I don't expect anyone to wait around for us to reopen. I understand you have families and responsibilities, and that's a priority. You need to do what you need to do."

I made little sense. This was a mistake. I should have had Art handle this. It felt as if I was trying to breathe through a coffee straw. I was being suffocated, and I needed to end this as soon as possible and flee.

"We've become like a family. That's how I always looked at it, and I hope it's been the same for you as well. I know you've spent more time at this restaurant than you have with your real families."

If we were a family, I was the asshole father who up and split one night. All I could see was resentment and anger staring back at me. I didn't know if it was real or imagined.

"You've sacrificed so much to help me make this dream possible."

Why was I doing this? Why didn't I stop and walk away?

"I'm so very sorry that this is how it's going to end."

Why was I apologizing to them? They enjoyed this. They wanted it to happen.

"Again, I expect this to be a temporary circumstance, and hopefully, soon—hopefully very soon—we'll all be working together again."

If I were to ever open another place, none of these people would be with me.

"I want to sincerely, from my heart, thank you for all your hard work."

I stood there, naked, searching for something. They waited for me to finish. I still needed to end with a semblance of grace and wisdom, wanting them to believe I was a good boss and a good guy. But I was done. I didn't see a point.

I nodded, then turned and walked through the door leading into the kitchen.

I looked forward to getting a hot dog at the ballpark all day. Sure, the hot dogs there were nothing special, and they were ridiculously overpriced, but I didn't care. They got the job done. Besides, it wasn't really about the hot dog itself. I looked forward to the experience. I hadn't been to a game this season, and I wanted the atmosphere of the ballpark. I wanted to sit there with Marina and her kid, relaxing, hanging out, people-watching, and soaking up the laid-back mood of an early-evening baseball game.

First pitch was set for six forty. Marina didn't get off work until five thirty. She had to get back to her apartment, get ready, and get her son ready. What did that mean? She could be ready by six, but I didn't think that was realistic. I knew Marina's idea of time estimation and management too well. Still, I figured we could get to the ballpark by six thirty. It wasn't ideal. We would miss batting practice and the team warm-up, but it would work.

As it turned out, I was the one who had the problem managing time. Ironically, with the final weeks of the restaurant looming, I was working harder than I ever had. We were still trying to save the restaurant. Richard and I were trying to negotiate a reprieve with the bank while searching for outside investment to help cauterize the wounds. Both options were Hail Marys, and we didn't have much hope either would happen. We kept going through the motions, attempting to save the business because we felt it was something we needed to do, but I'd finally accepted we were long past the point when anything substantial could be achieved.

The one element I had direct control over was the kitchen. I fired our produce supplier and set up a relationship with a local farmer's co-op. The price was higher, but that wasn't a consideration anymore. The quality of the food was unquestionably better. One Saturday, I gathered the kitchen staff—not only Art, but all the line and prep cooks too. That weekend, we went through the menu item by item. We discussed each element and went through ways in which we could improve each dish. We collaborated on dishes we could add. I told them we might as well jump out of the plane and figure out the parachute on the way down. Together, we came up with a new menu. I told them we would no longer have a fixed menu. We would experiment and collaborate, not plan more than a couple of days ahead, and see where our ideas took us. The collaboration and creativity energized me. They reignited a fire in me. There was nothing to lose. My marriage was in a helpless tailspin, and there didn't seem to be any way to fix it—and I wasn't sure I wanted to even if I could. The restaurant, that dream, was over. I had nothing else, and I threw myself into the work.

Again, the irony hit me like a hard right cross to the face. If I had been this dedicated in the first place, I might not be in this situation. What happened? What doused that initial fire, that brazen passion, that confidence I had all those years ago as a young cook? I'd had the enviable job of working for Nicolas Chang, my mentor, the man who stripped away my culinary school education and taught me how to be a cook. I'd walked away from his two-Michelin-star restaurant in San Francisco to go out on my own, moved back to Phoenix, and opened a place where I could cook my food.

With my first restaurant, Trono, I wanted to create a refined style of Mexican food. The goal was to have something like Pujol in Mexico City and bring it to Phoenix. The concept of the restaurant was to take Mexican street food and elevate it. I poured everything I had into that restaurant, but it turned out the Valley of the Sun was not interested in haute cuisine Mexican food. The restaurant made a splash at the beginning. There was a nice profile in the *Republic* and an amazing review in the *New Times*. There were also a few mixed reviews from critics that didn't seem to understand what we were doing. We never took off. I had been told I was too young to open my own restaurant, but there was no way I was going to listen to that. I was in over my head. I was classically trained and had worked in several great kitchens, but I had no experience running a kitchen at that level. I didn't care. I was steadfast, impervious to change. I didn't work well with others and wasn't willing to see the signs of a failing business. I worked in a bubble with a white-hot fury as I tried to express my ideas, trying to take Mexican food into bold new areas. I had an anger, a desperate need to be heard, for people to bear witness to food that was delicious, fun, emotional, and provocative. The world greeted it with a collective shrug, and the restaurant closed after a bitter three and a half years of intense struggle.

The closing of Trono was painful. I sank into a deep depression. Heidi, my first wife, and I were not two years into the marriage. Joslyn was eighteen months old, and Heidi was three months pregnant. I didn't have the luxury to not work, but I didn't want to go back to being a cook at someone else's restaurant. There were offers to come on as head chef to several places. I tried to pick one that fit best with my sensibilities, but my heart was never in it. I never had complete autonomy. I was never completely happy, never satisfied with the work I was doing, the food I was making. Cooking became a job, something I was doing because of family and, by extension, monetary obligations.

There were a myriad of reasons Heidi and I split up, countless slights and indiscretions large and small. My drinking didn't help. It also didn't help that I was having an affair with Christine, the manager to the restaurant where I was working as head chef. It is near impossible to distill our relationship down to its essentials, but I would suggest that Heidi and I had no business getting married at all. We'd had a romantic weekend that became a marriage. It got away from us before either had the wherewithal to stop and think about what we were doing. In lightning-fast order, we had one kid with another one on the way, crushing debt, and an underwater mortgage. We were both unhappy and couldn't afford a divorce.

It's one of my life's bigger absurdities that the breakup of my marriage led to me accidentally stepping into a creative invigoration. Christine and I had moved in together. I was cooking at a high-end seafood place in downtown Phoenix, bored out of my mind. We began inviting friends over for Sunday dinner. The idea was to replicate the Sunday dinners I remembered my family having. That was when I had my road to Damascus moment. Instead of the artistry of cooking, these dinners focused on the craft of cooking. It was such a simple concept, but it changed everything. The dinners became so popular, and Christine and I turned them into an underground restaurant. We called it Casa de Baca. It made the most sense. On Saturday and Sunday nights, we opened our apartment to eight to ten guests. Reservations were by referral only, meaning a previous guest had to recommend you. Two days before the reservation, Christine called each of the guests with the menu and pairing suggestions.

Our illegal restaurant became an enormous success. So much so that after a year, we brought Casa de Baca out into the open, keeping the same philosophies and standards, the promise to put craft over pretentious style, to bring people better food. It resurrected me as a chef. I was happy, and I cooked my best food.

I can't pinpoint a specific moment when my enthusiasm waned. It happened gradually. There was also no clear reason for my change in attitude. Or, put another way, there were all kinds of reasons for it, and no reason at all. I didn't want to cook anymore. I was never religious, but I believed cooking good food brought people closer to God, whatever that might mean. I guess I had lost my faith. It happened bit by bit—bad reviews where I was labeled as self-indulgent, lackluster business, no appreciation. It became hard to see the point in what we were doing. I was less angry. I didn't feel as if I had anything to prove. We'd found success, but I didn't care. I spent less and less time cooking and relinquished control over the kitchen to Art and over the business to Mark.

But now it felt good to be back in the kitchen again. I let Art run the kitchen while I worked more as a cook. And it felt good to cook. My decision to walk away wasn't a decision at all, but a forfeiture of a decision. I rediscovered a certain peace in cooking. All I had to worry about was my station. I knew everything I needed to do, and I controlled everything. I found myself nervous again, and I hadn't felt that in the kitchen in a long time.

All of that is to say I was running late to pick up Marina and her kid because I couldn't break free from the kitchen. Marina didn't mind. I knew immediately something was off with her. She smiled and hugged me. Her son, Danny, a small mop-haired kid who kept to himself, was excited for the game. Marina said he was more excited for the cotton candy. She tried to put on a smile and her usual cheery demeanor, but I could tell there was something on her mind, weighing her down. I kept asking what was wrong, what was going on, if she was all right, and she insisted everything was okay and she was fine. Traffic was light, and we made it to the ballpark before the national anthem. The Diamondbacks were in first place, so the stadium was packed and electric. We stood in line for concessions. I was finally about to get that overpriced hot dog when Marina told me she was thinking about getting back together with Danny's father.

It surprised me, but I didn't have much of a reaction. I nodded, studied the concession menu, and asked her how this had come about. She was vague, not wanting to get into it. I gave her space and left it alone, but the more I thought about it, the more it gnawed at me, and the more questions I had.

Our seats were on the seventh row on the third level. They gave us a good view of the field. Danny focused on his plastic batting helmet filled with popcorn. He'd already asked three times about cotton candy, and couldn't care less about the game. I prodded Marina about getting back with her boyfriend. I thought his name was Dwayne, but I couldn't remember and didn't want to ask. I didn't know the guy and didn't want to know him. To hear Marina tell it, he was a piece of work. He worked in construction of some kind, mostly new home builds. They'd known each other since grade school, but other than that I didn't know the details of their story. I knew he was another in a long line of physically and emotionally abusive assholes she was perpetually drawn to. She got pregnant, but that didn't change his ways. He'd continued to beat her for any perceived slight or indiscretion.

On the one hand, it was none of my business. Marina could do whatever she wanted. This outing notwithstanding, we weren't together, not in any meaningful way. We were not a couple and weren't exclusive. I didn't know what she was up to or who she was with, but I was certain there were other men in her life. That was fine. But this felt different. I had conflicting feelings. I couldn't give a fuck what she did, and yet it still bothered me she might go back to this asshole. I felt pangs of jealousy, which made little sense, but there they were. I didn't like the thought of her sharing a bed, or laughter, or time with a guy who clearly deserved none of it. I didn't deserve it either, but he sure didn't. Why now? Why was this happening now? My life was getting systematically flushed down the toilet, and my brief and sporadic time with Marina was one of the few elements that gave me some tiny semblance of pleasure and contentment.

"We're just talking," she said. "Nothing's happened yet. I shouldn't have told you."

"Why did you tell me?"

"I don't know."

I couldn't take the smell of the hot dog anymore. The mix of the beef, onion, and mustard was fetid. I remembered a grade school joke about biting into a hot dog and pulling out a vein. I had to set the dog down on the cardboard tray under my chair.

"What would be different?" I asked. "What makes you think anything would be different?"

"I know he's trying."

"Trying how?"

"He's going to counseling. Anger-management-type classes."

"He said that?"

"Yes."

"Bullshit," I said. "So that cleanses everything? Washes it away. You guys can be a happy family now?"

"No," she said. "I'm not saying that."

"I don't know what you're saying."

"He's Danny's father. It's not like I can write him out of my life."

"You imagine how great it can be, but you easily forget about the bad times, the times he screamed at you, or laid a hand on you. What's different? What kind of person is that? What kind of father is that?"

Marina rolled her eyes so hard she almost sprained her neck. "Spare me the 'good father' speech. I don't need to hear that, especially from you."

"I've never hit anyone. Never. Not one time. And I'm not holding myself up to be some paragon of fatherhood. I've made a laundry list of mistakes, but I'm trying to be better."

"That's what he's doing," she said. "He wants to try."

"The situations are slightly different."

"I'm not going back to him. I don't know what I'm going to do. I'm trying to figure it out, but I don't need a lecture from you."

I reached over and grabbed a handful of Danny's popcorn. He shot me a death-ray look that I pretended not to see.

"Well, hey," I said. "Go back to him. That could be the answer to all your problems."

"Maybe it would be."

"The perfect solution."

She sighed. Neither of us wanted to be at this game anymore.

"What's wrong with us?" I asked.

"What do you mean?"

"Don't we have fun together?"

"We're fine."

"Why do you want to screw that up?"

She shook her head and made a face like she had tasted something sour. "Screw what up?"

"This," I said. "Us."

"What us?" Marina asked. "Are we in some kind of relationship now?"

"I don't want to lose you."

I blindsided her with that, and she didn't know how to react.

"I don't want to lose being with you."

The inning ended with a pop fly that flew to right field. We sat in clumsy silence as the teams switched. An announcement blared about tickets for the 50/50 raffle. The pitcher for the Diamondbacks climbed the mound and tossed warm-ups to the catcher. A severely overweight man drenched in sweat carried a rack filled with cotton candy. I held up my hand, and he acknowledged me with a nod.

"No matter what happens," Marina said, "we'll always be together in some capacity. We will always be friends. I'll always want you in my life."

I paid the man the seven dollars, and he handed the bag of spun sugar to Danny, who clapped his hands and thanked me. He asked his mom if he could eat it. She told him he could, and she helped him get the bag open.

"I'm serious about that, Ben," Marina said. "I'll always want you in my life. That won't ever change."

I sat in my office stinking of meat and chili. With my hands laced behind my head, I stared at the calendar taped to the wall. I wasn't looking at it. I was comfortably lost with no clear thought.

"Hey."

I looked to the voice. Joslyn stood in the doorway. Her head was tilted, and she wore that slightly crooked smile of hers. She looked bright eyed and fresh faced in a pair of summer shorts and a tank top, hair pulled back into a ponytail. Often when I looked at either of my daughters, I couldn't imagine they came from me, that I'd helped create them.

"Hey there," I said. "What are you doing here?"

"Running errands, thought I'd stop by."

"You hungry?"

She shook her head. "You look tired. How is life treating you?"

I shrugged and didn't answer. I offered her a chair. "Sit down."

"I can't really stay," she said, sitting in the chair across from me.

"How's it going with you?" I asked.

"A week left until I walk the plank."

"Yes, yes," I said with a big smile. "And isn't that exciting?"

"Not really. Well, a little, I guess. You're going to be there Wednesday?"

I didn't know what she was talking about and didn't want my expression to betray that.

"Yes. Of course," I said. "What makes you think I wouldn't be there?"

Joslyn shrugged, and I finally understood she was talking about her graduation.

"Just asking," she said. "Wanted to remind you."

"I'll be there."

She nodded and took a moment before asking, "Is Christine coming?"

I guessed this was the true reason for my daughter deciding to drop in on me.

"I honestly don't know," I said. "Isn't Doug going to be there?"

"Yes," Joslyn said. "He is my stepdad."

"Christine is your stepmom."

"I guess," Joslyn said, and I couldn't miss the look she made.

"I don't know what's so bad about Christine. She's never treated you bad. She tried, anyway."

Joslyn let that go without comment. She looked at me, curious to see how far I would defend my wife.

"I suppose your mom doesn't want her to come."

"Oh, I don't know," Joslyn said. "It might make things a little less . . ."

"Right. Well, if I'm honest, I don't think your mom has to worry."

"She's not worried."

"Oh, of course she isn't," I said.

"It's just, you know, it's my graduation. I want it to be a nice night."

"I know you do."

"Free of conflict. No fights or tension. No bullshit."

"Did you tell your mother?"

"Yes," Joslyn said with an emphatic nod. "I have. Repeatedly. She's going to behave."

"Well, I don't think anyone is interested in ruining your night."

"So, you'll behave too?"

It burned that she felt the need to ask.

"I won't do anything to upset or embarrass you."

"No?"

I buried my annoyance. "I promise."

"Thank you, Daddy."

There it was. The one word that could melt most of my ire. "Of course."

We sat in silence. Joslyn had accomplished her agenda, and there wasn't much left to say.

"What time is it?" I asked, even though I knew the answer.

"Five, but you'll want to get there a little early."

"And dinner after?" Again, I already knew their plans after the ceremony. "Top of the Rock?"

Joslyn nodded and stood from the chair. "We'll drive there after the ceremony."

I nodded back. "Okay," I said with a smile that was too broad and fake.

Joslyn looked back at me, and after a moment, she smiled.

The timer gave a shrill buzz. It got the job done. I turned it off and opened the oven. I checked the foil. It was too hot to take out without help. I withdrew my dinner with an oven mitt and carried it to the kitchen table. I peeled the plastic. A billow of steam escaped. The food didn't smell too bad. The frozen dinner came with three pieces of chicken, mashed potatoes, corn, and a brownie for dessert. It was a staple meal of my childhood. I must have eaten it three times a week. I didn't feel like cooking, and I had a craving for it again.

I sprinkled salt and pepper over the spread and waited for the food to cool. I opened the newspaper and put the sections in the order I wanted to read them, starting with the sports. I browsed the stories as I spooned the corn into the compartment for the potatoes and stirred them together.

I heard the garage door open and tensed. Christine was home. My shoulders hunched and knotted. I leaned over the newspaper, no doubt looking as if I might fall over into it. I couldn't pay attention to anything anymore. I didn't know how this would go. Would we talk? Would we ignore each other? I didn't know how I would react to her. A part of me wanted to retreat into the office or the spare bedroom and avoid my wife altogether, but I didn't see the point. We couldn't avoid each other forever.

I blew on a forkful of food, listened, and waited. I could hear the car door open and then close. There were other indistinct noises. The door opened and Christine walked in.

She set her keys and purse on the table. I watched her, trying to gauge her mood.

"Where have you been?" I asked. It was probably a mistake to engage, but I couldn't help myself.

"Out," she said.

"Practicing your backswing?"

"You're the concerned husband all of a sudden?"

Christine opened the refrigerator and pulled out a cherry-flavored diet soda.

154

"I was thinking of a trip," I said. I hadn't been thinking about a trip. I said it with little thought at all. "How would a weekend away sound?"

"Where?"

"I'm not sure. Where do you want to go?"

"I don't really want to go anywhere."

I looked down at my food. While it tasted okay, the chicken looked as if it had been pieced together from leftover parts from a grotesque experiment. I closed my eyes.

"There's no hope, is there?"

Christine did not hesitate with her response.

"I think we both know that passed a long time ago."

"All we have left is hatred, resentment."

"I don't hate you, Ben. I've never hated you." After a beat, she added, "I just can't be married to you anymore."

I picked at the pieces of corn baked into the overcooked brownie.

"What would you think about going to Joslyn's graduation on Wednesday?"

"I'm moving out at the end of the week."

I turned around to face her. "Do I get to guess where you're moving to?"

"I just thought I'd let you know."

Christine walked out of the kitchen. I watched her disappear into the darkness of the living room and hallway. I turned back to the paper and my dinner. I tore a strip of meat from the malformed breast. It was grey and fatty, but tasted good.

It was late morning, and the club was empty. Some young kid I'd never seen before was stocking the bar. Someone else vacuumed the carpet. I sat at the bar with a whiskey in front of me.

"I'm just a little surprised, is all," Ernie said, lighting a cigarette. "This kind of talk isn't like you."

I shrugged. "I'm backed up against the wall. I don't know what to do."

"I don't know if there's much of a choice, compadre."

"I know," I said. "That's why I'm here."

Ernie took a drag from his cigarette. He flicked the ash into a glass ashtray. He was clearly trying to avoid eye contact with me as long as he could. He took another deep drag.

"It's too late," he finally said, amid a plume of smoke.

That wasn't the answer I'd expected.

"What do you mean?"

"You should have come to me six months ago, a year ago, when there was a hint of this."

"I didn't know then," I said. "I knew, but not the extent. I tried to put a tourniquet on the thing myself. I wanted to fix it without any outside help."

"But now it's impossible."

"Why is it impossible?"

"It's throwing good money after bad."

"No," I said. "This is my last hope."

"This isn't hope. That's what I'm telling you."

"I need your help," I said. "I really need this, Ernie."

Ernie crushed out his cigarette and lit another. "Situation you're in, what you're talking about, cops and insurance will be up your ass so quick, you won't know what to do."

"But if it's done right. That's what I'm saying. You can do it. You can do it the right way. There won't be any questions."

"There are always questions," Ernie said. "Especially with those insurance cocksuckers. There are always questions."

"No, no, no," I said. "My place goes up in flames, that's a million and a half. This isn't fucking nickel and dime bullshit."

"I know, *compadre*. That is exactly why everyone's bound to take a sharp interest if there's all of a sudden a fire. You're desperate."

"Yes, I'm fucking desperate."

"I understand. That much is obvious, but this isn't the answer."

I ran my fingers through my hair. I was in desperate need of a haircut. I wanted to down that drink in front of me. I wanted to down a hundred more and curl up into a ball and sleep until next summer. I wanted to disappear.

"Listen," I said. "I'm losing my ass here. It's not just the restaurant. I'm done. I'm coming to you, hat in hand, as a friend. What would it take? I know you have a price. I know you have a number. What would it take, friend? Come on now. You're a businessman. This is business. This is a way. This is a way out. What would you need to make this happen?"

Ernie took a drag and gave me a sideways look. When he finally spoke, it was slow and deliberate, as if he were talking to a child.

"There's too much risk."

I slammed my fist onto the bar. "Fuck the risk!"

"Hold on a second."

"Fuck yourself."

"The fuck do you think you're talking to?"

"Who am I talking to?" I asked. "I know who you are. What are you worried about? It's not the job. This would be a piece of cake for you. You know it would be. You worried about me? Don't. I'm coming to you like a fucking arrow. You don't have to worry about me. Insurance, cops, all the rest of those motherfuckers, I can handle it."

"Yes," Ernie said, crushing out his second cigarette. "You clearly look as if you can handle it."

"I'll give you half."

"I don't need it that badly."

"We've been friends a long time," I said.

"I know we have. That's why I'm telling you, as a friend, this isn't the answer. Anything else you need, anything else you need done, I'm there."

"This," I said. "This is what I need."

"I can't do it," Ernie said. He took out another cigarette and held it between his fingers. "I'm telling you this. You need to believe me, especially if you try to go to someone else, or try some stupid shit on your own. This ain't the way. This won't be any fucking good for you."

I downed the drink and slid the glass down the bar.

"Thanks for nothing," I said.

"I'm sorry, *compadre*," Ernie said. "I wish I could help you."

After the lunch rush, I told Art I needed to step out. I walked around the block to a small dive bar named Red's. I parked myself on a stool and ordered a drink. An afternoon ball game played on the television above me. Two hours in, I called Art and told him I would be late. An hour later, I called again and told him something had come up and I wouldn't make it back at all.

I tossed back the last of my whiskey, slammed the glass down on the bar, and ordered another. The genial afternoon bartender, a meathead named Dustin, was replaced by the night girl, a surgically enhanced bottle blonde who called herself Lisa. She wore jeans and a tank top tied in the back to highlight her buxom figure. Her arms were covered in intricate tattoos. At first, they looked like colorful abstract designs. On closer inspection, they revealed themselves to be interlocking fish.

"You're burning it pretty hard for a Tuesday," she said, placing the fresh drink in front of me.

"Is it Tuesday?"

"If you go by the calendar, it is."

"Every day's the weekend for me," I said. "Every night's the party."

"Is that so?"

I sipped the drink. It was light on whiskey.

"Why not?" I shrugged. "There doesn't have to be an occasion. Life's the occasion. What better occasion is there?"

"Maybe there isn't one."

"You're right," I said. "You're goddamn right."

"But maybe," Lisa said, with a strained bright smile, "maybe you should take it just a little easy."

"That's all I do," I said, hands raised like I was a referee signaling a touchdown. "That's my life's motto. Take it easy. You have to take it easy."

The after-work crowd dissipated. I stood at the jukebox looking for something to listen to. I didn't recognize many of the artists, and of the few names I knew I wasn't familiar with their music.

"You guys don't have shit here," I said, turning around as if to talk to someone, but there was no one paying attention. "What about the oldies? Actual music. Where a band played instruments. What is this shit? I've never heard of half of this shit. How can a bar not have a single song from the Rolling Stones? How about some boom bap rap? Beastie Boys. Something."

I continued to search, making noises of derision and annoyance.

"What are you looking for?" Lisa asked.

I twirled around to face the bar. It took a moment for me to find her.

"Something I can dance to."

"Why don't you come back and sit down?" she asked. She took a glass and filled it with ice and water.

"I don't want to sit down," I said. "I want to find a song I can dance to."

"This isn't the kind of bar you dance in."

I turned my attention back to the jukebox. "Are you telling me that I'm not allowed to dance?"

"No," Lisa said. "I'm saying this isn't the bar for dancing."

"Okay," I said. "Here we go. This is something. This could get the job done."

I had a few crumpled bills and a handful of change. I stared at the money, not sure what my plan of action should be.

"How much does this even cost?"

No one answered me. I went through my paper money and pulled out the dollar bills. I then flipped through those and found the ones that weren't too creased. I picked the best one and put the rest in my pocket. I tried to flatten it out as best I could, careful to work the edges. I fed the bill into the jukebox. The dollar didn't get halfway in before the machine spit it back out.

I tried again. The machine spit it out.

I took the dollar and tried to smooth it out by holding the sides and going back and forth along the edge of the jukebox like I was trying to shine a shoe.

I fed the dollar back into the machine. This time it took the entire bill. Then it made noise as if it were processing the dollar. I waited for my credit to appear on the display.

The jukebox spit the dollar back out. It looked like it was sticking its tongue out at me.

"Fuck!"

I ripped the dollar out and pulled the wad of bills from my pocket. I looked for another, but none were any better than the one I'd already tried.

I stumbled to the bar.

"Can I trade you for a cleaner dollar?"

"What's that?" Lisa asked.

I held up a dollar. "Can I trade this in? That fucking machine won't take it."

Someone asked, "Why don't you sit down?"

I pivoted to the voice. It had come from a guy built like someone who made a living with his hands, sitting at a table for four across from a beefy Hispanic woman with teased hair and penciled-in eyebrows.

"I'm sorry?" I asked, leaning closer to the man.

"Sit down," he said. "No one wants to hear your music."

I looked at him, face scrunched like I had tasted something sour, trying to process what he was telling me.

"But I want to dance."

"I don't give a fuck what you want to do."

"Excuse me?"

"No one gives a shit."

I stared at the man, still trying to figure out what was being said and how I should react. I turned to the bar. Lisa was no help. She stood at the far side cleaning glasses and pretending not to be paying attention.

The man and the woman continued to talk as if I weren't there. I wanted to say something to the man. I needed to clarify that all I wanted to do was play a song that would allow me to dance. That's it. It was a simple request. I didn't want to bother anyone. I just wanted a good song that I could dance to. Why was that so hard to understand?

I pointed my finger and was about to explain myself when I was hit with a small bit of self-awareness that told me it was not a good idea. I dropped my hand and slunk back to the bar. I climbed onto the stool and wrapped my fingers around my drink.

An hour later, a sudden, tidal wave feeling I needed to vomit crashed over me. I slipped off the stool and shuffled as fast as I could to the bathroom in the back of the bar. Thank Christ, it was empty. I stumbled into a stall, propped myself up with my hands on the wall, and hovered over the toilet, mouth open, spit dripping from my mouth.

I knew it was coming. I felt it churning inside. My body needed to rid itself of this poison. I couldn't remember why I thought coming to this bar was a good idea. As thin ropes of slobber hung from my gaping mouth, the reasons were vague and elusive: I couldn't be in the restaurant. I'd needed a break, but had nowhere to go. I'd considered a hotel room, something with ice-cold air-conditioning, but first I needed a drink. Whiskey sounded good. Whiskey always sounded good. One had led to another, as they do, and now it was close to midnight and my body was revolting.

I closed my eyes. My head spun like a dervish. I wanted to get home. I didn't care if Christine was there or not. I didn't care if it was uncomfortable. I wanted to fall into my bed and sleep. I needed to get out of this bathroom first.

I adjusted my position and opened my mouth wider, hoping it might hurry this along. I thought about sticking a finger down my throat. I would if I needed to, but only as a last resort. If nature did not take its course, I would nudge it along.

I closed my eyes again. I was so tired. My body ached. Maybe the restaurant closing would be a good thing. Maybe it would allow me to rest. But was that really what I needed? Maybe I was only in this situation because I had spent so much damn time resting. Did I deserve more time to relax and take it easy? I pushed these thoughts away. I didn't want to deal with it right then, standing over a toilet in a dive bar near downtown Mesa.

It wasn't going to come, and the need subsided. I would be okay.

I ripped paper from the roll and wiped my mouth. I took my time, leaning against the wall, slowly breathing. I felt better, like I had averted a crisis. I exited the stall and went to the sink. I let the tepid water run over my hands. I glanced at my reflection in the mirror above the sink and realized how much I looked like my dad.

I wiped my hands and face with a paper towel.

The nausea hit me like a sledgehammer. It was as if someone had tried to open a bottle of soda after shaking it. It was coming, and there was nothing I could do about it.

I stepped outside the bar and into a piercing sunlight that caused me to wince and jerk my head back.

"What time is it?" I asked no one in particular.

I checked my watch. It was four o'clock. That made little sense.

I found shade under a storefront awning and checked again. Maybe I had read it wrong. No, it was four. That meant I'd been in the bar for only a few hours. I had a moment where I questioned if it could be four in the morning, but that was clearly not the case. What in the hell had happened? Time had somehow stretched, or my perception of it had altered. I had made multiple phone calls to Art. I'd watched day turn to night through the bar window. It could not have been two hours. That was impossible, and still, there it was.

I walked back to the restaurant. I had a headache. My throat and chest burned from the vomit. I was exhausted. If it was only four, I could work, but I sure as hell didn't feel like doing that.

I saw no one milling about outside the restaurant. That was a nice bit of luck. I didn't want to be seen, and the last thing I wanted was to have a conversation with anyone and have to make an excuse about where I'd been and why I was leaving.

I hurried across the street at a half walk, half run that created a shrieking pain in the front of my head. I fast-walked through the parking lot to my car. I kept expecting to see someone stepping out for a cigarette break, or someone working the evening shift pulling into the parking lot.

I got to my car, unlocked it, and fell inside. The relief was instant. I sat there a moment, knowing if I closed my eyes I would fall asleep. I took a deep breath, then inserted the key and started the car.

I fought the afternoon rush hour traffic all the way home. My eyes kept closing, and I was drifting off. I had to shake my head and slap my face to keep myself awake. I saw Christine's car parked in the garage. *This should be fun.* I thought maybe I could slip into the spare bedroom unnoticed and fall asleep there.

I walked in through the garage. Every light in the house was on. I walked down into the living room. The leather couch was gone. The impressions of the couch's legs were still embedded into the carpet. I walked to the bedroom and found Christine packing clothes into a large suitcase. A very tall young man assisted her.

"I'm not interrupting anything, am I?"

They both looked. Christine sighed, and the man tensed and reacted as if I had caught them.

"No, you're not interrupting," Christine said, "but I am sorry you're here."

"You didn't expect me home?"

"Obviously not. We're not going to be much longer."

I eyed the man. He was in his late twenties, perhaps early thirties. He stood at six foot three, and had a lean, athletic build and a bronze tan.

"Maybe I should—" the man started, but I shook him off.

"No," I said. "Stay. It's all right. You're Dave, right?"

He nodded.

"Dave the tennis instructor. Famous Dave. You're the guy who's been dicking my wife. How's that going for you?"

"Benjamin, please," Christine said, disgusted.

"I really should—" Dave began again, but I waved him away.

"No, no. Stay. It's all right."

"Can you just go into the living room until we're finished?" Christine asked.

"Where would I sit? You took the fucking couch. Besides, there's no fun it that."

"Listen, sir," Dave said, taking a step toward me.

"Sir?" I asked. "Go fuck yourself. What are you taking besides the couch?"

"Nothing that isn't mine," Christine said. "Nothing you would care about."

"I care about the couch," I said. "I like sitting."

"The couch is mine."

"How do you figure that?"

"I bought it."

"With what money?"

"You never liked that couch anyway."

"No," I agreed. "I hated that fucking thing."

"There you go."

I locked eyes with Dave. He tried to hold my gaze, but I made him uncomfortable.

"What do you do besides play tennis?"

"You don't have to answer that," Christine said.

"You know," I said. "Whatever makes you happy. Who am I to judge? I've fucked around on her."

This stung Christine.

"I get it," I said. "I'm not a hypocrite."

"That's brilliant," Christine said. "That truly is. Please leave."

I told her no, and she gave me a look—that tilted-head, pleading look of hers.

"It's still my house," I said, walking to the small dresser on my side of the bed. To Dave, I said, "You might appreciate this."

I pulled out something I had wrapped in a red bandana, uncovered it, and tossed it onto the bed. Dave flinched at the sight of the .38 over-under pistol.

"It's pretty, isn't it?"

"What are you doing?" Christine asked. "This is pathetic."

"Pick it up," I said.

Dave looked from the gun to me.

"Go ahead," I assured him.

"What are you going to do?" Christine asked. "What are you trying to prove?"

"Pick up the gun."

"I don't think it's a good idea," Dave said.

"You don't need her permission," Ben said. "If you learn anything, learn that now. You don't need her permission for anything."

"Why don't you step outside and wait for us to be done?" Dave asked.

"Pick up the goddamn gun."

"Do you think this routine is scaring anyone?" Christine asked.

"I don't know," I said. "Is this routine scaring you?"

Dave just stood there, not knowing what to say or do.

"Just pick up the gun," I said.

Dave's eyes went again to Christine, then he reached down and picked up the gun.

"It's loaded, so be careful."

Dave held the tiny pistol in his hand.

"That gun," I said. "That gun is about a hundred years old. Hold it like you're going to shoot it."

Ben gripped the handle.

"That's it," I said. "Feels good, don't it? Now point it at me."

"Benjamin!" Christine called out. "For Christ's sake."

"Shut up!" I yelled. The ferocity of my voice surprised and scared her.

"You got what you wanted. Let your boy do me a favor."

I looked to Dave. He stood with the gun in his hand, nervous, trying not to shake.

"That's my grandmother's gun," I said, my voice now calm. "My grandfather was a sheep herder. Depending on the time of year, he might be gone for months at a time. My grandmother kept that baby under her pillow at night. It's a firecracker. Kicks like a bastard. Anything farther than eight feet and you won't be able to hit it for shit. You have to put it up close. If you do, you can blow a hole right through someone."

I let that sink in before asking, "Do you want to give it a try?"

Dave licked his lips and swallowed. "No."

"Do it," I said.

"This is so stupid," Christine said.

"Point it at me. Pull the trigger."

"What is wrong with you?" Christine asked.

Dave tossed the gun back onto the bed.

"No?" I asked, laughing. "You don't want to?"

Christine zipped her suitcase.

"You need help," she told me. "You need serious help."

"What do you care?" I asked. "You're leaving. You're free."

Dave took the suitcase from the bed. They moved past me toward the hallway.

"No hard feelings," I said.

I picked up the pistol from the bed and fired it into the wall. The sound was like a thunderclap. Dave and Christine jumped. She screamed. I'd made a large hole in the wall.

"You can leave now," I said.

"You are a small, pathetic man," Christine said through gritted teeth.

I shrugged and watched them walk out of the room. I stood there, staring at the floor. I heard them in the kitchen speaking to one another although I couldn't make out what they were saying. A door opened, and a moment later it slammed shut. And at once I was submerged in guilt and disgust. I had to take a deep breath. I didn't want to do this anymore. I didn't want to take another step forward. I'd had enough. I put the pistol to my head. My face contorted. Tendons on my neck stood out, taut like cables.

I gasped for breath and dropped the gun. I couldn't do it.

I began to sob, mouth open in a soundless scream. I put the gun back to my head. My breathing was quick. My heart raced. I closed my eyes. My hands shook. I opened my mouth in a silent scream and cocked the hammer.

The telephone rang. It was loud, like the wailing of a dying bird, but it still sounded far away. The ring was endless, on and on and on. It paused a moment, then started again. This happened over and over. I felt displaced, as if I were watching myself from an old tube television with spotty reception. I could see myself lying on the floor, my eyes open, my body lifeless. It didn't look as if I were breathing. I could see the imprint of the gun barrel on my temple.

My eyelids fluttered. I stirred, slowly, as if emerging from a long, deep hibernation. I lifted my head and looked around. I didn't know where I was, and it took me a moment to realize I was still in my bedroom. I worked my way up onto my elbows, then turned my body around and worked my way onto my hands and knees. I felt as if I were moving through thick syrup. I used the bed as a prop to help myself up to my feet. My legs were unsteady, and I thought I could fall back to the ground. The phone continued to ring. I put weight on my foot, and an intense pain shot up from my right ankle. I limped to the nightstand like a wounded animal.

I answered the cordless phone.

"Dad?" the voice asked. It took me a moment to register it was my daughter, Joslyn, on the line.

"Hey," I croaked.

"Did I wake you?"

"I don't know. I think so."

"You think so? You don't know if you were sleeping?"

My head was a fog, my thoughts unclear.

"No," I said. I wasn't sure how long I took to answer. "I think it was a deep sleep. I'm having a hard time coming out of it."

"Well, I'm sorry to wake you then," Joslyn said. "I'm sure you needed the sleep."

"No, it's okay."

"I didn't mean to keep calling. I kept expecting the machine to pick up."

"Oh," I said. "I didn't realize it was off. I'm sorry about that."

"What are you sorry for?" Joslyn asked. "Listen, why I called, I know we talked about it, so please don't be pissed or anything, but I wanted to make sure you were going to be there tomorrow."

I didn't know what she was talking about, but I said, "Of course I'll be there."

"Great," Joslyn said. "That's excellent. I have to get there early. If you want, you can come to the house and just head on over with everyone else, or you can just meet Mom at the school."

"What would your mom prefer?"

"She's fine either way."

I rubbed the back of my head. It felt as if a bird was tapping on my skull. "I'll think about it and let her know."

"Okay."

"I don't want to cause any tension."

"I don't think you have to worry about that," Joslyn said. "Not this night, anyway."

I nodded and thought I said, "Good," but wasn't sure.

"Daddy," Joslyn said. "I'm glad you're going to be there. It means a lot to me."

"I would never miss it."

"I love you," she said.

"I love you too."

The line clicked and the call cut out. I dropped the handle. It banged against the corner of the nightstand and fell to the floor.

I hobbled to the bathroom sink. I turned the water on and hunched over the basin. I checked the temperature, then splashed the water onto my face.

Dark, heavy clouds crawled over the mountains to the north. They resembled waves about to crash into the valley. As an overture for the pending summer storm, a cool breeze brought a pleasant respite from the usual oppressive heat. A stream of cars filled the school parking lot, and family and friends packed themselves into the football bleachers.

"It was good of you to come tonight."

I glanced at Doug and said, "She's my daughter."

He nodded, not sure if I was joking. I wasn't about to let him off the hook. Doug was a nice-enough guy. He wasn't too exciting, which I guess was what my ex-wife liked about him. He was safe and stable. He worked as the manager at a car dealership. He'd brought with him two kids of his own—a boy and a girl, I could never remember their names—who lived with his ex-wife. As far as I knew, that divorce was amiable, or as amiable as one can be. Doug was still on good terms with his ex-wife. They had grown apart and decided they were better off split up and friends than together and enemies. My daughters both liked Doug. He was nice and funny, and he treated them well. Doug was a solid guy, a good guy, a steady presence for my daughters. I suppose that is what one hopes for with a stepfather. Our relationship had always been cordial. We could talk about food, cars, and sports. I found Doug annoyingly affable.

"I hope it doesn't rain," Doug said.

I tapped my younger daughter, Samantha, on the knee. She was sitting next to me but her attention was elsewhere.

"You know," I said. "I used to play football on that field right there."

"You played football?" Doug asked.

"I know, Dad," Samantha sighed. "Number seventeen."

"You've heard that one before?"

"We've all heard that one before," Heidi said. My ex-wife sat on the other side of Doug. "I've heard it about a million times," Samantha said.

"That many times, huh?"

"At least."

"When you're at a game some Friday, or maybe running the track during PE, do you ever look at the field and think about your dad playing on it?"

"No," Samantha said, but she couldn't help but laugh.

"Not at all?"

"Not one bit."

"Well, I'm going to keep telling you that story until you do."

"I can't wait."

I let that settle, and then in mock anger said, "I can't believe you don't think of me playing on that field."

"You can't believe that?"

"That's right. You know what that is?"

"Is it unbelievable?" Samantha asked.

"It is unbelievable."

"You can't believe that, huh?"

"It's outrageous."

Samantha shrugged. "It is what it is."

"Or," I said, "it is what it isn't."

"What does that mean?" she asked with that amazing condescending tone and expression she'd mastered as a toddler.

I tapped my temple. "Think about it."

"It doesn't make any sense."

"It makes all the sense in the world."

Samantha tutted in mild irritation. "You're such a dork."

I laughed. It was the exact reaction I'd been pushing for.

The ceremony began twenty minutes late. By that time, the wind picked up and the air had the smell of imminent rain. After some brief remarks by the school's principal, the salutatorian gave a long and boring speech about the future and living one's dreams. The speech was not only cliché but naive. As I listened, I wondered if the role of the parent or the adult figure was to slam reality down on these kids, or sit back and let them figure it out on their own. I could never work out the proper balance. It was a constant push-pull. I prided myself with being honest with my kids, sometimes brutally honest if needed, all the while knowing this was a blatant lie; I wasn't truthful at all. I only had to parent them on a sporadic, often patchy, basis. Heidi bore most of the burden as a parent. I knew well enough that as much as it pained me, as hard as it often was to be apart from them, absent from the day-to-day goings-on in their lives, my daughters were much better off with Heidi than with me.

The valedictorian talked about the need to be selfless and globally aware as the new graduates ventured out into the world. My attention wandered. I noticed that Heidi and Doug held hands, their fingers laced together. I realized I would have to tell my daughters, and my ex-wife, and fucking Doug, that the restaurant would be closing. I knew I would put that off as long as I could, and I would want to spin it as a good thing, something I wanted to happen, had even planned to happen. I doubt anyone would buy that. Heidi would see right through it. She might say nothing, but I knew she would give me that look of hers, that cold look of abject disappointment. When we were married, receiving that look was always far worse than any argument we ever had.

They began to announce the names of the graduating class, but there were nearly five hundred seniors, so there was still a long way to go. Kids snuck in flour tortillas that they tossed like Frisbees as the names were called. An inflatable beach ball appeared, and the graduates bounced it around. The principal repeatedly stopped the ceremony to admonish whoever the pranksters were and warned if caught they would be kicked out and would not be receiving their diplomas. This rebuke only encouraged the students to continue.

When they called Joslyn's name, we all cheered and clapped. Samantha stood up and yelled, "Way to go, J Dog! That's my girl!" Joslyn waved and gave a big smile as she walked across the stage to receive her diploma.

The tortillas and inflatable balls continued. The students seemed to have an endless supply. Short of ending the ceremony altogether, the principal did not know what to do. He gave up trying to stop it, but once they called the final name, he stood at the podium and told the class how disappointed and ashamed he was and that this was by far the most ill-behaved graduating class he had ever seen. The students erupted in an uproarious cheer.

I stood with Heidi and Doug in the large foyer of the dimly lit restaurant. I had my hands buried deep in the pockets of my slacks.

"How's the restaurant business going for you?" Doug asked.

"It's good," I said.

"That's always nice to hear."

"Things are well."

"I know it was rocky there for a while."

How did he know? My instinct was to assume this was a passive-aggressive dig, Doug patronizing me for my lack of success, but looking at his face with that dopey grin, I knew he was being sincere.

"We were maybe a little slow there for a while, but we're actually thinking about expanding."

"Expanding, huh?"

I caught the look Heidi gave—at first surprised and then skeptical of this news. She looked at me like a teacher listening to a student give an excuse to why they did not do their assignment.

"Right now it's in the early stages," I said. "More exploratory. We're thinking of another place. A north restaurant. Scottsdale maybe."

"That would be amazing," Doug said.

"And you," I said, eager to change the subject. "How's cars?"

"It's a bit slow lately, honestly."

I knew Heidi would not be thrilled with Doug's honesty.

"I was thinking of a new car," I said. "Maybe something for Christine. She needs an update."

"Well, come on by," Doug replied.

"I might actually do that."

"I better hit the bathroom before they seat us," Doug said.

He gave Heidi a kiss and then asked the hostess for directions to the bathroom.

Heidi and I stood silently. We were never uncomfortable with silences. It was one of the nicer facets of our relationship.

"You look very nice," I said.

"Thank you."

"I wish I could lie and tell you differently."

This made Heidi laugh. "I know you probably do."

Heidi had a great laugh. I loved her laugh because I knew it was genuine. Every reaction Heidi gave, whether it was a laugh, a compliment, an orgasm, anything, it was earned. She did not fake anything, and never even bothered to try. I treasured this when we were dating, but it became problematic as we were knee deep in trying to make our tenuous marriage work. Now we were no longer together, I could enjoy it once again.

"I can't believe we made it here," I said. "That our girl has graduated high school."

"It happens quicker than you think it will."

"Indeed, it does. And she's happy?"

"Yes, she's very happy."

"That's all you," I said. "I know you know that. I mean, it's obvious enough, but I want you to know I know that too. For whatever that's worth, which is probably not too much."

"No," Heidi said. "I appreciate you saying it."

"It's true," I said, looking at my shoes.

We stood in silence. It wasn't awkward, but it was felt.

"We don't get to talk too often," I said.

"No, we don't."

"Life by you is good?"

Heidi hooked her hair behind her ear and crossed her arms. "We're all pretty happy."

"I can tell. And that's good. I'm happy for that. I mean it. I really am."

Doug returned just as the hostess told us the table was ready. She led our group through the elegant dining room to a large table that had a beautiful view of the nighttime city skyline.

They brought us salads that looked more like architectural achievements than something one might eat. I picked at mine. It was too much pomp for what was actually a simple and rather bland Caesar salad.

"No, no," Joslyn was saying. "I just expected to feel a little different."

"And how do you feel?" Heidi asked.

"That's the thing. Like, nothing. Nothing different, anyway. It doesn't feel as if I'm done with school at all."

"You're not done with school," Doug said.

"No, I get it," Joslyn said. "College. I'm going to college in the fall, but I don't have to. It's not mandatory. If I didn't want to ever step foot into another classroom again, I wouldn't have to."

"I'm not going to college," Samantha said.

"It's just a weird thing to think about."

"I'm not going to college," Samantha said, a little louder.

"What are you talking about?" Heidi asked. "Of course you are."

"I don't think so."

"Yes, my dear, you are."

"Janice's sister is a dancer, and she makes at least five hundred dollars a night."

"What kind of dancer?" Doug asked.

"The stripping kind," Joslyn said.

"A stripper?" Heidi asked, a little too loud.

"It's more of a cabaret kind of thing," Samantha said.

"Are you trying to push my buttons?"

I moved the romaine lettuce around on my plate. I smiled as if enjoying myself, content to listen and not offer much to the conversation. I'd been distracted ever since we sat down. I kept hearing a voice, pieces of a conversation, that swam in and out of reach. I recognized the voice immediately but could not place it.

I kept looking around the restaurant but had no luck finding the face to match the voice.

"I'm not trying to push your buttons," Samantha said with a smirk. "I can dance."

"Stop now," Heidi said.

"I'm a very good dancer."

"Seriously? Are you being serious right now?"

"No, Mom," Joslyn said. "She's not serious."

"I seriously don't want to go to college."

"It's not funny now," Heidi said.

I continued to hear the voice. It nagged me like a nettlesome fly. It felt like it hovered just below the hum of conversation, but it was clear. I turned again and scanned the dining area, but recognized no one. Whose voice was that? Where did I know it from?

"Are you going to let your daughter talk like this?"

I snapped back and realized all eyes were on me.

"It's respectable," I said. "If that's what she wants to do."

"Thank you," Samantha said.

"Dad!"

"Oh, Benjamin, please," Heidi scolded.

"I'm sorry, what?" I asked. "What are we talking about?"

A large white cake filled with pink and purple flowers lit up by a dozen candles sat in front of Joslyn. Even from across the table in this low light, I could see my daughter blush. She smiled and tilted her head down. She looked like a little girl again.

"It's not a birthday, you guys," she said.

"You can make a wish on your future," Doug told her.

I heard a laugh. It was unmistakable. I could not see where it was coming from, but I knew the voice. I was sure. I just couldn't place it.

"Congratulations, sweetie," Heidi said.

Joslyn closed her eyes, took a breath, and blew out the candles. One candle in the middle flickered but did not go out. The table collectively groaned. Joslyn leaned forward and blew on the flame. Samantha and Doug clapped. Joslyn tried her best not to look disconcerted that she had not blown out all the candles in one go.

"My God, it's beautiful."

It clicked. I set the final piece. It was so obvious, I could not believe it had not come straight away. I twisted my body around and searched the dining room. She had to be there. I knew it was her.

My eyes swept the tables. I saw her. It was that easy.

Sara sat on the far side of the dining room at a small table for two.

Sound fell away. It was as if someone had dialed the world down and everything moved in extreme slow motion.

She was older, but I could never forget that face. She sat across from a man in his mid- to late forties. They were dressed up—he in a nice suit, and Sara in a white and silver dress. It looked as if the man had just given her a present. It was a piece of jewelry, perhaps a necklace. I couldn't tell for sure. Whatever it was, it caused Sara to respond with enthusiastic excitement. She leaned across the table and kissed the man on the mouth.

"Dad."

"Are you okay?" Doug asked.

It felt as if I had a storm raging in my brain.

I looked at Doug with a plastic smile and said, "I'm fine. Why?"

Heidi said, "Your face. It looks as if the color completely drained from your face."

"We asked if you would like to say something," Heidi said.

I didn't know what she was talking about.

"Are you on drugs?" Samantha asked, laughing.

"Yes," I said. "I would like to say something."

I raised my glass of water in a toast. My mind was blank. I didn't know what I was doing.

"I just want to say . . . ," I began. "I just want to say, and congratulate you on everything, your achievement. For you, my daughter, I wish you nothing, nothing but the best. I love you very, very much."

Joslyn clasped her hands together and mouthed "I love you" to me.

Doug reached under the table and pulled out a small box.

"This is for you," he said, setting the box in front of Joslyn.

"Holy shit!" Samantha exclaimed.

"Please," Heidi said. "Language."

"I can't believe they bought it for you."

"You've earned it," Doug told Joslyn.

Joslyn unwrapped the gift. I could not focus on any of this. I kept turning my head to catch a look at Sara. I wanted to make sure she was still there, that she wasn't an apparition, or this wasn't some kind of hallucination. She was still there, sitting across from a distinguished-looking man, drinking wine and laughing. The edges of my vision closed in like the iris in an old movie.

Joslyn was about to open the box. I excused myself from the table.

"What's wrong?" Heidi asked.

"Are you okay, Dad?"

"Yes, yes. I'm sorry. I just need to, um, yeah."

"You don't look too good," Doug said.

"I just need to use the bathroom."

"You sure you're okay?" Joslyn asked.

"Yes, of course," I said. "I'm sorry. I'll just be a minute. I'm sorry."

I stood, and for a split moment I thought my legs would buckle and I would fall to the floor. I took a cautious first step. When I realized I could still walk, I moved across the dining room, weaving in and around tables, almost crashing into a waiter carrying a tray full of entrées. My eyes locked on Sara, always Sara, and the man at her table.

I shoved the bathroom door open and darted for a stall. I slammed the door behind and locked it. I hovered over the pristine bowl, hands propped on the wall, staring down at the clear water. My mouth was open. I was ready to vomit. I almost welcomed it, but nothing came.

There was a gentle tap on the stall door.

"Are you all right in there, sir?"

"Yes. No. Thank you."

"Are you sure?"

"Yes, I'm fine. Thank you. I'm fine."

I listened as the attendant walked away. I continued to stand, staring down into the water, mouth open, hoping to vomit, to purge, to do something that might make me feel better. When it was clear nothing would happen, I sat down on the toilet.

The night had taken a hard left turn. It confused me. I was scared, not knowing what the hell I should do, how I should act, how I should feel. Sara sat out there in the dining room. How was that possible? I didn't know what to think. I felt as if I'd been shaken. This was a dream. This was a nightmare. It had been so many years. There hadn't been a day where I didn't think about her in some small way. I wondered if she was alive or dead, what she might be doing, what her life had become. There were so many times over the years when I'd wanted to see her again, talk to her, see that smile, hear her laugh, make sure she was all right. But I'd never believed it might happen. She was gone. She was out of my life forever.

But here she was, sitting right outside these bathroom walls. It wasn't a sick joke or a dream. It was very much real. She was sitting with a man who looked as if he were cast as an older character from a daytime soap opera. By some mind-boggling providence of fate or luck, my path had once again crossed with Sara's. Even if it was in only the most tangential way, she was back in my life, and my first instinct was to run, to hide in that bathroom stall. I wanted to pretend that I never saw Sara, that the fiancée who had disappeared so many years ago was not sitting out there pleased as punch, enjoying her night out. She was alive. Sara was alive. After all that time, all the heartache and pain, the eternal darkness of not knowing, I had an answer to a question I'd asked myself countless times, and I didn't want to face it. I didn't want to face her. I didn't want to face her. There was a part of me that wanted it to be a dream, but it was very real.

Did I just want to sit there? The time, the years, everything I had gone through since her disappearance in that airport, did I really want to hide like a scared child? Yes. That's the truth. That's exactly what I wanted, but I knew I couldn't hide. I'd imagined this moment so many times in so many variations. I could never imagine that I would see Sara again in this way, but that was how it was being laid before me. I didn't want to face it, but I had to. There was no choice. I didn't know what I would do, but I had to do something. I could not live with the consequences of doing nothing.

I took a deep breath like a diver preparing to jump into the water. I opened the stall and headed for the bathroom door. I kept my focus straight ahead. I didn't want to make eye contact with the attendant, who was in actuality indifferent to me.

I stood in the foyer of the restaurant. I could see my family on the far side of the dining room laughing and enjoying the cake. The waitress poured coffee for Heidi and Doug. On the other side of the restaurant, the distinguished-looking man gave his bill a quick glance and signed it. He slid his credit card back into his wallet, then he and Sara readied themselves to leave. The man downed the last of his wine. They stood. Sara wrapped a cashmere shawl around her shoulders. There was small talk. They smiled at each other. Sara took the man's hand. He leaned over and kissed her on the cheek.

I presumed this man was her husband although I wondered whether a husband would kiss his wife on the cheek like that. I supposed some might, but it felt more like the sweet gesture of a man courting a woman. It was impossible to tell either way the nature of their relationship.

They walked toward the entrance. The waiter approached them and had a brief exchange with the distinguished man. They shook hands. The man smiled and patted the waiter's shoulders.

I kept my attention on Sara. I wanted to take her in, burn her into my memory: her expensive dress, the way her still-slim body moved beneath her clothes, the jewelry on her ears and around her neck, the giant diamond on her left hand, which settled the husband question, the way the distinguished man placed his hand on the small of her back and followed her through the dining room.

She walked poised with her shoulders back and head high. She carried an unmistakable confidence, completely secure with herself. Her hair was the same dirty blonde, with streaks of sunshine running through it, cut about an inch below her ears. She styled it in a way that made me think it took time to make her look as if it took no time at all. She had a flawless, natural tan. She was still so beautiful. I stood there, slack jawed, looking like a cartoon character struck by lightning. As she approached, I felt a nauseous heat in my stomach. Again, I wanted to run. I didn't want to face her. It felt as if I had stepped into a fantasy, or a TV-movie version of my life. I felt drunk even though I hadn't had a drink all night.

They came straight toward me. I stood frozen as if my feet were nailed to the floor. I could not move if I wanted to. I was terrified and nervous, but all of a sudden I no longer wanted to run and hide. I wanted to face her, head-on. That needed to happen.

Sara and the distinguished man walked up the steps from the dining room. I tensed, my stomach clenched into a fist. I forced a smile. I wasn't sure what I would say, or if I would even have a voice to speak.

They walked right past me. Neither so much as glanced my way, not once, not even for a moment. It was as if I weren't standing there.

The hostess thanked them and wished them good night. They both thanked her, and they walked out the double glass doors into the night.

I watched as the distinguished man handed the valet his ticket and the valet took off after his vehicle. I looked back to the table. Doug had his arm around Heidi. Samantha held court, dominating the conversation.

I turned back outside. Sara and the distinguished man held hands. I noticed my own hands were shaking.

A dark-green Mercedes pulled up to the curb. The same valet popped out of the car like a jack-in-the-box and skipped around the hood.

I looked back to the dining room. Doug wiped his face with a napkin and stood from the table. He excused himself and walked toward the entrance.

The distinguished man handed the valet a tip. It looked like a ten-dollar bill. A nice tip. The valet opened the door for Sara. She smiled and thanked him and got inside the car. The distinguished man walked around the back of the Mercedes.

Doug was halfway through the dining room.

I took a few steps toward the front door.

"Thank you for joining us."

I eyed the hostess. She was young with a big smile and a mess of curly brown hair. I gave her a tight-lipped smile and a single nod, and I walked to the double glass doors.

The Mercedes pulled away. I pushed through the door and hurried to the valet. I handed him my ticket. The valet thanked me and said he would be just a moment. He then took off for my vehicle.

The Mercedes turned down the drive leading to the main road and disappeared.

I looked back. Doug crossed the foyer walking toward the bathroom. He didn't so much as glance outside.

The bitter smell of rain was strong. I closed my eyes. What was the plan? What was I doing? I didn't know, but I knew I needed to follow the Mercedes. That was as far as my plan went.

The valet brought my car. I hurried around the back of the car to the driver's side and handed the valet a bill. I didn't know what it was. I hoped it was something small. I got inside the car and took off after the green Mercedes.

I maneuvered the steep road that led down the mountain from the restaurant. I drove faster than I should have, taking turns faster than I should have, veering into the oncoming lane. If another car had come up the opposite way, it would have been hard to avoid them. My hands gripped the steering wheel so hard my knuckles were white. Some soft rock bullshit was playing on the radio, but I didn't want to shift my concentration even a little to change the channel.

I was too late. I knew I would be too fucking late. I would lose my chance. Sara would disappear into the night and drop out of my life—again. This was it. I had lost my chance.

I bit my bottom lip. My heart was about to explode. Why had I hesitated? Why had I stood there like a goddamn idiot and let her drive away?

I made a big right turn, going wide around the base of the mountain, past tennis courts and a bungalow that belonged to the high-end resort associated with the restaurant.

The Mercedes sat at a red light.

I deflated. I could breathe again. I slowed behind the car, so relieved that I had not lost it. I turned the radio off. I needed silence. I could see shadows of vague shapes in the front seat of the Mercedes. I wondered what they were talking about.

I could feel my heart banging in my temples. The air conditioner roared at full blast, but I was still sweating.

The traffic light turned green, and the Mercedes eased forward and then turned left. I followed. The Mercedes forced its way across three lanes of traffic. It looked like they were headed to the freeway. I made my way over. The Mercedes turned right, pulling onto the freeway on-ramp. I merged into the turning lane and sped down the ramp after it. Traffic wasn't too bad. I saw the Mercedes move over to the middle lane. The distinguished man wasn't a speeder, and it was easy to catch up. I didn't want to get right behind him. I thought it unlikely anyone outside a movie or a novel would notice someone was following them, but there was no need to risk it by being too obvious. I stayed two lanes to the right and a good fifty feet behind the Mercedes.

We continued in this way for a few miles. As we approached the split for Highway 60, I saw the right blinker come on. The Mercedes made its way over and took the exit for the highway. I was careful to keep my distance as I followed them. Although, in a way I wasn't following them; I figured they must live in the East Valley, as did I, and this was the route I would have taken on my own, anyway.

Traffic on the 60 was light. I was careful to keep my distance. My heart continued to race. My blood pressure was out of control.

A few drops of rain hit the windshield, then a few more. I noticed up ahead, about a mile down the freeway, what looked to be a sheet of rain. When the Mercedes hit the rain it all but disappeared as if it had driven behind a curtain. The rain was fierce. I flipped the wipers to high and they still had a difficult time keeping up with the onslaught.

I lost the Mercedes. It was impossible to tell which blurred red brake lights were the ones I needed to follow. I had to slow down. The rain was intense. Giant pools of water had already accumulated in the lower areas of the road. I kept both hands on the steering wheel and maneuvered as best as I could.

I moved to the far outside lane so I could pay careful attention to the cars heading down the off-ramp in case the Mercedes had pulled off. The windshield fogged. I rubbed it away with the sleeve of my shirt before I remembered—no shit—that I had the ability to defog them.

I worked my way through the torrent for damn near ten miles going only thirty-five miles an hour. I was sure I'd lost the Mercedes and there wasn't a damn thing I could do about it. God had played a trick on me, offered me the chance for answers and absolution, and then pulled the rug out. I kept my attention focused, but it didn't make much difference. I didn't have a chance in this rain.

Then, as if a faucet had turned off, the rain cleared, then stopped altogether.

I got excited. The wipers continued to flap back and forth. I searched for the Mercedes. I didn't see it. I had lost them. Son of a bitch. I slammed my hands against the steering wheel.

And then I saw it. The car was almost a quarter of a mile ahead. I hit the gas. The four-cylinder engine made a high-pitched scream. The Mercedes' right blinker was on. Where were we? The next exit was Val Vista. We were in Mesa.

The car moved into the far right lane and ascended the off-ramp. The light at the top was green. I knew there was no way I could catch up and make that light. I hit the gas anyway, racing down the rain-slicked freeway. I hit the ramp just as the light turned yellow. The Mercedes' brake lights flared red. They would not run it. They could have made the yellow. It might have gone red halfway through the turn, but they would have made it. Again, thankfully, the distinguished man was a cautious driver.

I pulled behind the Mercedes. If one were suspicious that a car was following them, it would be now, off the freeway, at that time of night when street traffic was sparse.

The light turned green. The Mercedes pulled left, heading north. I needed to stay back. I turned left but moved to the far outside lane so I would be behind them. It might be a funny situation for Sara to look over and see me sitting in the car next to her, but that was not what I wanted. I didn't know what I wanted, but it wasn't that.

We headed north past streets that had strip malls on each corner so similar I felt as if I were caught in a loop. As we continued, the stores and the fast-food restaurants gradually gave way to orange groves and residential neighborhoods. The streetlights became few and far between. There were acres of dark orange groves. I didn't know how much longer I could continue along the same route as the Mercedes and not risk suspicion.

The Mercedes' left blinker came on. I tensed. What the fuck was I going to do now? Did I risk following them? How could I do that? It was a sure way to get caught. I could continue past the street for a distance and then turn around. That would risk losing the car in the neighborhood. If I lost them, I could look for the car. However, if they slipped into a garage, there would be damn near no chance of me being able to figure out which house was the one.

I had to decide. The Mercedes slowed, pulling into the left-turn lane. I had to decide now.

I tapped on the brakes, slowing the car. I took it down below thirty. The Mercedes turned. There was no one else on the road. I didn't have any more time to think.

Fuck it.

I sped up, moved to the inside lane, and turned down the same road as the Mercedes.

I saw the brake lights ahead.

I exhaled, relieved. I'd gotten lucky.

This wasn't a neighborhood of cookie-cutter stucco tract homes. This was a nice, very upscale neighborhood with houses made of brick set far back from the road. The front yards were expansive and immaculately manicured.

The left blinker came on again. The distinguished man was a conscientious driver even in a residential neighborhood with no traffic. A good Boy Scout. It was as if he were leading me directly to them. Later that night, I wondered if this was incredible serendipity guiding me along. Right then, it didn't matter.

The Mercedes pulled into the driveway of a house. I slowed the car. I wanted to be very careful. I didn't want to roll past the house as they were getting out of their cars to go inside. I didn't want to risk either of them noticing my car.

I counted to ten, and then sped up, just a touch. The house was a large red brick ranch-style number with a yard filled with large trees. There was a light on in what I guessed was a living room or a den. I eased the car past the house as the garage door was coming down. I turned in my seat and watched it close.

I parked down the street from the house. I was close enough to see it, but not so close as to arouse suspicion. There was still a decent-sized risk I would be noticed. This looked like the neighborhood where any resident looking out their window would wonder what that strange car was doing out in the street.

A light rain fell. I periodically flicked the wipers to clear the windshield. I could still see the buttery light coming from the front room. Other than that, the house was dark and looked peaceful.

I didn't know what I was doing, but I knew I couldn't leave. This couldn't be it. This could not be the end. By some astronomical twist of luck, or fate, or whatever one called it, I had seen Sara again. I'd followed her to this house on a mad impulse. Was that the end of the story? I refused to accept that. I couldn't drive off. I couldn't stand such a disappointing conclusion. There had to be more.

I checked my watch. It was almost eleven. They could still be awake. It was a Friday night. Many people stayed up late on Fridays.

The entire neighborhood was quiet. I had already been sitting in my car for almost thirty minutes, and I hadn't seen another car drive by. I wondered what kind of money one needed to buy a house in this neighborhood. I guessed it was half a million dollars easy, and it would not surprise me if it was quite a bit more. What kind of job did one need to buy a house in this neighborhood? Were Sara and the distinguished man a two-income household? If she worked, what did she do?

What was I going to do? I couldn't sit here all night.

I opened the door and stepped out into the rain. I jogged across the street to Sara's house. I stood in the driveway, the rain already soaking my clothes. I glanced around. There could be someone watching, spying on the strange man standing in the driveway to one of their neighbors' houses.

I walked along the sidewalk eyeing the house. The front window with the light peeking through had a heavy curtain. There were two smaller windows to the left. I assumed they were bedroom windows. The blinds were closed, and it was dark inside. I came to a path made of red brick that led up to the front door. It looked like a tongue snaking out of an open black mouth. The brick was a passage to the front door, but I could not help but think the door could open to something else, something still unknown and mysterious and out of reach. It could open to something dangerous.

Who was I kidding? Opening that door would be like picking a scab, an old wound that the person on the other side would not expect and would not want to deal with. Was there any chance the distinguished man knew about me? Had Sara confessed that piece of her past to him, or would she have kept it a secret?

I could not envision the possibility that Sara would open that door and gush with happiness to see me. It was impossible.

Seeing me again would cause dismay, and confusion, and pain. It would be painful for her. She had moved on and created a different life for herself.

Maybe that was true, but I could not walk away. That idea was just as impossible. I needed an answer. I needed something from her. After all these years, I needed a remedy for all the questions and the pain I had endured.

I hurried up the path toward the front door. It was blocked by an iron gate I hadn't seen from the sidewalk, but when I tried the gate, it was unlocked. I opened it and stepped onto the front porch. I spotted a gap in the front curtain that allowed me to see inside. I crept closer to the window.

There was a dark leather couch and an oversized chair. The walls were adorned with Navajo rugs, and a large oak bookshelf was filled with hardback books and blue glass figurines.

I took a step closer to the window, hoping to get a better look.

I heard a noise and almost screamed. I crouched down and retreated into the shadows. A car passed. My heart was lodged in my throat. I turned and watched it slowly drive down the street. When it left, I allowed myself to take a deep breath. I couldn't believe it had scared me as much as it did. I was about to move back to the window when the porch light came on.

I froze. I was trapped. I heard the deadbolt for the front door unlock. I tried to push myself as far as I could back into the corner of the porch, pressing myself up against the wall. It was impossible for me to know how much the shadows hid me from view, if at all.

The door opened and the distinguished man stepped out. He wore a bathrobe pulled tight. He reached down and picked up a pair of muddy tennis shoes that were lying next to the door and retreated inside. The door locked again. The porch light went off.

I dared not breathe. What the fuck was I doing? That would have been a hell of a thing getting caught sneaking around the outside of the house. But it would have been the perfect way to introduce myself again to Sara and this man.

I peeled myself off the wall and stepped back onto the porch. I noticed the doorbell. There was a little circle of light around the small white button. I could push the button. It would be easy to do. Simple. That would force the situation.

I reached up and hovered my finger over the button. Sara was on the other end. I stared at my finger and the halo of light around it. All I had to do was apply a little pressure, and the doorbell would ring.

I sat in the recliner in the living room. An old movie with John Cassavetes was on TV, but I wasn't paying attention to it. I clinked the ice in the tumbler I held. I needed to replenish it, but I couldn't bring myself to stand and go to the bar for more whiskey. The phone rang. I turned my head and looked at it with a half-lidded gaze. I'm not sure how long I let it ring before I reached out for it.

"Thanks for the disappearing act," Heidi said, using her stern, exasperated voice.

"Hello."

"Should I even bother asking? I wonder if it's possible for you to give a story that would be good enough."

"I'm sorry," I said.

Did I sound drunk? Was I slurring my words?

"It's not me you should be apologizing to."

"I'm not."

"Of course you're not."

"I wasn't feeling well."

Heidi sighed—a big, exaggerated noise. I could see her shaking her head on the other end.

"Every time I think you might step up and play father, you manage to disappoint. At least you're consistent in that."

"It's been a rough night," I said. "Can you fuck off a little?"

"Do you remember our agreement?" Heidi asked. "You're fucking this up. I don't know why I continue to care. A part of me wants to watch you flame out, but those girls love you too much. They don't know any better."

"They'll learn," I said.

"I can count on you to hammer the point home for them. They're your daughters."

"I'm aware of that."

"Don't make the biggest mistake of your life."

Sara wheeled a cart overflowing with white plastic bags filled with groceries through the parking lot. As she headed to the Mercedes, the trunk popped open. She parked the cart, careful to position the wheels so it would not roll away. When she finished putting the groceries into the trunk, she put the cart back into a corral with others, and headed back to her car.

"Excuse me."

I reached my hand out and touched Sara on the shoulder. She turned toward me. There wasn't the slightest hint of recognition on her face. I waited for it. I waited for some sign, a sign, however small, that she knew me.

"Yes?

"Sara? Sara Turner?"

"I'm sorry. Excuse me?"

"You're Sara Turner."

"No. I'm sorry. I'm not."

"Yes," I said.

Sara looked puzzled. Perhaps she wasn't understanding what I was asking.

"My name is Joanna," she said.

"Joanna?"

"That's right."

"No."

"Excuse me?"

"Sara. Sara Turner."

Sara chuckled. "No. I'm sorry. My name is Joanna."

"Joanna?"

"Joanna Corey."

She made a face, almost like a wince, and I thought maybe she regretted saying her full name out loud.

"Don't you recognize me?" I asked.

Sara took half a step back, made a quick study of my face, looking as if she were attempting to place me.

"I'm sorry. I don't."

"You don't recognize me?"

"I don't believe we've ever met."

"We've never met?"

"I don't believe so."

"How can you say that?"

She stood there looking at me, trying to figure out the puzzle.

"It's Benjamin," I said.

That didn't do it.

"Ben."

Nothing.

"We sure knew each other at some point."

"I don't think so."

"Yes," I said. "We have a pretty extensive history."

"I think you might have it wrong."

"There's no way I have it wrong," I said.

"How do you think we would know each other?"

"Is that a joke?"

Sara made a move to her car. I came forward. She flinched, bringing her arm up.

"That's not necessary, Sara."

"I don't know you," she said. "I don't know what this is."

"Listen to me," I said.

"No."

"Just listen for a second."

"No."

"It's Benjamin. How can you seriously not recognize me, or remember who I am?"

Sara opened the driver's door and got inside. I stepped forward, blocking her from shutting the door.

"What is your problem?" Sara asked. Her voice taut, on the edge of a scream. "I don't know you. We've never met. You're harassing me."

"Harassing you?"

"You've made a mistake. I'm not the person you think I am."

"Yes. Sara Turner."

"No."

"Yes. I'm Benjamin Baca."

"I'm going to start honking this horn and screaming my goddamn head off if you don't back up."

"Listen to me."

"Get back! Now!"

She started the car, grinding the engine. I stood there, staring down, trying to figure out a way to flip this conversation in a new direction.

I took a step back. Sara reached over, grabbed the door handle, and slammed the door shut. She jammed the gear into reverse and jerked the car back. Once out of the space, she gave me a quick look. I saw the fear in her eyes, and I wanted to laugh.

She pulled away, and I stood there in the parking lot watching her go.

A soft midmorning light blanketed Sara's house. The lush front yard still twinkled from the remnants of rain the previous night. The garage door rose. Sara stepped out of the house wearing an immaculate black business suit. She hurried to the daily paper in the middle of the driveway wrapped in a plastic bag. She picked it up and shook off the water.

If I was going to make my move, I needed to do it now. As she headed back toward the garage, I ran up the driveway. Sara must have heard me. She turned her head and was so startled to see me charging up behind her, she didn't have time to react. She took a step back, tripping, and let out a half scream. I held up my hands and watched her fall back, her head bouncing off the concrete.

I stood frozen, hands up, mouth open. I'm not sure how long I stood there. It couldn't have been more than a second or two. Our past flashed in my mind like faded Polaroids, and a glimpse of our future—where this might go—blurred just out of reach. I could leave, run away, drive away, and disappear. It wasn't too late. But that wasn't the ending I wanted. That wouldn't give me any clear answers, any satisfaction. I had to continue. I had to see this to the end, no matter the consequences.

I put the gun inside the waistband of my pants. I got behind Sara, lifted her by the arms, and dragged her back into the garage. I hustled to the back and hit the garage door button. It slowly made its way back down.

I emerged from the bathroom off the side of the kitchen. Sara's body lay twisted on the tile floor. She looked as if she were taking a nap. She still had those small freckles that peppered the bridge of her nose and cheeks. I checked the back of her head. She wasn't bleeding. She was still out. I didn't know if that was because of the fall, or shock, or a combination of both.

I opened the refrigerator. There were some staples—a carton of eggs, milk—and then a mishmash of odds and ends. It didn't look as if Sara or her husband cooked.

The dining room was just off the kitchen. A small bar connected the two. I found a set of elegant Baccarat cocktail glasses and a nice variety of alcohol. Someone in the house was a fan of single-malt Scotch. I counted five different varieties.

I moved to the living room. The beige carpet was thick and soft. The color must've been a nightmare to keep clean. There was a leather couch and a piano in the corner. They also had what looked to be a high-end stereo system with two speakers as tall as a grade school kid. I couldn't figure out how to turn the stereo on. I scanned the CDs on a bookshelf. They had a diverse collection of classic rock, '70s and '80s country music, and older jazz records. Nothing too obscure. On the bottom shelf was a small collection of vinyl records. I didn't bother to flip through these.

I walked into a long hallway. The temperature dropped. There were large, double wooden doors to the left. I tried the handle. The door was unlocked, so I pushed the door open. Inside was a large master bedroom that had a small office or seating area just off to the side. I caught a faint hint of perfume. There was a king-sized bed at the back of the room that was neatly made and filled with a diverse assortment of throw pillows. The furniture was dark wood and looked like a modern variation of a farmhouse style.

There were photographs everywhere. Most were in frames placed either on the furniture or hanging on the wall. There were photos of Sara and the distinguished man: wedding shots taken years ago, both of them looking young and beautiful, as well as travel photos taken at the Grand Canyon with a sunrise background, and on a cruise ship, and standing in front of the Colosseum in Rome. Most of the photos were of the children. It looked as if there were three of them, a boy and two girls. There were baby pictures, and school pictures, pictures of the kids playing in the rain, or standing on the end of a pier with the ocean behind them. The boy had Sara's blonde hair, but his features came from his father. The girls were practically exact replicas of Sara. They weren't twins, but it wouldn't surprise me if they were often confused for such. They were close in age, maybe a year and a half apart, and they had the same long blonde hair, periwinkle-blue eyes, and sunshine smiles.

I entered the kitchen of the restaurant. Carlos was busy mopping the floor. He moved fast, efficiently swinging the mop back and forth across the floor. I realized that when the restaurant closed I might never see Carlos again, or his wife, Martha, or any of his children or family. I was so caught up in my own bullshit, I hadn't stopped to consider in any more than a passing way the people I would lose.

Carlos had become an indispensable workhorse at the restaurant. The beauty of Carlos was his versatility. He worked primarily as a prep cook, but he could handle any job in any part of the restaurant, and his work ethic was unmatched. Martha worked in the kitchen. She handled prep and made countless tortillas six nights a week. She also made the most perfectly proportioned tamales like a machine. Their kids, all six, had worked at the restaurant at various times. They were more than employees. They were family, and I'd never appreciated them as much as I should have.

I drove my thumbnail into my middle finger and gritted my teeth. I didn't need tears right now.

I waited for the emotions to pass before I asked, "What are you doing?"

Carlos glanced back in my direction, and when he recognized me, he lit up with a big smile.

"Mr. Baca, what are you doing here?"

"I would ask you the same thing."

"Oh, it was so busy here last night."

I sighed. Of course it was.

"I didn't get a chance to finish up," he said.

"How long have you worked for me?"

Carlos tilted his head, counting the years. With a smile he said, "In total, almost nine years, Mr. Baca."

"All that time, I've told you over and over, when are you going to start calling me Ben? My name is Ben. Mr. Baca is what they called my father, and my grandfather."

"Maybe next time," Carlos said.

"I appreciate you coming back."

"Of course."

"You always come back."

Carlos shrugged. "It's my job."

I would miss Carlos so much.

"You can go home, though."

Carlos didn't understand.

"I'm serious," I insisted. "I'll finish this up."

"No, Mr. Baca. I'll finish."

"It's okay," I said. "We're closed today. Go home. Enjoy the rest of the day off. Spend a night with your family for a change. Get some rest. You deserve it."

Carlos considered it, then finally put the mop back into the bucket.

"You know, Mr. Baca. I want to say, I did love working for you and the restaurant."

"Did you?"

Carlos nodded. "I did. Very much so. You taught me a lot about cooking."

"No, my friend. You're the one who taught me."

Carlos smiled.

"Hopefully, this isn't the end," I said. "The plan is you'll be back with me soon."

"God willing," Carlos said.

"You believe in God?" I asked.

"Of course, Mr. Baca. He is the reason for everything."

I wanted to ask him if he was sure about that. Instead, I told him to hold on a second, and went back to the bar and pulled a bottle of Gran Patron off the shelf. I returned to the kitchen and offered it to Carlos. We went back and forth, Carlos saying he could not accept the gift and me insisting he had to. He finally took the bottle and lavished me with over-the-top gratitude.

I walked Carlos outside. We shook hands and then I hugged him, patting him hard on the back. The gesture surprised Carlos, and he didn't know what to do. I didn't care. I thanked him again for all his hard work, and he thanked me again for the opportunity.

I watched Carlos walk to his truck. The man gave me a final nod goodbye, then got into his truck and pulled away.

I waited until Carlos turned the corner. I walked to my car and opened the trunk. Sara was inside with her hands tied behind her back and a pillowcase over her head. She knew something was happening even if she couldn't see what it was.

I leaned in and took her by the arms. There were muffled screams. She tried to squirm and shake me off, but it didn't do much good. I pulled her out of the car, threw her over my shoulder, and walked across the parking lot and into the restaurant.

I carried Sara through the kitchen, then through the doors into the dining room. She wasn't heavy, but she sat in an awkward position on my shoulders. I wasn't in the best shape either. Carrying her was a challenge.

I took her into the bar, pulled out a chair from one of the small tables, and sat her down. I took a step back, sweaty and out of breath. Because her hands were still tied behind her back, it made her position on the chair awkward.

I moved around the bar and took two glasses and filled them with ice and water. I brought the glasses back around the bar and set one in front of Sara. I sat down opposite her with the other glass.

I wiped the sweat from my forehead and took a sip of the water. It tasted good, but it wouldn't cut it for much longer. I would soon need something much stronger.

This was it. In for a penny, in for a pound. There was no turning back now. I would plunge ahead, jump from that bridge, sink or swim, fuck or walk. I would not stop until I had answers.

I leaned over and grabbed the corner of the pillowcase and yanked it off.

Sara's eyes fluttered open. She winced, eyes darting around the room before settling on me. I could almost see recognition slap her in the face.

"You thirsty?" I asked.

Sara looked at me wide eyed, and I wasn't sure if she'd heard me or understood what I was asking. I pointed down to the glass of water. She looked at it and nodded. I again leaned over and reached up to the tape across her mouth. Sara turned away.

"You thirsty, or not?"

I understood her trepidation, to a degree. She considered it and gave me a slight nod. I gripped the edge of the tape and pulled it. It caused her pain, and when her mouth was free, she gasped for air.

"I don't want you tied up," I said. "I also can't risk you doing anything. I can't have you acting up, or trying to scream, or any nonsense. I want to keep your mouth uncovered, and I want to untie your hands. Can I trust you?"

She looked at me with those eyes, those big, beautiful eyes. My heart ached. I couldn't believe this was happening, that this was how it would play out.

"Can I trust you?"

She nodded, and I stood and moved around the table. Her body tensed as I took her hands and undid the knot. I did a terrible job. I was never any good at knots, and if she had worked at it, she could have freed herself.

I slid the glass in front of her and sat back down. Sara studied the water as if trying to determine if it was safe to drink. I waited. I thought it best she realized on her own that I didn't have bad intentions.

She reached for the glass and drank.

"I'm sorry about your head," I told her. "I didn't mean to scare you."

She held the glass with both hands, letting it rest in her lap, and averted her eyes as if she couldn't bear to look at me. I had the thought again that maybe it wasn't too late. I wasn't past the point of no return. I could call this off and drive her back home.

"I didn't want this," I said. "For it to be like this, for us to meet like this. I just wanted to talk."

I wanted to hug her and tell her I missed her and I was glad she was okay. Her life looked as if it had turned out well. I wanted to tell her I was happy for her. I also wanted to impale her with a hard look.

"All these years," I said. "All these years and here we are. Here you are. We're in each other's life again. Never would have guessed. Never in a million years would I have guessed that would happen again."

I needed courage. I needed whiskey. It took me a while to say anything more. We sat in silence for a long time.

"The thing about life," I finally said, "the thing I've always found interesting, is it just never stops. The world keeps turning. It doesn't stop for anything. I guess that's obvious enough. You have those moments, those big life moments—death, some kind of tragedy—those moments that even when they're happening you still have the wherewithal to identify them as something big, life changing. You can feel it. And I always wished I could push 'Pause,' freeze the frame, stop everything, and give myself some time. Time to gather myself, get my thoughts together, and press 'Play' when I was ready to go on. It's impossible, obviously enough. Maybe it's a childish thought. It doesn't matter. Life goes on no matter what's happening to you."

Sara's lips began to tremble. Her body shivered as if she were cold. Her fear was palpable. My heart ached for her, but I felt annoyed too. Why was she scared? It was unnecessary. What did she think I would do? I suppose, in fairness, at that point, she didn't know what I had planned. Was she scared because I had caught her? That had to be an enormous shock to her. Whatever the reason, I could concede it was natural for her to be scared, but that didn't make her fear any less irritating.

I ran my fingers through my hair. What was I babbling on about? There was so much I wanted to say. I had imagined this conversation with Sara many times over the years. I'd never imagined anything like this. Through the years, I had gone through near-countless permutations of how this conversation would go, but sitting there in that moment, I didn't know where to begin. I felt buried by conflicting thoughts and emotions, deeply felt things I needed to express. I wanted to be clear and concise. I wanted more than anything for Sara to understand. I didn't want to ramble or vomit a deluge of random bits and pieces.

I pushed the glass of water away and leaned forward.

"When you disappeared, and it got to the point where we weren't going to find you and there was nothing we could do, nothing more that could be done, I finally got home, back to our home, and I felt as if I'd been left to face the world by myself. And I was lost. There's no other way to put it. I didn't know how I was going to be able to pick myself up and continue. But the world turns. Everything moves on, and you have no choice but to stand up and deal with it one way or another. How was that going to happen? I didn't have a clue. I didn't know. And I just . . . I just couldn't do it. None of it. School. Friends. I pushed it all away. I felt like I'd been hit with a tidal wave, and it was pressing down on me, and there were times when I felt as if I couldn't breathe. There were so many days when I couldn't find an excuse to get out of bed."

I grabbed the glass of water and gulped the rest down. I didn't want to do this. I didn't want to be here anymore. It was a bad idea. It was a colossally bad idea. What the fuck had I hoped to accomplish by this foolish lunacy? What was the end game?

"You can't do that," I said, my tone a touch more severe. "You can't stay in bed. There's life. There's responsibilities.

You still need to pay rent. There are bills. The laundry still needs to be done. You still need to get through all the stupid little bullshit of life. When you vanished, my life went with you, but I still had to live."

I couldn't wait anymore. I stood and walked around the bar. I pulled a bottle of aged whiskey from the shelf and poured myself a shot. I threw it back, and it felt like fire burning down my throat and warming my stomach. I poured another and gulped it down.

"I don't suppose you want a drink?" I asked.

Sara looked at me with those big eyes.

I threw back a third shot. I could already feel the drink's tendrils massaging my brain.

"I guess you'll stick with water," I said. "For now."

I figured I might as well bring the bottle back to the table with me. I didn't want to get drunk—I needed to keep my thoughts clear. I simply needed to dull the edge. I considered another drink but knew it would be too much too soon.

"The hardest thing with you, when you disappeared, was not knowing. That was the bitch of it."

I poured another drink anyway. I left the bottle but carried the drink back around the bar and sat down.

"It took me a long time to realize that I might never get any answers. That's a harsh reality to come to, that the mystery is going to remain just that. It eats at you. I started to replay events over and over and over again. They became these disjointed scenes from a movie. Then after a while it felt more like I was watching a movie from a television show I'd recorded with an old VHS tape. And it always came back to the fact that I didn't know what happened. I'm never going to know what happened—not in any way that satisfies. I can't solve the mystery. I can't answer all these questions. If I'm not making my point, you'll have to trust me when I tell you it's a motherfucker indeed."

Sara kept her eyes averted, staring down at the tile floor.

"I would tell myself that maybe you were still out there. Maybe something had happened. Maybe you were out there, somewhere, living a life. And I would look for you. I couldn't help myself. I'd look for you in crowds. I know it's absurd. The chances of picking you out of a crowd were astronomical, but I'd look anyway."

"I thought I saw you twice. The first time, funny enough, was at an airport buying coffee. I eventually gave up. It happened slowly, but it happened. Time is funny that way. I always thought that idea that time heals all wounds was bullshit, but I don't know, maybe there's something to it. Maybe time does heal. It's a nice thought. I don't know about that, but I will tell you this: if it does heal, it sure does not forget. No. Not at all. Not by a long shot."

I paused. The tendrils of the whiskey dug deeper into my brain. I closed my eyes. I couldn't escape the feeling that this wouldn't be worth it. This game would lead nowhere—not anywhere positive, anyway. It could only cause more problems, more pain. It wouldn't offer any relief.

"And then the other night, it was this perfect evening, a nice milestone kind of night for my family. It was one of those nights you could never forget. My daughter had just graduated from high school. We were out to dinner. My family. Or what used to be my family. Everyone was more or less getting along. It was a good night, a happy night. And then I heard you. I was sitting there, and I heard you. The laugh. It was your laugh. That infectious laugh of yours. God, how I used to love that laugh. My whole day used to be built around trying to make you laugh.

It took me a moment, but I couldn't mistake it. I could never forget it."

I wrapped my fat fingers around the whiskey. I could smell it. I wanted it, but I held off. I needed to maintain some control.

"Do you know what that's like? Can you imagine? It was like seeing a ghost rise from the dead. Because you were dead. I'd convinced myself of that. There was no other way. I hope you can understand that. I had to bury you. I couldn't go on with the mystery. Whatever really happened to you, I had to bury you in order to move on. It took a long time. It wasn't easy. I just had to resign myself to the fact that I would never know. I buried you in here."

I tapped the temple of my forehead and smiled.

"I guess I didn't bury you deep enough."

I downed the drink and held the whiskey in my mouth. I swished it around like it was mouthwash before swallowing.

"That laugh. You were laughing, and here you are now. Sitting right in front of me. Alive. Am I surprised? Yes. Shocked? Yes, I am shocked. You could say that. It'd be the understatement of a lifetime."

I wanted another shot. I wanted more. I wanted to drink until I blacked out. I wanted to sleep a long, deep sleep, a death sleep. I wanted this constant, dull pain, this endless, permanent ache, to leave me.

"Nothing?" I asked. "Are you even listening to me?"

Sara tilted her head up and looked at me with those green eyes.

"It's been all these years, and you have nothing to say? Not one thing?"

Sara opened her mouth, about to speak, but stopped herself. She swallowed, then reached for the glass of water and drank.

She set the glass down, and we sat for what felt like an interminable amount of time.

"I don't know who you are," she said.

I didn't know how to react to that. "What do you mean?"

She swallowed and repeated, "I don't know who you are."

I smiled. "Right. Of course you don't. Why would you?"

"Sir, I really—"

"Stop," I said, holding up my hand to cut her off. "First of all, cut the sir."

"I'm sorry," Sara said. "But I don't know who you are. We've never met, and I don't know what this is about. I don't know what you want from me."

"What do you mean, we've never met?"

"I've never met you before."

I had to laugh. It was just too absurd.

"We've never met?"

She shook her head. "No."

I didn't know what to think. Yet again, this was not going how I thought it would.

"I'm not sure what you're doing here, Sara. I don't know what your end game is, but you need to know that I'm not playing games with you. Do you understand?"

"Yes," she said. "I understand, but I'm telling you the truth."

"Sara, what are you doing?"

"I don't know you."

"That's bullshit."

"No, sir. It's not.

"What is going on?"

"We don't know each other. I've never seen you before."

I sat up straight and put my hands on my knees. I shook my head to clear the whiskey. Sara's hands were in her lap. She was having a difficult time looking at me directly but kept giving me quick peeks.

"I don't understand what you're doing," I said.

"I'm not doing anything."

"Why do this? Why try to lie? Why pretend we don't know each other? I don't get it."

"I don't know you."

"Listen, if this is the way you're going to be, if this is the way you're going to act, it's going to be the longest fucking night of your life."

Sara opened her mouth to speak, but reconsidered. She swallowed again.

"I don't know who you are," she said, her voice barely above a whisper.

"Enough!"

I slammed my fist onto the table. It created a loud noise and caused immense pain in my hand. Sara shrank back, and her hands shook. She was nervous and scared. That wasn't what I wanted, but if it was needed for her to come around, I was okay with it.

"I don't know what you're doing," I said. "I don't want to listen to it. I'm not going to listen to this bullshit. Just stop. Stop it, please. You goddamn fucking well know who I am."

Sara shook her head.

"Yes."

"I'm sorry, but I don't."

"I know you," I said. "You're Sara."

"That's not my name."

"Sara Turner."

"My name is Joanna Corey."

"It's not."

"It is."

"Who do you think I am?" I asked.

"I don't know."

"What?"

"I don't know who you are."

"We know each other."

"We don't."

"Come on!"

"How do you think we know each other?" she asked.

"Stop it. Please. I'm Ben. Benjamin. Look at me. You know me. We were engaged to be married."

"Engaged to be married?" It came out as both a question and an exclamation of shock.

"Yes. You know this. Cut the shit. You know me. I was your fiancé."

"That's crazy."

"Twenty fucking years ago."

"That's impossible."

"It's not impossible. It's the truth."

"I've never met you before in my life."

"We were living in California. We were set to be married. We were on our way back to get married, and you pulled a high-wire disappearing act on me."

"What do you mean?"

"You disappeared. We were at the airport, and you disappeared."

"I'm sorry, but you're confused. I don't know who you are."

"Benjamin Baca."

"My name is Joanna Corey."

"Bullshit."

"Listen," Sara pleaded. "Listen to me. I'm married. I've been married to the same man for twenty-two years."

"Twenty-two years?"

"Yes."

"That's impossible."

"It's true."

"Listen," I said. "There is no possible way that could have happened. The math doesn't add up. You're lying."

"It's not a lie," Sara said, becoming more and more animated as she spoke. "It's not a lie at all. I've been married to the same man for twenty-two years. His name is Pete. Peter Corey. That's my husband's name."

"Pete?"

"Yes," Sara said. "I have kids."

"Stop."

"No. My children—"

"Stop it."

"I have three kids. Three. My name is not Sara. It's Joanna."

"Shut the fuck up!"

Sara flinched.

I took a moment. I needed to think this out. I breathed through my nose, sounding like a bull in the ring.

"I'm not going to listen to this shit," I said. "It's over. The fucking con is up. All these years, and now you're caught. Deal with it. You are caught. It's over, so stop it. Let's just move on."

I was out of breath and felt a hitch in my chest and side. I'd thought this would be easy. I'd thought Sara would realize the situation, recognize who I was, maybe feel guilt or shame, and confess. Maybe confess is not the right word. I thought she would tell me what had happened to her. It seemed reasonable enough. I couldn't understand why she continued to lie. Why keep up the ruse, pretending she was someone else, and that she didn't know me and had never seen me before? What was the point? I couldn't figure out the benefit of doing that. What did she hope to gain?

I walked to the bar, stood on the bottom rail, reached over, and grabbed a bottle of whiskey. I took it back to the table and sat down. I took my time. My movements were slow and deliberate. I unscrewed the cap and filled my glass with whiskey, then I stared at the beautiful golden liquid, trying to figure out what I would do next.

"Sir—" Sara said.

I stopped her with a look.

Sara retreated. She took a breath, regrouped, and then started again.

"I am sorry. I'm really very sorry. I don't know what else to say other than that. I'm truly very sorry. I don't know what to say to you. I can't tell you anything other than the truth. I don't know who you are. That's the truth. To the best of my knowledge, I've never seen you before. We've never met. I don't know who you think I am. I don't know how you think we could have met or had this relationship. I don't know. I'm sorry, but that's the truth."

I listened. I took a sip of my drink, swallowed, and then downed a third of the whiskey. I listened, and I seethed. Her words only stoked the fire.

"You don't know me?"

Sara shook her head. "No, I don't."

"We've never met?"

"No."

"We didn't date? We weren't engaged to be married? We weren't on our way back to St. Catherine to finalize that wedding?"

Sara shook her head again.

I nodded and took another sip. I took my time before saying anything.

"I really don't understand what you're doing. I don't get it. We're done. The jig is up. And I don't know how you have the nerve to sit there and continue to pretend, to really fucking lie to me. Treat me like I'm the asshole. I'm crazy. Like I don't know what I'm talking about. I'm the one making a terrible mistake. I don't see how you can do that to me. I don't deserve that, do I? Or maybe I do. I don't know. You never expected to see me again. Okay. Fair enough. I get that. It's a shock. It's clearly a shock. You're just as surprised as I was. Probably more so. But now you're here, sitting there. We're face to face. I don't know how you can continue to lie, continue to pretend. Why do we have to play this game? Why do we have to do this charade, and go round and round like this? What's the point? Just admit it, admit you're caught, and we'll move on."

I was tired. It hit me all of a sudden just how tired I was. I again had this feeling I didn't want to do this anymore, but I was already so far in, I didn't know how I could stop either. I was well past the point where I could turn around.

"Your name is Sara. Sara Turner. You're the daughter of James and Sheryl. I don't care what you call yourself now. New name, new life, husband, kids, timeshare by the beach—I don't give a fuck. Maybe we'll get to that eventually. But right now I want the past. Your past. I want what you did to me. You left. You left me there in the airport. It devastated me. My life. I want to have a conversation. What I really want is simple. It's really very simple. What I want, what you're going to give me, is why."

I could see the conflict in her. I could see her weighing her options, trying to figure out how to respond. I waited.

"I don't have that answer," she said. "I don't know the why. I don't know why this woman did whatever she did to you. I don't have the answers. I don't know why because I'm not the person you think I am."

I nodded, and turned it over. I filled my glass with whiskey, then I said, "You continue down this path, and it will not end well for you."

"But I don't know why," she pleaded.

"Make no mistake: I don't give a fuck. That's where I'm at."

"I don't know."

"You better figure it out."

Sara could not hold back any longer. She tried to stay strong, but this was too much. She cried. Her eyes filled with tears, and I could see she wanted to fight them back. She didn't want me to see it. She wanted to be tough, but that resolve evaporated.

I watched her, unmoved by her tears, and sipped the whiskey.

"I want your side. Don't you get that? I'm not going to do anything to you. I'm not going to hurt you. I just want your side of the story. I know there is one. I want to hear it. I always wanted to tell you mine. I want to have a conversation. A dialogue. Do you have a clue, just a little clue how bad you hurt me, how my life was completely turned upside down by you? It was. There's no other way to put it. It was a mystery I was never going to be able to solve. And that being the case, it was easy to imagine that something terrible had happened to you. I hoped not, of course. But the odds were that something terrible had happened. But I could never truly know. I could never really truly know for certain, and it became easy to assume that something bad had happened, that you were dead. That didn't really satisfy me, but it was all I had. But now that you're here, sitting right there, it had to be something else."

I picked the glass up, gave what I hoped was a dramatic pause. I wanted her to give thought to what I said.

"With that in mind, those tears, that's ripe. I want answers. I want you to start giving me some answers. That's it. That's as simple and as painless as it can be. You want upset and tears, all the rest of the bullshit? If that's the direction you want to go, I can accommodate that. Let's make this as difficult as possible. That's fine too. Do you want to see your kids again?"

That got her. I saw it and pounced.

"Your husband. That perfect fucking house in the middle of those orange groves. You'll never see any of it ever again. If that's how you want it to go, we'll go there. It doesn't matter to me. So, think carefully. You better start talking to me. Tell me what happened. From here on out that's all I want to hear from you."

"I can't tell you what I don't know."

"You better learn to lie."

Sara wiped the tears and glanced around the bar. Her eyes fell to a print of Manet's *Bullfight* framed on the wall. I didn't know much about art or artists. It was a present from Christine when we were about to open the restaurant.

"How about a guess?" Sara asked, her eyes moved from the print to me. "A man who would attack a stranger. Attack a woman. Kidnap a woman. Hold her against her will. Maybe that's the kind of man a woman would want to leave, would want to run as far away from as she possibly could. How about that? Did you think of that?"

I blinked and my head snapped back as if someone had shot me in the forehead with a pellet gun. I had to laugh. I couldn't help myself, because no, in fact, this stupidly obvious point had never occurred to me before. She was right, and I got to laughing so hard, tears came to my eyes.

"You're right," I said. "Of course you're right. This is stupid. It's a grotesque act of intense stupidity. That's fine, but it

216

didn't happen in a vacuum. It's not as if I jumped directly to this option."

"The grocery store."

"That, yes," I said. "I tried to do this a different way."

"You've been calling my house. Hanging up. Then you kidnap me."

"Listen," I snapped. "This isn't what I wanted. Not at all. But I couldn't just let you go. Why is that so hard for you to understand? I couldn't just shrug my shoulders and move on. I couldn't live with that. One way or another, we were going to have a conversation."

She gave me a tough grin.

Why did I need to explain this to her? It was so tiresome, so much more difficult than it needed to be.

"How do you think you're going to get away with telling me that you're not Sara? How do you think that's going to work?"

Sara gave a slight shrug of her shoulders, like a little girl.

"I'm not her," she said and almost laughed. "I don't know what to tell you. I'm not her."

"I'm not going to say you're not different," I said. "You're older, obviously. You can't do much about that. Believe me, I know well enough that time can be a son of a bitch that way. You're older, but time hasn't changed you that much. It's you. I know. I know who you are. I honest to God thought we'd get through this part rather quickly. I didn't expect this round and round bullshit, denying what is plain as day. It's stupid, Sara. It's over. You're caught. What's the point in refusing the obvious? No more lies. I've lived too many lies. God knows I've lived way too many goddamn lies. Because in the end, it's not the color of your hair, some wrinkles, signs of age. It's that laugh. The laugh. It could never let me be. And it's your eyes. It's that I can look in your eyes and know. I know who you are."

Sara opened her mouth to speak, but I held up my hand.

"Before you protest. Before you open that mouth and try to sell me on more bullshit nonsense, I want you to think a moment. There is undeniable proof you are Sara Turner."

I waited for her to ask, but she didn't.

"It's your tattoo," I said, and I saw her body go rigid. "The little red heart tattoo that you have behind your left ear. At your house, when you were out, I checked. The tattoo is there. There isn't a doubt in my mind. Now, I want you to think about how you want to continue, about what you want to say, and how you want this to go. It doesn't have to be this hard. It really doesn't. I'm not looking for a battle. Honest to Christ, as stupid as I know this may appear, all I really wanted was a conversation."

Sara reached for her glass. She took a sip, then finished the water.

"Do you want more?"

Sara shook her head.

We sat in silence. I don't know how long it lasted. Maybe less than a minute, but it felt longer.

"What time does this husband of yours get home from work?"

"Six."

I checked my watch. "He'll expect you to be home?"

"Yes. I'm sure he will."

"You're usually home when he gets in?"

"Yes."

"And you're the kind of wife that makes sure you have dinner on the table so you can eat as soon as he walks in?"

"We were supposed to go out tonight."

"Date night?"

"We're supposed to go to a movie."

"What do you think will go through his mind when you're not there?"

"I'm sure he'll wonder where I am."

"What about the kids?"

"My children don't live at home anymore."

"No?"

Sara shook her head.

"The pictures I saw, they didn't look old enough to be on their own."

It wasn't a question, but I expected some kind of response. I waited for it, and when it was clear Sara would not give one, I asked, "You two have to knock around that big house just the two of you?"

"It's our home."

"When I saw you in the parking lot, when I came up to you, there was nothing. No reaction. No recognition. I started to think maybe it was amnesia. You looked at me like I was a stranger."

"You are a stranger."

I let that go. "Have you suffered from amnesia?"

"No."

"How would you know?" I asked. "If you slipped, say, in that bathroom at the airport and hit your head. If you had an accident, something that affected your memory. However it happened, how would you know? You see the point? You wouldn't. But no. That's not the answer, is it?"

Again, Sara did not respond. She looked at me with those big green-apple eyes.

"We're just going to continue to play this game. This stupid, needless game."

"I don't know what you want from me. I'm not this woman. I'm not Sara."

"You're Joanna."

"Yes."

"Where were you born, Joanna?"

"Stockton."

"Stockton?"

"It's a small town."

"Small town where?"

"Kansas."

"Kansas?"

"That's right."

"You were born in 1979."

"1974."

"Jesus Christ!"

"It's true."

I leaned forward, forearms on my knees. Even though there was a table between us, Sara stiffened and leaned back in the chair.

"Your dad died of cancer when you were twelve."

"No," Sara said. I could see a slight pickup in her tone as if she was getting the handle of this back and forth and maybe saw a way out.

"Listen," she said, "both of my parents are alive. They live here in Sun City. They are alive. I'm not who you think I am. Do you see? It's a mistake."

"No," I said. I bit my bottom lip and shook my head and said it again. "No."

"You're wrong about me. It's all a big mistake. You're wrong about it all."

"No."

"Yes. Please, you have to understand."

"You're Sara Turner."

"I'm sorry. I truly am. I'm not Sara. I'm just not."

"Enough."

"You need to listen to me. Please, Ben. Right? Benjamin. I'm not who you think I am. You need to let me go. Please. Before it's too late. Before this goes too far. Right now, this is a misunderstanding. It's just a terrible misunderstanding."

"Stop."

"You can let me go."

"No."

"Please. You need to let me go."

I ran my fingers through my hair and said, "I don't know what's going on here."

"I'm begging you."

"I don't know what you're doing. I don't know why you're doing this. I don't know what happened to you."

"Nothing happened to me," she said. "It's not too late to end this. You can let me go. I'm not going to say anything. I don't want to hurt you."

"I don't know what you're doing, what the game is, but it has to stop."

"It's not too late, Ben. We can end this."

"I'm so sick of your fucking lies."

"It's not a lie," Sara said. "I'm not lying. I have no reason to lie."

"You have every reason to lie."

"You're not listening to me."

"I am listening to you. That's the problem."

"You're not hearing what I'm telling you. It's not a lie. Please, I'm begging you. You need to believe me."

"I know, Sara," I said, my voice now calm. "That's the thing: I am the one that knows. That's the problem you have right now. I do know."

"I don't know you," she said. "I don't know how many times I have to tell you. I know what it's going to take. You're wrong. You're making a mistake."

"No," I said. "You're the one who's made the mistake."

Sara dropped her head, chin to chest, and let out a loud, mad shriek. The tendons on her neck stood out like drawn wires. She then tilted her head back and screamed as loud as she could. She wanted a release, a way to expel the anger and frustration. I felt sorry for her because it wouldn't help. It would only exhaust her and give her a headache.

I let her carry on. I wasn't in a hurry. Not yet. I had time. I took my wallet out of my back pocket, unfolded it, and withdrew a small photo, the same photo Marina had found. I unfolded it, looked at the picture, and held it up.

"This is you," I said.

Sara buried her face in her hands and wept.

"Look at the photo. Calm down for a second and look at it."

Sara brought her hands down and looked at the photo.

"Tell me this isn't you. Look at it and tell me I'm wrong."

I waited, and then said again, "Tell me this photo isn't you."

Tears ran down her cheeks. Her eyes burned red. She looked at the picture, then leaned forward and appeared to study it. She wiped her tears again and smiled.

"Twenty-two years old," I said. "I took the picture at the beach. Now look me in the eye and call me a liar."

Sara looked at me directly in the eye, and said, "That's not me."

"Are you a fucking child?" I erupted.

"That's not me in that photo."

"You don't . . . you don't goddamn want to listen."

"I can lie to you," Sara said. "If that's what you want, if that will end this, I can lie. I can tell you whatever you want to hear."

"I don't want a lie," I snarled. "That's the goddamn point. I want your lies to stop."

"I can't give you what you want."

"You're fucking torturing me, you bitch."

Sara had to damn near stifle a shocked laugh.

"All these years, you continue to torture me."

"I don't know what you want me to say."

"Do I need to hurt you?" I asked. That wiped the smug grin and attitude from her. "Would that move this along? Is that where we're headed?"

"No," Sara said. "I don't want that."

"I don't give a fuck anymore. Do you understand me? I'll kill you."

She tensed.

"I'm not in the mood for this shit anymore. You'll never see those kids again. Your husband. You think our past clouds this situation. I'm not someone to be fucked with."

Sara sat with her head down and her hands folded in her lap. She looked like a kid being scolded.

"Why are you doing this? I don't believe you don't remember. I don't believe you don't know. How dare you try to tell me that's not a picture of you. How dare you try to pass that off like I'm a fucking idiot. I can't figure out what you're doing. I can't figure out why, unless you underestimate me."

"Please," Sara said, her voice soft.

"You still want to play me like an asshole."

"That's not it."

"What is it then?"

"Sir—"

"No more lies. No more bullshit from you. You better start talking, and you better start now."

"Sir, please."

I slapped her, hard. It sounded like a whip crack. She lost her breath. I stood and walked to the bar, reached over the countertop and withdrew a pistol, then returned to the table. Sara watched me, eyes wide, helpless. She trembled.

"No," she said, or simply mouthed the word. She was so quiet it was hard to tell.

"Talk."

"I can't."

"Talk!"

"I can't."

I pulled the hammer back. Sara flinched.

"Don't push me," I said.

She closed her eyes.

"I don't know what to say," she cried. "There's nothing I can tell you."

My anger felt like acid. I wanted to pull the trigger. I wanted to kill her. I had so many unanswered questions. Contradictory feelings and emotions beat my body and mind like pugilists. I wanted it to end. I wanted the pain to wash away. Perhaps the only way to do it was with a gun and a bullet. This had veered so far out of hand and so far from my intentions. I thought it would be easy. That was the most idiotic part of all this. The resolution would be so different. What was I thinking? It was reckless and dangerous, and really so fucking stupid, to bring her to the restaurant of all goddamn places. I wasn't thinking. This had no chance of ending well. That was painfully obvious now, but at the time it felt like a sound decision. It felt like the only reasonable solution left.

I loved her. I still loved her so much. I'd always loved Sara. The years, the emotion, the tears, the heartache, the pain, the battles, the scars—all the wreckage had not dulled the edge of my love for her. Maybe there were no answers. Maybe there was no way to answer all the questions. Some mysteries linger forever in memory and are never solved, at least not in any satisfactory way.

I lowered the gun and took a step back. I looked at Sara and the ache I felt in my heart was overwhelming. I wanted acknowledgment, some tiny indication she recognized me and remembered our time. We were together once, happy, with the hope of a bright future. That hope might have faded, but it was there once. Maybe hope reignited when I heard that laugh, that irresistible, unforgettable laugh once again. No. I was foolish and pathetic—Christine was right on the money about that one—and my anger bubbled into a bitter shame, a shame so powerful and overwhelming I wanted to disappear.

I lowered the hammer and dropped my head. Then I turned and walked away.

Red chili simmered on the stove, its aroma intense. It smelled like childhood. My grandmother, a small, frail bird of a woman, always had a pot of red chili on the stove. She made two dozen tortillas every single day, year-round. When I was a kid, one of my most favorite things to do in the world was to ride my bike to her house after school and eat a fresh tortilla hot off the griddle with melted butter, or with creamy peanut butter drizzled with honey. My version of red chili was a slight variation on hers. I made a conscious effort not to replicate her recipe. I knew well enough that even with all my training, skill, and experience, I would never come close to what she'd created. I didn't want to try. Chefs like to talk about the story they are telling through food. I believed in this, but I also knew every time someone tells a story, it becomes less true. My food won me praise and awards. I found it amusing. If people only knew what my grandmother had done, what she could do with food in that tiny kitchen of hers, they would not bother to applaud me. Even though I constantly went back to those old recipes and traditions, I knew they were gone forever. The chili, the salsa, the thick flour tortillas, the tamales, all the food she made, the effort and love she put into her food, passed away with her.

I stirred the chili. It was ready. I surveyed the rest of the ingredients prepped and laid out on the table. It was time to assemble the meal.

I brought two plates from the kitchen into the bar. I set one in front of Sara and one for me. I sat down and poured a decent red wine for each of us.

Sara stared at the food. It was cheese enchiladas, rice, and beans. Simple food, a combination platter found at any Mexican restaurant, but cooked with a level of precision and craft few could match.

"It's not poisoned," I said with a smile.

Sara gave me a skeptical eye.

"Try it."

Sara took her fork. She paused, trying to think this out, then scooped up some rice and ate it. She then cut a piece of the enchilada and tried that too.

"You like it?" I asked.

She nodded and said, "It's good."

We ate in silence, sipping the wine between bites.

"Are you surprised by the restaurant?" I asked.

"It is quite good," she said.

It was clear she was being genuine, and I felt a pain in my heart. I know this might not make any sense, but it was important to me that she liked the food. It meant something. It meant a great deal.

"It's one of those odd turns my life took when you left. When I was back in California, I couldn't go back to my job. I knew I needed a change. I didn't know what I would do, but I couldn't go back and sit in that cube anymore. It felt more like a prison. It took a while to figure it out. I decided I might as well go with something I'm passionate about. "

I poured more wine.

"Did you know that your mom buried you?"

Sara stopped eating. She sat there, fork in hand, and stared at her plate.

"It was an empty coffin. Actually, they filled it with pictures, little odds and ends of yours. I don't know all of what they put in there. Things they thought would mean something to you. Or represented you. They buried you in that pissy little town. I wasn't invited, which I guess wasn't much of a surprise."

I finished my glass of wine and poured more.

"Is your mom still alive?"

Sara looked frozen. I waited for an answer, or some acknowledgment of the question. Neither was forthcoming.

"There's never going to be any satisfaction, is there?"

No response. Nothing.

"What am I going to do here?" I asked. "What am I going to do with you?"

The question hung there, until Sara said, "You can let me go."

I poured more wine for her even though she didn't need it.

"Why don't you tell me what's been going on with you and your life?"

"Like what?"

"This perfect life you've created for yourself."

"It's not perfect," Sara said.

"It's not?"

"No," she said, putting her fork down. "Does that make you happy?"

"Why would that make me happy?"

"Maybe that's what you feed off of."

"Is that what you really think this is?"

"Maybe I should give you a line-item description of every hardship and tragedy I've ever had to go through. Would that satisfy you enough to stop this?"

"How long have you been married?"

"Twenty-two years."

"Love at first sight?"

"No," Sara said. "We didn't really get along at first."

"Do you remember our first date?"

"No."

"We went to the museum. The Joslyn Art Museum. We ate lunch at that little garden café. We saw Key Largo at Indian Hills. They brought it back for some anniversary, I think. My oldest daughter, we named her Joslyn. I came up with it. I never told my ex-wife where the name came from."

Sara sipped the wine. She set the glass back on the table.

"What great things have happened to you in your life?" I asked.

"There's been no great adventure."

"What does your husband do?"

"He teaches at the university."

"Peter."

"That's right."

"What does he teach?"

"Art. Painting. Sometimes figure drawing and photography."

"He's an artist?"

"More a historian."

"And you, Sara, what do you do?"

"Nothing," she said. "I've been a mother."

"That's not nothing."

She shrugged.

"Three kids?"

She nodded.

"You really did change," I said.

"How did I change?"

"When we were together, you never wanted children. Not for a while, anyway. You wanted to travel. You wanted to experience the world."

"It didn't quite happen that way," she said.

"You lost the ambition," I said.

"Is that what happened?"

"You were full of plans and ideas. All the things you wanted to do. The future."

"Maybe they were childish things that needed to be put away."

"You settled down, became a mom, a family woman."

She shrugged again and said, "I guess so."

I considered this, rolled it over, then shook my head. "It doesn't fit. It doesn't fit the person I know. Then again, so many years have passed, we're more strangers now anyway, so what do I know?"

I guess neither of us had much of an appetite. I didn't want to talk anymore. I didn't know how to end this. I downed my wine and noticed that the bottle was empty. Sara wasn't drinking hers, and I considered asking her if I could have it.

"You don't have the slightest regret?" I asked. "Don't you feel just a little sorry for what you've done?"

"I have a lot of regret."

"Is that so?"

"More than I could ever sit here and distill for you in this restaurant."

"And you?" I said. "What did you do with all your regret?"

She looked at me with a piercing gaze that gave me a suffocating sense of familiarity. She said, "You live with it."

I kicked the bathroom stall door. It slammed against the side and came back. I kicked it again, breaking the hinges, causing the door to fall to the ground. I ran my fingers through my hair. It wasn't enough. I punched the stall. My hand stung, but I didn't care. I kicked the shit out of the stall. I didn't stop until I was hunched over and out of breath.

I walked to the sink and turned on the water. My hand was a pulpy mess. I put it under the faucet and washed off the blood and bits of loose skin. I caught my reflection in the mirror. I didn't look good. My eyes were bloodshot, and my skin was pasty. I looked sick.

I charged into the bar. Sara sat with her hands folded on the table.

"Listen," I barked. "I just want to know why."

"Why what?"

"Don't fuck with me anymore. I'm begging you. Please, don't do that."

"I can't tell you why."

"No more bullshit, okay?" Sara shrank from my anger. I retreated. "I'm sorry," I said. "Listen. I need you to please listen to me here. I need to know why you left me. I don't care about anything else. The rest is bullshit. Why did you leave that day?"

"But I didn't leave."

I slammed my hand on the table. "No! No! No! No! That is unacceptable. You left. You obviously left. What else could have happened? Why? That's all I want to know. Why?"

"I didn't leave."

I turned from her and buried my palms into my eyes.

"For Christ's sake," I pleaded. "Please don't fucking do this to me anymore."

I turned back to her. Sara looked at me, wide eyed and frightened.

"I need to know. Please. Don't do this. You can't. You can't just sit there and look at me like that. You can't string this along forever. What was it? Why? You saw something that day. Maybe it had been building for a long time. Maybe you had an epiphany. What was it? What did you see?"

Sara just sat there.

"What did you figure out? You saw your life. You saw a future with me and decided you couldn't do it. Tell me. What was it about a life with me? What did you see?"

Sara lowered her eyes.

"Listen to me. Give me the answer. Tell me. This will be over. I'll take you home. Tell me what happened. What did you see that day? What was it? Or did you decide before? Goddammit, you have to tell me. Because here's the thing, this is what I want you to know: you were right. You did the right thing. You were right to leave. I just need to know why. Do you understand? I need to know why."

Sara opened her mouth, but I could tell she'd only give me more hemming and hawing and bullshit. I couldn't listen to that anymore. I picked up the table and tossed it. Sara screamed. In the action, I twisted my back something fierce and could already tell I had hurt myself. I didn't care.

"Tell me. Tell me why. Look at me. Look! You were right. You should have left. I deserved it. You needed to leave. I know that. I've known all along. You did the right thing."

I went to the bar and took the pistol.

"No!" Sara cried. "No. Please, don't."

"Why did you leave?" I asked. "What was there? What did you see?"

We stared at each other. There were no answers. There would never be any answers. I backed away from Sara. I couldn't look at her anymore. I felt shame. I was embarrassed, and I felt compelled to apologize and try to explain myself, but the time for that had passed. I turned to make sure there was a chair nearby. I pulled one from another table and sat down. I cried. I didn't want to cry, but I couldn't help it. It burst from me.

Sara sat there and watched me blubbering like a fool. She didn't know what to do, and maybe this is crazy or delusional, but I sensed that she wanted to offer comfort. She didn't, though.

"I loved you so much," I said. "I loved you so goddamn much. I want to know what happened. I don't know what happened. I don't know what happened to me."

"Nothing happened to you," Sara said. "You were there all along."

She picked up the wine bottle, and with shocking quickness covered the distance between us and slammed the bottle against my head. It happened so fast, I didn't have time to react. The bottle didn't break. It bounced off my head, and I could feel my skull vibrating like something out of a Chuck Jones cartoon. I screamed out and dropped to the ground. My vision blurred and went black at the edges. I felt something wet above my eye. My hand went to it. I had blood on my fingers.

Sara jumped up and took off running. She wove between tables and chairs and disappeared into the darkness of the dining room. I heard her trying to open the front door. I knew it was locked and there was no way she would get out that way. She struggled with it, yanking on the handle, banging the thick wood with her fists, grunting and shouting.

I couldn't shake the sound of ringing bells from my head. I struggled to move. I listened as Sara searched for a way to open the front door. I dragged a chair closer and used it to prop myself up. I had to keep wiping the blood from my eye, smearing it across my face. I felt as if I were pulling myself out of a tar pit, but I got to my feet just in time to see Sara tear through the dining room and burst through the door to the kitchen. She would not find a way out that way either, but she could find a place to hide or some other kind of trouble.

I had to go after her, and I needed to be quick about it, but I couldn't get my feet to move. I could feel my heart racing through the gash above my eye, pumping out blood with every beat. I probably needed stitches.

I hurried to the kitchen. Or I hurried as much as I could. I made it there just as Sara burst through the door leading to the back parking lot. She'd figured out how to unlock it after all.

That lit a fire in me. I ran after her, my head pounding. I could never run very fast. I hit the door and burst into the night. Sara turned back and screamed. She held a large steak knife in her hand. She'd figured out the dirt parking lot in the back of the restaurant was enclosed by a chain-link fence with barbed wire at the top. It was a necessary precaution of the neighborhood.

She surveyed the fence and parking lot, considering her options, then ran to the back fence and tried to climb. I admired the determination, even if it was comical in its execution. She screamed out for help, a high-pitched, wild scream. Chances were there wouldn't be anyone around to hear her, but I couldn't take that risk. I ran across the lot to her. She'd gotten about two feet up the fence. It would be easy to reach up and pull her off. But as I grabbed her shirt, Sara jumped back off the fence. That took me by surprise. She attacked, charging me, knife up. I pushed her away, taking the hand with the knife and squeezing her wrist, twisting it, as hard as I could until she dropped it. She slapped me with her other hand. It stung. I pulled her down and pushed her to the ground. She tried to scurry away like a crab, but I was on top of her, reaching down and grabbing a handful of hair. She screeched, over and over again, sounding like a wounded animal. I took her by the arm and pulled her back up to her feet. She wanted to fight, but she didn't have it in her. I walked her back toward the restaurant, looking like a cop leading their perp. As I reached for the knob on the back door, Sara shook free. I caught her shirt, pulled her back, and slapped her as hard as I could. Her knees buckled, and I had to hold her up. I got the door open and pushed her inside.

I manhandled her back through the kitchen, through the dining room, and into the bar. I shoved her into a chair.

What was I doing? What was the plan? The gun. What did I do with that damn gun? My eye went to the bar. I didn't see it. Did I leave that fucking thing in the bathroom? I couldn't leave Sara to check.

"The bullshit stops," I shouted. "Now. I'm done with this."

"Fuck you," she barked.

"That's cute."

"I'm not the person you think I am."

I shook my head and twisted around. I felt a jab in my lower back as if I'd been poked by a stick. I reached back and found the gun wedged between the waistband of my pants and my back. I didn't remember putting it there. My mind raced. It felt scrambled. I could hardly keep up. I needed to take a deep breath, but instead I took the gun and lunged forward.

I pointed the gun at Sara. She flinched, screamed out, and turned her head.

"The bullshit stops."

"No," she pleaded. "Don't."

"There's a slight amusement to watching you string your bullshit fantasies about your family, your life, all of it. I admire the stones you've got to stick with it like you have. Look at me. Look at me!"

Sara raised her eyes to meet mine.

"The bullshit and the games stop now. I'm through. I'm through fucking around with you. You start talking. You start telling me what happened. You start now."

"But I can't," Sara said.

I cocked the hammer and leaned forward. "Why are you doing this? How does this benefit you?"

Sara began to cry again. "I can't."

I came closer, pointing the gun at her head. She made a whelping noise.

"Tell me why. How did it happen? Where did you go that day? How did you disappear from that airport?"

Sara's mouth hung open in a mute cry. Snot ran from her nose.

"Tell me. Tell me what happened."

"I can't."

I placed the barrel of the gun against her forehead.

"It ends right now, one way or another," I said.

She just sat there, head down.

I pressed the gun hard against her temple. I then pointed it away, toward the bar, and fired. The shot from the small gun sounded like a cannon going off.

Sara shook like her whole body were dry-heaving, and she cried, "All right, all right. Stop. Please. Stop." She worked to catch her breath. "Just stop. I'll tell you. Okay? Stop, and I'll tell you what you want to know."

I didn't know what to say. She broke. This was it. My body tensed. After all this time, after all this effort—the stress, the years of pain, the heartache, the frustration of living with the mystery, with the unknown—it was all going to end. There would be answers. I realized I was scared. Terrified. I felt it in my heart and my stomach. Standing there in front of her, I suddenly wasn't sure I wanted to know the answers. I know that doesn't make much sense. I felt panicked, like I wanted to flee. I didn't know what she would tell me, and it terrified me. I wanted to know the answers, but I didn't know if I could face them.

I lowered the gun and took a step back. I waited for Sara to regain her composure. She dropped the farce, her stupid little charade, and I was willing to give her time to gather herself before she talked.

"May I have a drink of water?" she asked.

"Of course," I said, and went to the bar. I took a glass, filled it with water, and brought it back to her. She took it with both hands. She sipped it first, then gulped half the glass down. She wiped her mouth with the back of her hand. I watched her shoulders as they rose and fell, up and down, with each breath.

She took another drink, then like a cobra, spit the water at me. I didn't expect it, and didn't react. It hit me in the face. Sara began to laugh. I looked at her as she laughed. It was more like a cackle, the clucking of a witch. She tilted her head back and howled with mocking laughter.

I can't tell you how long I stood there, water dripping from my face, and watched her laugh. I didn't know what was left to say. I didn't know what to think. I didn't know what my next step would be. All I knew was that I wanted this to be over.

I raised the gun and fired. The laughter stopped. The blow jerked Sara back, and she fell off the chair. She was on her hands and knees, blood leaking from her chest, whining. I took a step forward to stand over her and fired again. She collapsed. I pulled the hammer back and fired again. Her body went limp, and the sound of the gun rang in my head for a very long time.

I entered the office and turned on the lights. The fluorescents flickered to life. I winced. I couldn't handle their harshness. I turned them off and instead pulled the switch of the lamp on my desk. It emitted a more soothing, buttery light.

I fell into my chair. My head felt like it were about to split open. I opened a drawer and pulled out a bottle. I twisted the cap and filled an empty coffee cup. I drained the cup and refilled it. I sat there staring off at nothing before I picked up the phone and dialed.

Ernie picked up the other line.

"Yes?"

"Ernie, it's Ben."

"Benny. What's going on?"

"I got a situation here. I'm going to need some help."

I stood back as two of Ernie's goons—I didn't know their names, and they hadn't bothered to introduce themselves when they arrived—laid out a heavy-duty brown tarp on the bar floor. They got on opposite sides of Sara, at her head and feet, picked her up, and placed her on the right-hand side of the tarp. Then, as if wrapping a grotesque burrito, they folded both ends of the tarp and rolled her up. They picked her up, and I held the doors for them as they carried her body through the restaurant to the back parking lot. They loaded her into the back of a beat-up white minivan. They said nothing. They didn't look at me or acknowledge me. They shut the door, got in the van, and drove off.

I got a bucket of scalding-hot water and bleach and carried it into the bar. I got on my hands and knees and cleaned the blood off the floor. It had already become thick like honey.

When I'd finished, I washed the pot and pans and all the utensils I'd used to make dinner, then I wiped down the steel counters.

When everything was clean, I stumbled back into the office. I sat down and poured myself another drink. I didn't think I had ever been so tired. I wanted to lie down on the couch and take a nap, but I didn't want to risk still being there when the crew came in for the day. Still, I didn't know how I would drive home.

I downed the rest of the whiskey. As I filled the glass again, I noticed tiny splatters of blood on the cuffs of my shirt. Sara's blood. I don't know how long I sat in that chair and stared at the stains.

I held up a glass of whiskey. The others did the same.

"I think I'm at a loss for words," I said.

The room gave me a courtesy laugh.

"I'm just . . . I'm just so grateful, and I really feel truly blessed that that we can gather here tonight, at this new restaurant, on the eve of my daughter's wedding."

Samantha sat a nearby table. Her fiancé, Scott, had his arm around her. She looked at me with a big smile, her blue eyes holding back tears. I smiled back.

"I honestly never thought this day would come. I never thought there would be a man out there brave enough, slightly crazy enough, to marry our Samantha."

More polite laughs.

"She's tough. I love that about her. She's a tough woman. She doesn't suffer fools. She demands, and frankly deserves, the very best in everyone. I've gotten to know Scott over the last year, and I know—I know in my heart—that he is just the man to give her his best. I stand here tonight and I could not be more proud. I wish you both nothing but love and happiness for the rest of your lives. May you live a life of no regret."

I held my glass a little higher. The room followed my lead. A few cheers and then applause. I walked over to Samantha. Scott stood and shook my hand. He had a firm grip but was confident enough with himself not to overpower you with it.

"Congratulations," I told him.

"Thank you, sir."

"Enjoy it," I said. "Enjoy everything."

"I certainly will."

I leaned over and gave Samantha a kiss on the cheek.

"Thank you, Daddy."

"Of course."

"Thank you for everything."

Heidi and I sat at a table by ourselves, having a drink.

"Tomorrow," she mused.

I nodded. "Tomorrow."

"Our baby is getting married."

"It's hard to imagine. I thought for sure the other one would go first."

"Are you going to be able to keep it together?"

"I doubt it," I said.

Heidi sipped her wine as her eyes scanned the room, a large private dining space in the back of the restaurant.

"I like the new place," she said.

"Thank you. Maybe in this case, the cliché is true and the third time really is the charm."

"Well, it's good," she said. "And I'm happy for you."

I think I sat up a little straighter and puffed up like a peacock. I loved hearing her say it because I knew it wasn't a bullshit platitude. She meant it. There were times when the new place was being built that I thought with a tinge of sadness, I wish Heidi were with me now, helping, experiencing this on a day-to-day basis. We were always our best when we were working on a project together. I had fucked that relationship up good, but then again, we wouldn't have been there in the private dining room in the back of my brand-new place if I hadn't.

"You know," Heidi said, "we've done a good job with the girls."

"Yes, but, let's be honest, it was more you and Doug."

"No," she said. "It was you too. Especially these last few years."

"Maybe people can change," I said.

"I don't know if you've changed. Maybe you have. I think you just remembered, is all, and you made a decision. You decided to be a better father. You decided to be a better person all around."

She embarrassed me although I knew it came from a good place.

"The other weekend, I was flipping through some of our pictures," I said, "and I came across one from that Christmas. We were headed to my aunt's for Christmas Eve. Samantha was pitching a fit about those white tights you wanted her to wear."

Heidi laughed and shook her head. "Right. Right."

"You hadn't put them on yet. She's wearing that green-and-white dress, the one with those red Christmas trees on it."

"She bent over to look at the presents under the tree."

"That little bare white butt mooning."

"You snapped that picture."

"I had to."

"We should've had it blown up and framed for tomorrow," Heidi said.

"We had so many years," I said. "You and I together. Even the most ordinary lives can have dramatic twists and turns. I love you. I want you to know that. I love you."

Heidi took my hand and squeezed it. "I know you do, Benny. And I love you too. I love you very much."

I stood with Ernie near the far corner of the room. The guests for the rehearsal dinner continued to drink and mingle. The staff was about to bring out the dulce de leche cake Samantha had asked for.

"My friend," Ernie said, slapping me on the back. He was already drunk enough that his legs wobbled. "You're a lucky man."

"That I am."

"I look at this." He motioned with his hand, not noticing when he spilled some of his drink. "I look at this, and I think how it has all turned out good for you."

I nodded, guarded by his strange tone.

"You have a new restaurant. A new life. You're standing up here, king of the town."

I smiled.

"No one knows the darkest secrets of your life," he said.

"What do you mean by that?"

"You know," Ernie said, pointing with his drink. "You know what I'm talking about."

I wrapped my arm around his shoulder and pulled him close. "What's going on with you, friend?"

"Yes," he said with a big insincere smile. "Friend. We are friends."

"Is there a problem?" I asked.

He shook his head. "No problem, man. No problem. This is a celebration. It's good times. It's good times all around. I'm just telling you, you're a lucky man."

"I am," I said, hoping my agreement would push him off this line. "I'm lucky."

"Yes. Very lucky." He swilled his drink. "And I want you to remember. One thing I don't want you to forget, compadre, is that I saved you."

"You saved me." The way I said it hovered between statement and question.

"I saved you. I did. Don't forget. Now that you're a big man of success. Don't get a big head. You didn't do this all on your own."

"I know I didn't. I would never claim I did."

Ernie gave me a sideways glance.

"Why don't we sit down?" I offered. "Let's sit down."

"I'm fine here."

"We can sit down, get off our feet."

Ernie shook me off. "No. I'm good here."

"Okay," I said, and then brought him closer. "Let's not be a jerk. Not tonight. This is a conversation for later, maybe. It's my daughter's night. So cut it out with this shit."

I held him closer for a dramatic beat, then let go, gave him a forced smile, and went to leave.

"I just want you to remember," Ernie said.

I turned to him. "How could I ever forget?" And then I walked away.

I was making my way through the room when someone grabbed my arm. I turned to see George. He was Scott's father, a tall, silver-haired man with a permanent bronze tan.

"There he is," George enthused.

"Here I am."

We shook hands and came together in an awkward hug that was more us touching our chests together.

"How are you doing tonight, George?"

"I couldn't be better."

"That's good."

"Beautiful night. Great dinner. That cake was one of the most amazing things I've ever had."

"Thank you."

"My son marries an angel tomorrow." He beamed. "Things are good. I'm thrilled to be here."

We went back and forth on the wedding and the possibility of playing a round of golf before he and his wife had to fly back to Minnesota. He thanked me again for the kindness and the hospitality I'd shown them. We shook hands again, and I told him I would say goodbye before he left for the hotel.

I broke away and left the private room. I walked through the now nearly empty main dining room. Busboys and a few of the waitstaff were cleaning up for the night. I couldn't keep the smile from my face.

I entered the small bar just off the entrance to the restaurant. I pulled up a stool and sat down. The bartender, an eager kid named Antonio, hurried over to me.

"How is the evening, Mr. Baca?"

"It couldn't be better."

"Would you like a drink?"

"Whiskey, neat."

I pulled out a cigarette and lit it. Not thirty seconds later, Antonio placed the drink in front of me. I thanked him. He nodded and went about his work.

I took a deep drag of the cigarette and glanced at the television where sport highlights played with the volume off. I enjoyed the drink and the smoke. I appreciated having a quiet moment to myself.

"Excuse me," the voice said. "Ben?"

I turned my head and froze. My heart seized. I felt like I'd been hit in the chest with a heavy mallet, and for a moment I thought I might pass out. Sara stood in front of me. There was no doubt. It was her. Age had changed her face and added streaks of silver to her hair, but it was her.

"I was sitting over there," she said, and I looked to a booth where a balding man in a golfer's shirt with a distinct paunch sat with a beer in front of him. "I saw you come in. I can't . . . I mean, I couldn't believe it. My heart, it almost popped right out of my chest."

She smiled that same warm, irresistible smile.

"I knew it was you. I immediately knew. How long has it been? All these years, and you just happen to walk into this bar, at this moment. Who could have guessed that would ever happen?"

I sat as if encased in amber. I didn't think I could speak even if I knew what to say.

"I almost didn't come over," Sara said. "It's stupid, but I had butterflies, you know? I got instantly nervous. Maybe I'm the last person you want to hear from. I had so much regret for everything. It was almost overwhelming. But then again, that was so many years ago. So much has happened since then. I have to say, I've thought about you a lot, wondering how life turned out for you. I guess we have a lot to talk about, don't we? I'm sure you have some questions for me."

She smiled and I wanted to die.

"And here you are. Here we are, together again. God, Ben, how are you doing? What happened to you? How has your life been?"

I sat and I looked at her. It was all I could do not to scream.